HIS BROTHER'S KEEPER

'She could see the scratch marks she had made on his face.

"Was it so bad?" he said.

She turned her head and spat at him . . .

On the flight she drank endless cups of coffee, thinking all the time not of the man she had been hired to kill; but of her hatred for the man who had raped her.'

Peter Rawlinson was an MP for twenty-three years and became Solicitor General, Attonery General and later a Peer. For many years he was a barrister at the top of his profession.

HIS BROTHER'S KEEPER

Peter Rawlinson

ORION

An Orion paperback
First published in Great Britain
by Chapmans Publishers Ltd in 1993
This paperback edition published in 1994
by Orion Books Ltd,
Orion House, 5 Upper St Martin's Lane,
London WC2H 9EA

A CIP catalogue record for this book is available from
the British Library.

ISBN: 1 85797 526 X

Printed in England by Clays Ltd, St Ives plc

To Judy – in Rome
To Bernard – in Paris
and
Patrick – in London

ONE

They sat waiting in the car, his arm round her, her head on his shoulder.

'Not long now,' he said. 'Another ten minutes.'

He could feel how tense she was as he held her warm body against his.

The plan to kill Edmund Hamilton had always required someone small and the man, Donal, had suggested they get a girl. Then, while they were waiting or returning, he said, they could act as lovers. So a girl had been brought from Marseilles, an olive-skinned, pretty girl with black hair tied in a pony-tail and the body almost of a child. A gipsy, Donal had thought when he had first seen her.

'Are you a tinker?' he asked, smiling at her. He was a tall man, well over six foot with light blue eyes. 'Is it in the circus you've been?'

'As a child.'

'What's your name?'

'Nadine.'

She was certainly a gymnast, as he saw when they rehearsed in a building on an abandoned factory-lot McGiven had found for them in Kilburn. Before that, Donal had made his final reconnaissance of the garden of the house, along the river and in the woods, and when the girl had arrived and the rehearsals were complete, the operation was ready.

Donal looked out of the window of the car and watched the clouds drifting across the moon. It was a Sunday night in early July, and an hour earlier they had driven to the entrance of a farm track off the country lane some two miles upstream from the village.

'Now,' he said, his eye on the clouds. He took his arm from around her and they got out of the car and made ready to cross the fields and reach the river. This was the danger time, for he had a large canvas bag slung across his back and the girl a heavy satchel. They climbed the gate and crouched by the hedge, watching and listening. When Donal was satisfied, they crossed the field and disappeared into the belt of thick shrubs along the river bank. Pushing through the undergrowth, he slid down the steep slope to the edge of the water and pulled on waders up to his thighs. With a small foot-pump he inflated the rectangle of rubber, which had been folded inside his bag, until it became a small dinghy. He slipped it into the river, holding it by a short cord. The girl lay in the shrubs, keeping watch.

He whistled, and she joined him. Standing in the water, he lifted her into the dinghy and climbed in after her. There was just room for the two of them. Slowly they floated downstream, she squatting with her satchel beneath her chin; he crouched in the stern. Shafts of moonlight broke through the branches of the trees, making silver slashes across the dark water, as Donal, using a small paddle, steered close to the shadow of the bank.

After twenty minutes, he looked at his watch and judged they were alongside the garden of the house. He stood on the gravel of the river bottom, pulling the boat under the trees, lashing it to a branch. He lifted the girl out and stripped off his waders, hiding them in the reeds. On their bellies they crawled to the top of the bank and with a night-glass he studied the lawn of Edmund Hamilton's house stretched before them in the moonlight.

A thick bank of cloud blanketed the moon, and with a slight pressure on the girl's arm he gave the signal for them to go on. With their bags slung over their backs, they entered a belt of trees and shrubs which bordered the lawn until they reached the sheds and a tall brick building detached from the main house. They approached it from the garden side; at its front the garage had double doors fitted with two mortice locks and secured by a heavy padlock gripping a thick chain connected to two hasps.

High up on the side where they were standing was a small window with a ledge, a fanlight hardly two foot square.

Donal laid down his canvas bag, took out a pair of aluminium folding steps which he mounted and, standing on the top rung and stretching to his full height, he began to cut the panes of glass from the frame. The girl handed his tools up to him, and took the glass as he cut it. When he was done, he lowered his hands. She jumped and he lifted her so that she gripped his waist with her legs and then climbed on to his shoulders. With her arms above her head, she grabbed the frame of the fanlight and, hoisting herself up, put her head and shoulders through the opening. With her belly on the frame, she slid head first down the inside wall. When only her feet were hooked on to the frame above, she was able to place her hands on the flat roof of the car. She swung her legs clear, balancing for a moment on both hands. Then she brought her legs down behind her and crouched like a cat, before straightening to her satchel which he pushed through the open window and lowered on a cord. She slung it over her shoulder and squeezed between the side of the car and the garage wall.

Laying the bag down by her feet, she crawled beneath the chassis, using a small torch to find the place where she had to fix the device. With the torch on the ground beside her, she took from the bag a dark rectangular plastic box with a magnet fitted on its top, and positioned it above the rim of the chassis, directly beneath the driver's seat. Then she primed it and slid back from under the belly of the car.

She slung the empty bag over her shoulder, gripped the torch in her mouth and clambered on to the roof of the car and jumped, grasping the ledge of the frame with both hands, hoisting her head and shoulders through the window. Donal, standing on the steps, helped her until she was able to leap to the ground. She sat for a moment with her chin on her knees, her eyes shut. When he flicked his fingers, she stood, handing him the glass which he replaced with the putty he had prepared. He rubbed on earth to dirty it until he could see by the light of his

9

torch that it would do; sufficient at any rate not to be noticeable for the short time that was needed.

Then he packed the steps and the kit into his bag and they turned back towards the trees. At the river, he pulled on his waders and they boarded the rubber boat. Once more they floated downstream. At a point where the river flowed through a thick wood, he guided the boat to the bank, disembarked, and carried the girl ashore. With his knife he slashed at the rubber until it became a flat square floating in the water, held by the cord. He pulled it ashore and put it into the bag with his waders. Then they clambered up the bank and into the wood.

There was no path, and he used a compass as they pushed their way deeper into the undergrowth until he signalled for them to stop. He took two small entrenching tools from his bag and they started to dig in the soft earth. When he signalled that the hole was sufficient, they buried their kit, and scooped back the earth with their gloved hands. He stamped it down and she scattered over it leaves and branches. In another place in the wood, he buried their gloves.

As they emerged from the wood into a field, he put his arm round her and she rested her head against him; she was so small that it scarcely reached to his chest. They climbed a gate on to the road and began to walk the several miles back to their car. If they had been seen, they were lovers in the moonlight, going home.

At the car the girl stripped off her shirt and the black gymnast's tights. Donal watched as she stood in her bra and pants, looking at her white thighs and small breasts. She took a short dress from the boot, pulled it on and got into the front seat. He climbed in beside her.

Suddenly he put his hand between her legs. She grabbed his hand, pushing it away and turned her head away from him, but with his other hand he jerked her chin and kissed her on the lips, squeezing her breasts. She struggled, but he held her to him, fondling her body.

'In the back,' he said.

She shook her head violently, but he bundled her over on to the back seat, falling on top of her, pinning her arms above her head. Then he was in her, brutally, savagely. At his climax, she got a hand free and tore with her nails at his cheek.

'Christ!' he shouted and started to shake her, banging her head against the arm-rest on the side of the door. Then he clambered off her and got out and stood fixing his clothes and wiping the blood from his face.

She stayed huddled in the back as he went to the driver's seat, lit a cigarette and started the engine.

'Get in the front,' he said, and she came and sat beside him, leaning away from him against the door.

He drove to the M11 motorway well north of Cambridge and there turned south, joining the heavy lorries on their way to London. An hour and a half later at the junction of the M25 ring road at Theydon Bois underground station, he stopped the car and got out. He put his head through the open window. She could see the scratch marks on his face.

'Was it so bad?' he said, grinning.

She turned her head and spat at him. When he had wiped his face, he disappeared into the station on his way back to the safe house in Kilburn.

The girl drove the car down the M25 to the M4 motorway and Heathrow, where she parked in the short-term car-park and caught the bus to the airport. She had been told by McGiven to post the car-park ticket in the stamped and addressed envelope he had supplied. He had spare keys and he was to pick the car up, see that it was clean of fingerprints and abandon it – or have it burnt out. Her keys she dropped in a waste-bin but she tore up the car-park ticket and the envelope. Perhaps when she was safely gone, the police might find the car – and him.

After check-in and immigration, she went to the deserted women's room and washed herself, scooping water on her face and between her legs, drying herself on the paper tissues. She looked at herself in the glass. Her mouth was bruised and the back of her head cut. She untied her hair and let it fall to her shoulders.

When the aircraft took off shortly after seven-thirty, the family in the house at Grantchester were just stirring, their car still in the padlocked garage in which she had been crouching only four hours earlier. On the flight, she drank endless cups of coffee, thinking all the time not of the man she had been hired to kill, but of her hatred for the man who had raped her.

TWO

When the watchers had arrived in the village among a group of tourists the previous September, they had seen that a police patrol guarded the house day and night and accompanied the man wherever he went. In October, two of them flew to Nice to report at the château in an oak forest in the hills overlooking the valley below the Gorges-du-Loup in the Alpes-Maritimes. The older of the two, a Turk called Andreas, was short and squat with a round face and thin black hair brushed across his balding head; the younger, a Greek, Manolis, was slim and equally dark with a slight cast in his left eye. 'The Unholy Alliance', Consuero called them.

It was an isolated place to which they went, approached through a gate and a gatehouse guarding a drive which for two kilometres wound through an oak forest. Where the trees ended at a cliff above the valley, the drive turned sharp right, down a slope to the 'château-fort', or small castle with towers at either end joined by massive walls of grey battlemented stone. Beneath the walls on the northern side, a narrow strip of lawn ran the length of the house from tower to tower, bordered by a parapet over which the tops of the trees growing on the side of the hill were just visible. From the parapet the valley fell sheer to the village far below, and beyond the valley towered the mountains and the great twin rocks of the Gorges-du-Loup. The south side, with the main entrance, was gentler. A large garden with tall trees and an olive grove stretched to the foot of a steep hill crowned by oaks; forty kilometres to the south lay the coast.

The two arrived shortly after noon and waited in the stone-flagged hall at the foot of the circular staircase as the manservant in a white coat closed and bolted the heavy oaken door behind them. Then he showed the two visitors into a double room off the hall, the first part of which was furnished as a drawing-room, with a sofa and easy chairs before an open fire; the second half as a library, with a vaulted ceiling decorated with a peeling fresco.

'The gentlemen from England, Señor Consuero,' the manservant announced before he withdrew.

Vincente Consuero, his long legs spread out before him, a bundle of papers on his lap, one hand resting on the short dark beard on his chin, did not rise on their entry. He did not even look up from the papers he was studying. 'Welcome,' was all he said as he waved them towards two chairs opposite him. 'I shall not be long.' The two sat and waited in silence. When he had finished his reading, Consuero slowly got to his feet. 'Before you tell me what you have to report, we shall eat.'

The three of them sat at the long, wide dining-room table, saying little. Then Consuero called for a light top-coat which he put on over his grey cheek suit, wrapped a bright yellow scarf below his short black beard, and took them outside.

'Now, you may begin,' he said as he lit a thin, black cigar and they marched in the pale, autumn sunshine up and down the narrow strip of lawn beneath the north walls and above the valley while they reported on the man who, eighteen months earlier, London had sent to Colombia to find the headquarters from where their cartel had been directing the traffic in drugs into Europe. As a result, they had been forced to abandon those headquarters and, ever since, Consuero had promised that, sooner or later, they would have their revenge.

When Andreas had completed his report, Consuero tossed the dead butt of his cigar over the tops of the trees. 'So, for the time being, we shall leave him to his work – and to his new wife,' he said. 'He will have a little more time to enjoy it – and her.'

The wind had now risen and black clouds were gathering above the mountains of the gorge, heralding one of the storms which came at this place so suddenly and so dramatically. Andreas looked at his watch. 'It's time to leave.'

It was when they were at the car and the first drops of rain had begun to fall that Consuero had quoted Talleyrand: 'Revenge is a dish that should be eaten cold.' Then he turned on his heel and disappeared through the double doors into the house. In the drawing-room, he drew the curtains and sat before the olive log burning in the wide grate, as the storm blew up over the mountains and the wind howled along the battlements of the château.

His visitors were driven away down the long private road between the trees whose branches in summer met in a tunnel of leaves. The bar at the gatehouse was raised, and forty-five minutes later they were at the international airport waiting to catch the late flight to London.

Throughout that winter, quartered in Cambridge and working in shifts, the watchers kept a log of the routine and movements of the guards around the house and of the escort which accompanied Dr Edmund Hamilton when he left each morning to drive into the city. They recorded the time he parked at the college in the forecourt of the Master's Lodge; they discovered the libraries where he worked, the halls where he lectured, the rooms where he gave tutorials, the usual time he returned home. Each week Consuero studied the log, and each week he returned the same message: Have patience.

In February the two came back to the château. This time they talked in the vaulted drawing-room while a snowstorm powdered the house and the forest. Nothing had changed, they reported. Time was passing.

'They will not protect him indefinitely,' Consuero comforted them. 'At some time the guards will go, and then it will be left to him to take his own precautions. Soon he will tire of that. Everyone does.'

'Everyone?' questioned the older man.

'Yes, Andreas, everyone. They tire of the trouble and

grow careless. Then will come the time. So remain patient – and plan.'

Plan they did. The front of the house was visible from the road, but at its back they had noted the lawn bordered by belts of trees and shrubs which fell away to the elders and rushes of the river bank. Which was why, when the time came, they had decided on the river.

With the arrival of the warmer weather, they saw Hamilton's wife, Teresa, walking and sitting in the garden, her small figure growing bigger with the child she expected. Then, suddenly in May, the guards were gone. Consuero had been right.

Maurice Turnbull, the head of the Special Protection Unit, had gone to see James Kent, the Chief or C, head of MI6, the Overseas Intelligence Service. Turnbull was a large bald-headed man with an untidy, comfortable figure dressed in an ill-fitting blue suit, which contrasted with Kent's neat and sleek appearance. Kent stared at him, his grey eyes inscrutable behind his large horn-rimmed glasses.

'My outfit is under great pressure,' Turnbull said. 'What with the Libyans and new IRA Active Service units with prominent people on their list of targets, my resources are over-stretched.' Kent nodded. 'We are short of trained men,' Turnbull went on, 'and I'm being obliged to review each case of individual protection. As Hamilton is one of your men, I thought I should speak with you.'

Kent removed his glasses and began polishing them with the white handkerchief he took from his breast pocket. 'It was my predecessor,' he replied, 'who arranged for Hamilton to have protection after the man had returned from a mission in Latin America. He is not, strictly speaking, one of my men, as you put it.'

Pernickety bastard, thought Turnbull. 'All I want to know,' he growled, 'is whether Hamilton's protection has to be continued. His name is not on any of the lists of targets we have. Is it on any other?'

Kent shook his head. 'Not that I am aware.'

'So is it essential that his protection should be maintained?'

'I'll make an assessment and let you know.'

'Please do – and as soon as possible. I could use the men guarding Hamilton. There are other cases which seem more urgent.'

When Turnbull had gone, Kent sent for the contemporary reports from the MI6 station chief in Bogota. There was no activity from the cartel Sir Godfrey Burne had sent Hamilton to investigate in Colombia. In the station chief's opinion, its continued existence was doubted. Opposite this, Kent had some time ago minuted in the margin: 'Its strength and importance was much exaggerated. It was always my opinion that Hamilton's mission was unnecessary.'

To a recent enquiry about the whereabouts of Consuero, the group's leader, the station chief had replied that this was unknown; there was no evidence that anyone of this name was active, certainly not in Colombia. Here again Kent had minuted: 'There have been no reports from any station about anyone of this or of any similar name.' That was all. Kent closed the file. Since there was no trace of any activity or even of the continued existence of the cartel, he would agree to Turnbull's request. On the following day, Kent informed the Special Protection Group that Hamilton no longer merited priority. The protection could, in his opinion, be safely withdrawn. He did not inform his predecessor Godfrey Burne, now living in retirement, with whom Kent had little contact. Kent did not see why he should. Edmund alone was informed.

The withdrawal of the guards was reported to Consuero, now in Palermo in Sicily.

'Keep up the watch, Andreas,' Consuero had said. 'Check the precautions he maintains himself.'

Edmund Hamilton had been relieved when his protectors were gone. His mission to Colombia for MI6 was now many months past; no one, he told himself, would bother with an obscure academic back at his humdrum work at his university, and the continual presence of the guards had been unsettling for the pregnant Teresa.

'At last,' he told her, 'we shall have some peace.'

The police advised Edmund to vary his route to and from work and, whenever he could, his timetable. He also ought to make daily checks on the car. Edmund replied that as Teresa grew more unwieldy, he could hardly expect her to kneel and examine the underneath of the chassis every time she used it, so they supplied him with a small mirror fixed to a pole. They admitted that the withdrawal of the guards meant that the authorities considered any danger remote. A patrol from the Cambridgeshire police would make routine visits. At first Edmund tried to use the pole, but he found it ineffectual. For any real examination, it was still necessary to get down on all fours and examine the underneath of the chassis. But the car was locked away in the garage when at home; in the town it was parked in the drive of the Master's Lodge which had a porter on the gate. So his inspections became more casual and he soon abandoned them altogether.

The watchers noted this as the weeks of early summer passed and when they reported to Consuero, now in Naples, he authorised them to go ahead. As he walked through the lobby of the Excelsior Hotel and took the lift to the second-floor suite for his appointment, Consuero thought with satisfaction that, very shortly, London would be taught to mind its own business – and keep its fingers out of his.

THREE

In the late afternoon of Sunday 8 July, Sir Godfrey Burne, the former Chief of MI6, drove his dark green Daimler up the A33. He was on his way to London to attend a dining club which met once a year and whose members were some of the most powerful men in the United Kingdom – not the ephemeral politicians, but the heads of the civil service – the past and present Permanent Secretaries in all the government ministries as well as the past and present Chiefs of MI6 and the Home Security Service, MI5.

'Do you really have to go?' his wife Angela had asked earlier as they sat on the lawn of his house in Wiltshire, basking in the sunshine. 'It's too good a day to have to go to London.'

Godfrey, his square face burnt brick red by the sun under his mop of grey hair, smiled. 'It keeps me in touch.'

'After the way they treated you, I can't see why you bother.'

Godfrey stretched his hands above his head. 'It wasn't the people I'll meet tonight who eased me out. That was the politicians, and none of them will be there.'

Angela got to her feet and he looked up at her. She is still very beautiful, he thought; the same clear skin of the girl I married thirty years ago. Only her figure had thickened and her fair hair was now almost white. He knew that she had resented his dismissal even more than he. Not for herself; but for him.

'I'll be back in the morning.'

'Well, don't drink too much port.'

'I never touch port.'

As he carried out the table for them to lunch on the terrace, he thought of the real reason why he was so determined to attend the dinner. He had heard that all was not well with MI6, of which, until eighteen months earlier, he had been the Chief.

The week before, he had been at the bar of the SOE Club in Hans Place when one of his former junior officers, Mark Somerset, had approached him. 'Are you alone, Godfrey?' Mark had asked.

'For the moment. I'm expecting a guest.'

They had gone to a table in the corner of the room and talked.

Mark was tall and gangling, in his early thirties, with a shock of unruly dark hair above an angular face as rumpled as his clothes. He was a half-brother of Edmund Hamilton, who was the senior by two years. Edmund's father John, then in the Foreign Service, had married a girl from Andalusia when he was in his middle forties and had died suddenly of a massive stroke when his wife was two months pregnant. Within a year of Edmund's birth, she had married Anthony Somerset. A year later, Mark had been born.

The two boys had been sent to the same schools, Mark always following two years behind Edmund. The two half-brothers were very close, but their personalities utterly different. Edmund was the scholar, easier and quieter than his younger brother and popular with his contemporaries. Mark was more lively, irreverent, ready to question every established nostrum, losing friends by the sharpness of his tongue.

'Mr Somerset,' his university tutor once reported, 'seems to regard show and panache as sufficient substitutes for research and industry.' Mark got to hear of his tutor's opinion and settled down to work. A year later, he got a First. But he did have 'show', which he made no effort to conceal. He had an air to him, provocative and rather mysterious, that women found very attractive. Unlike his brother he had no time for team games, and on holiday would go off by himself or with a single companion, walking and rock climbing in the Lake District or, in the summer, in Switzerland.

When they were both at Cambridge, Mark a freshman and Edmund in his last year, a tourist bus, cornering at outrageous speed the steep bends on the coast road just south of Barcelona, collided with the Somersets' car and the boys' parents were killed instantaneously. The effect on Edmund was the greater. He had been the first-born, and very close to his mother. Thereafter he came to rely more and more on his half-brother, and the two became even more inseparable. So when Godfrey, on the look-out to recruit a scholar to the service, had invited Edmund to join MI6 direct from university, it seemed almost inevitable that Mark would follow. And he did, two years later.

In MI6, they were known as 'the twins', and in London shared a small house in Kensington until three years previously, when Edmund had left London and MI6 and returned to Cambridge and an academic career. Mark had stayed on in Whitehall, although it had always seemed improbable that he would ever fit into a structured government service, for he was an awkward subordinate, and according to James Kent, then Godfrey Burne's Deputy, lacked deference for the system and its official hierarchy. There had been troubles early in his service. Once he had been climbing on the Eiger and, when summoned home because of a crisis in the department, had at first refused to break his leave. It had taken a stern telephone call by Burne to get him home. Then, more serious, there had been the affair of the British naval officer.

The officer, then serving with NATO in Naples, needed money and was being blackmailed. He was suspected of selling secrets of the performance of the latest Allied sonar devices and torpedoes to the Soviets. Mark had been sent out from London to work with a local, a man called Alessandro, who had been employed to shadow the officer and locate his dead-letter drops. When the trap had been sprung and the officer taken back to London for trial, Alessandro's claims for money for his expenses were questioned. Alessandro maintained that Mark Somerset had authorised them and produced a signed chit.

'You had no right to authorise these,' said Morgan, the Chief Clerk in charge of administration at MI6, when Mark had returned. 'The claim is outrageous. Parts appear to me to be fabricated, or at the very least grossly exaggerated. How could you have authorised it? What checks did you make? We are dealing, Somerset, with public money.'

'Don't be so pompous,' Mark had replied. 'We nailed the bastard, didn't we? And we wouldn't have, if it hadn't been for Alessandro. Don't be so bloody mean! Pay him. He deserves every cent.'

When the Deputy, Kent, complained, Godfrey had said, 'All right, James. Leave it to me. I'll deal with him.'

Mark was reprimanded, but Alessandro got his money.

Kent again went to Godfrey. 'It's not good for discipline, C. Young Somerset is bloody-minded and too insubordinate.'

'I know,' Godfrey had replied wearily, 'but he's an original. I don't want to lose him. And he's good at the job.'

Indeed Mark was, and even Kent had to accept that he could not be dismissed merely because he was not polite enough to his superiors.

On Edmund's departure to Cambridge, Godfrey heard that Mark had installed an Australian girl, Jakes Hunter, in the mews house. Then, from the special mission to South America which Godfrey had prevailed upon Edmund to undertake, Edmund had brought home an Argentinian bride, Teresa. According to what Edmund told Angela Burne, all four got on well.

So, when Mark took Godfrey aside at the SOE Club and began to talk about MI6, or 'the friends' as they were known in Whitehall, Godfrey was prepared to listen.

'Our new boss is a disaster,' Mark began. 'Instead of uniting the team after those political sods got rid of you, he's gone out of his way to emphasise who are "Burne's men" and who are his. And promotion he keeps for his.'

Godfrey smiled. 'Sour grapes?'

'Of course. I'm a bloody sight better than most he's promoted! No, I'm serious, Godfrey. Kent's not up to it. He's not a leader; he behaves like a prima-donna in the office.

He's always worrying about his status and authority and he's obsessed with red tape and regulations.'

'Which, translated, means he's caught you out breaking the rules.'

'Often! No, Godfrey, there's more to it than that. He's also incapable of making the slightest decision without scampering across the river to the politicians to get permission, say, even to pass a file to a station in the field. The Foreign Secretary is practically running the whole damn show. I'm not the only one who feels like this. I can tell you, "the friends" are on the verge of mutiny.' He went on like this until Godfrey's guest arrived and they parted.

Godfrey had made allowances for the mutual dislike of Mark and Kent; also for any over-reaction he, the discarded Chief, might be tempted to feel on hearing reports on the short-comings of his successor. But he had been troubled by what Mark had said about the political influence. It was not good to have C and the Overseas Intelligence Service in the pocket of a political minister – and certainly not this one. If Mark was right, the situation could be serious. How serious, this evening would prove an opportunity to discover.

'I suppose Kent'll be at the dinner,' Angela had said as they ate their lunch.

'Of course.'

No two men could have been more unlike than the former and present Heads of MI6. Godfrey Burne had the build and face of a countryman and invariably dressed in tweeds or light grey checks which he had worn even in MI6 headquarters at Vauxhall Cross or attending formal meetings at the Cabinet or Foreign Offices. When he had been C, he was not known as Whitehall's best administrator but he had aroused great loyalty among those who served him.

His successor and former Deputy, James Kent, was the complete opposite – a townsman, with a pasty complexion and heavy horn-rimmed glasses. Now fifty-three, only two years younger than Godfrey, there was no trace of grey in his sleek, dark hair. His figure and movements were neat and tidy; his clothes, summer or winter, invariably sub-fusc. He had always been contemptuous of Godfrey's leadership and instinctive reaction to problems – what he called Godfrey's 'hunches'. Order and method were Kent's idols. Intelligence, he claimed, was a matter of system, of industry, the cross-checking of files and reports and, above all, of analysis. It had been his patron, the present Foreign Secretary, who had intrigued energetically to get him the post on Godfrey's enforced retirement.

'And Edmund Hamilton?' Angela went on.

'Edmund? Oh, no,' Godfrey replied. 'He's back at Cambridge.'

'I thought he might be coming as a guest. Are you taking anyone?'

'No, the better to talk to old friends.'

'I keep thinking about Edmund and Teresa. She must be due in a month or two.' The Hamiltons had visited them during the winter, soon after Teresa had known that she was pregnant. 'When the baby has arrived, I shall ask them down. She'll need a change.'

'And you can spoil her to your heart's content.'

'Of course.'

He left at three o'clock, wondering as he drove whether there was anything he could do – or indeed ought to do – were it confirmed that all was really not well in MI6 under the leadership of James Kent.

It was a few minutes past eight o'clock when Godfrey mounted the staircase to the room where the diners were to assemble. When he was halfway up the stairs, Tom Blakely called him from below. 'Godfrey! Wait for me.'

Blakely was the Permanent Secretary at the Home Office, and an old friend. They took their glasses of champagne and stood apart from the others, in front of the empty fireplace.

'Before we're interrupted, Tom, tell me about my old people. How are they all?'

' "The friends" are not happy. James Kent is not exactly proving a great leader of men. He certainly does everything strictly by the book – that's no bad thing, but it is being said that he only does anything after too many bobs and bows to the Foreign Secretary.'

They were joined by others, and soon the whole party, with three women among the formally dressed men, filed into the dining-room with its long, polished table furnished with the club's silver and tall candlesticks beneath the eighteenth-century portraits of Charles James Fox and his friends. The curtains of the windows overlooking St James's Street were open. We'd make a useful bag for a terrorist, Godfrey thought as he made his way to the table.

The head of the civil service, the Cabinet Secretary, was presiding. When he saw Godfrey, he waved and called across the room, 'Glad to see you, Godfrey. The country air suiting you?'

Godfrey smiled and nodded. There was no seating-plan and when he had pulled out a chair, he found himself next to the Permanent Secretary at the Foreign Office, Andrew Templeton, a tall sandy-haired man with gold-rimmed glasses in front of a pair of sharp grey eyes.

It was only when the main course had come and gone that Godfrey said casually, 'And the new Foreign Secretary – how's he fitting into the Office?'

Templeton looked at Godfrey over his glasses. 'He's proving a powerful minister, and unlike his predecessor he has the confidence of the Party, especially the backbenchers.'

Godfrey pushed the lemon sorbet around his plate. 'And my old service?'

Templeton turned to him. You mean, his look said, how are they getting on without you. Then he shifted his gaze towards the far end of the table to where the neat, almost anonymous, figure of James Kent had modestly seated himself. 'Not getting the credit they deserve,' he said, 'but, as you well know, it'd be a bad day for all of us if "the friends" were to become popular with the media.' He pointed to the portrait of Charles James Fox above them, and smiled. 'Or, as he would have put it in his day, if they were to get the approbation of the public prints.'

I'd almost forgotten the pomposities of Whitehall, Godfrey thought as Templeton added, 'The Foreign Secretary and James Kent get on well together.'

'Not too well, I hope?'

Templeton drank from his glass of Sauterne. 'Some suggest so. But that's just Whitehall gossip.'

So there was gossip. That was all Godfrey knew he would get out of Templeton.

After the single toast to the Queen, the diners took their glasses and began to circulate. Godfrey made his way down the table to talk to the Director-General. As he sat, he saw Kent was standing behind him.

'Good evening, Godfrey. You're looking well.'

'That's because I lead such an idle and agreeable life. How are you enjoying yourself?'

Kent pursed his lips. 'Enjoyment' was not a description he considered appropriate for his important responsibilities. But then that was typical of Burne. 'There's a lot going on. We have two new IRA teams active on the mainland.'

'And the Libyans?'

'Quieter.'

'The drug barons?'

'Nothing unusual. By the way, they've withdrawn protection from Hamilton. Turnbull of the Special Protection Unit came to see me. He's under immense pressure. Every case has had to be reviewed.'

Godfrey looked at him sharply. 'Are you satisfied that Hamilton's no longer in danger?'

'Oh, yes. That's all in the past. It's a question of priorities. I had to make a recommendation and it seemed appropriate, in all the circumstances.'

'You've advised that the protection can be withdrawn?'

'Yes. I have.'

Godfrey was silent for a moment and then said, 'I'm glad you're so certain.'

'Quite certain. One has to make a judgement, and of course I have the advantage of the most up-to-date information.'

By which you mean, thought Godfrey, that I have not. He got to his feet. 'I hope you're right,' he said. 'I hope to God you're right.' After a few words with the Director-General and then with Tom Blakely, he left.

I've no real place here, he thought. If Mark and 'the friends' are unhappy with Kent, there's nothing I can do. Outside, he summoned a taxi and was driven to the SOE Club in Hans Place.

At about that same time, the man and the girl were in the boat on their slow, silent voyage down the river towards Edmund Hamilton's home.

FOUR

'You hate me because I'm fat and ugly.'

'Of course. I hate you because you're very fat – and very ugly.'

They were lying together in bed. It was seven-thirty on Monday morning, just when the girl was boarding the Rome flight at Heathrow.

Teresa had her head on Edmund's chest and he kissed the top of her hair. 'It's very lively this morning.' He had his hand on her belly.

'It's not an it. It's a he.'

'How do you know?'

'I just do.'

'Why didn't you want to have the test?'

'That would spoil everything.'

He buried his face in her hair, loving the scent of it.

'You're so sure it's a boy?'

'Of course.'

He took his arm from beneath her warm body, and stretched. 'I must get up.'

'It's still early.'

'I have to give a tutorial at ten and I must get to the college and do some work.'

He got out of bed and she watched him as he drew the curtains and stood in front of the open window in the early morning sunshine. He's very handsome, she thought, as he stood there in his light-blue pyjamas. And he's mine.

Edmund leaned forward, his hands now on the sill and his head out of the window. 'I can see Brownlow in his garden. At least I can see his hat. Even at this hour he's wearing his panama with the regimental band.'

'He's proud of it,' Teresa said sleepily. 'I like Colonel Brownlow. I like him better than some of the dreary old dons.'

'He'll need that hat later. It's going to be hot.' He turned and came to the foot of the bed, his dark hair tousled, smiling down at her. 'Sleepy-head,' he said. 'Lazy-bones.'

'You're a bully!' She pushed aside the bedclothes and heaved herself up clumsily. 'I suppose moving about will get worse and worse.'

'Far worse. Wait until you get really big.'

She stretched. 'My poor back,' she groaned, taking her white dressing-gown from him.

She went slowly down to the kitchen. When Edmund appeared in the dining-room dressed in his light summer suit and blue tie she was struck again how handsome he was; and how much she loved him. The coffee, toast and fruit were on the table.

'We have that dinner tonight,' he said as he ate. 'The College Summer Feast.'

'I know. The Master, the Bursar . . .'

'And the Chaplain, and the Admissions Tutor . . .'

'And their wives, who look me over and ask questions.'

'Of course they do. It's so long since it happened to them.'

'Why haven't you asked Mark as your guest? He could have brought Jakes, and she and I could have had a good gossip. We haven't seen them for weeks.'

'I asked Mark, but he couldn't come. I got the impression that something's wrong between him and Jakes.'

'All the more reason to get them down.'

'I know. I suppose they're having a row, but it's been going on a little too long.'

He finished his coffee. 'Let's have iced tea this afternoon in the garden by the river.' He got up from the table and came and kissed her before walking to the door. Suddenly he stopped and came back and kissed her again, this time full on the lips. 'I won't take the car. I'll leave it for you, and call a taxi from the village.'

'Good. I have to go into Cambridge to have my hair done.'

'Pick me up at half-past three at the college.'

When Edmund had gone, she stayed at the table, her hand under her chin, looking out of the dining-room window. She heard him on the telephone in the drawing-room ordering his cab. The front door banged behind him. It was good of him to leave the car for her. From where she was sitting she could see Mrs Allen, their cleaning lady, walking up the drive holding Ann, her four-year-old daughter, by the hand. She often brought the child, who played while her mother did the housework and gossiped with Teresa. In four years' time, Teresa thought, I shall be walking my son like that. She put her hand on her belly where Edmund had put his when they had been lying together in bed.

'We are receiving reports of an explosion in a car in a village outside Cambridge . . .'

It was shortly after nine o'clock when Godfrey heard the words in the calm tones of the announcer. The Daimler swerved violently. He braked hard and pulled into the side of Cromwell Road, forcing the traffic behind to swing past, the cars hooting angrily. He turned up the volume of the radio, but there was nothing more. He leaned back in his seat, both hands stretched out on the wheel.

A house outside Cambridge! He remembered what Kent had told him and pressed the buttons of the radio, searching for another channel. Nothing. He sat for a moment and then decided. He would go there at once. Please God, he prayed, it was not them. He made a U-turn, arousing more fury, and drove fast, north to Camden Town, and then east until he joined the M11 for Cambridge. He kept the radio on but heard only the regular repeat of the short and ominous message.

As Godfrey turned the bend into the village, he saw the police

30

tape strung across the entrance to the Hamiltons' drive. Newsmen with cameras were already gathered.

The local policeman standing by the gate was a man Godfrey knew from his visits to his college, St Peter's. 'You can't go in, Sir Godfrey. No vehicles, that is.'

Godfrey looked through the car window over the man's shoulder at the screens further up the drive. 'A car-bomb?'

'Yes. It's very bad. Bystanders too. A woman and a child. They were blown to bits.'

Godfrey looked down at his two hands gripping the steering-wheel. At last he brought himself to ask, 'Who was in the car?'

The policeman saw the look on Godfrey's face. 'It was him, sir. Dr Hamilton.'

So it was the young, handsome Edmund, whom Godfrey had recruited and then, when he had left Whitehall, Godfrey had asked to undertake a special mission in South America. Godfrey had no doubt who was responsible for his murder.

'I'm a friend of his. I'd like to go in.'

'I know, sir. I've seen you together at the college. I'm very sorry. Park here, please, sir.'

As Godfrey walked past the screens around the burnt-out car, police sifting through the wreckage looked up. The Chief Superintendent of the Cambridge CID knew him by sight and came up. 'It's a bad one, Sir Godfrey.'

'Was he alone?'

'Yes. He was bringing the car from the garage to the front door to leave it for Mrs Hamilton.'

'Where is she?'

'They've taken her to hospital, to Addenbrooke's. She saw it from a window. Two others were also killed, a woman and her child. They've taken them away – what was left of them. Those Irish bastards!'

Godfrey knew it was not the Irish. 'Was it remote control?'

'They don't think so. A bomb underneath, on the chassis.'

'Is anyone in the house?'

'A neighbour and his wife. They came when they heard the explosion.'

'I'll telephone my wife to ask her to come. She knows Mrs Hamilton.'

Like Godfrey, James Kent first heard of the explosion in the car taking him to his office in Vauxhall Cross. Cambridge. He, too, remembered his conversation last night with Godfrey. When he was in the hall, Mark Somerset, wild-eyed, ran to him. 'You've heard?'

'Only that there's been an explosion at a house near Cambridge.'

'It's a car-bomb. At Grantchester.'

'Is that confirmed?' asked Kent.

'Yes.'

'Casualties?'

'We've not heard yet. It can't be Edmund. He had protection.'

'It had been withdrawn.' Kent began to walk to the lift.

Mark grabbed his arm. 'What do you mean, it had been withdrawn?'

'What I said.' Kent walked on, with Mark beside him.

'For God's sake, why was it withdrawn?' Mark asked.

Kent did not reply. He entered the lift and pressed the button, but Mark put out his hand and stopped the door from closing.

'I'd like to come with you to Grantchester.'

'I shall not be going. I am due at the Cabinet Office in half an hour.'

'Send the bloody Deputy to the bloody Cabinet Office! Edmund was one of us.' Mark had raised his voice. Others, waiting for the lift, had gathered behind him, watching the scene.

'If I went, I'd be recognised,' said Kent quietly. 'That would broadcast his connection with the service. You go to Grantchester. Then report to me. Now, please, take your hand away.'

But Mark still held the door to prevent it from closing.

Kent could see over Mark's shoulder the faces of the small crowd waiting for the lift.

'You won't go?'

'No, as I said, you are to go.'

Mark dropped his hand, and the lift doors closed.

In the house at Grantchester Godfrey went to the drawing-room. The neighbour, a tall, grey-haired man with a white military moustache, was standing looking out of the window; an elderly woman, her face very pale, was sitting in a chair.

'I'm Godfrey Burne, a friend of the Hamiltons. I heard the news over my car radio. I understand they've taken Teresa to Addenbrooke's.'

The man turned. 'Yes,' he said.

'The doctor wouldn't let me go with her,' said the woman in the chair, staring blankly at Godfrey. 'There's no hope for her baby.'

'I'm Brownlow, and this is my wife,' said the man. 'We live on the other side of their garden. I was walking past the entrance to their drive on my way to the post office. There was this tremendous explosion and parts of the car and of the . . .' He stopped, then went on, 'Everything was flung into the air. 'It was like the war – my war.'

'Did you see Mrs Hamilton?'

The man now had his back to Godfrey. 'She came running out of the house in her dressing-gown and knelt beside the car, sobbing and clutching at what was left. When I got to her, she was all covered in blood and dirt.'

Godfrey walked to the telephone. 'I'm going to ask my wife to come. She knows Mrs Hamilton well.'

As Godfrey dialled, Brownlow said, 'He had police protection until a short time ago. He never told me why, and I never asked. But yesterday I asked him why the police had gone and he said it was because it was all right now – there was no need for it.'

'He also told you the police said he ought to check under his car each morning,' said Mrs Brownlow. 'He couldn't have done that.'

'He said he'd been told there was no danger now,' repeated her husband.

She asked Godfrey, 'Why did they take the guards away?'

Godfrey had the telephone in his hand, waiting for Angela to pick it up at home. 'I don't know.'

'That poor girl,' she said. 'She wanted a son, she said. Like his father.'

'Angela,' said Godfrey into the telephone, 'I'm at Grantchester. You've heard the news? Yes, I'm afraid it is Edmund. Teresa saw it. They've taken her to Addenbrooke's. Can you come immediately?' He paused. 'It'll take you some time. I'll meet you at the hotel, the University Arms.'

'It's the Irish, I suppose,' said Brownlow.

I am responsible, thought Godfrey. I asked him to go to Colombia.

'I'd hang them – every one of them,' said Mrs Brownlow.

'No, hanging's too good for them.'

'I shall be outside,' Godfrey said to Brownlow.

'She's a foreigner, you know,' Mrs Brownlow went on. 'God knows where her family is.'

'She hasn't any. That's why my wife is coming.'

Godfrey went out to the police. Some were searching the garden by the drive, collecting the debris, the bits of metal and the bits of human remains, placing what they found in polythene bags. He could see the newsmen and their cameras at the end of the drive. A man in plain clothes was standing by the wreck of the car supervising the examination. He recognised Godfrey.

'I'm Sinclair. I've just taken over the bomb squad. Were you staying in the house with the Hamiltons, Sir Godfrey? You're not here officially?'

'No. I heard about it on my car radio. He worked for me in the past. I'm a friend of his.'

'You were,' Sinclair said grimly. 'And there are the others.'

34

'Is it the usual pattern?' asked Godfrey.

'Looks like it – the kind the Irish use, planted underneath the driver's seat and held by a magnet. He'd been on the list of protected persons until recently. Why did they withdraw protection?'

'I don't know.'

'We're examining the garage,' the superintendent said.

The two walked to the garage. Another officer in plain clothes was standing by its open doors.

'This is Lacey, Special Branch. He was on the protection team for Dr Hamilton.'

'We should never have been taken away,' Lacey said. He turned to Sinclair and pointed to the front of the garage. 'We had a light there on a sensor which illuminated and set off an alarm when anyone approached the front. But not at the sides.' He beckoned them to follow him to the far side of the building. A policeman on a ladder was examining the small window. 'That's where they got in. The glass has been removed. The putty's quite fresh.'

'Not easy for anyone to get through that window,' said the superintendent.

'Someone small could have.' They all walked back to the front of the garage.

'Any reports of strangers in the village?' Godfrey asked the superintendent.

'The usual, but a lot of people come through here, summer or winter. Tourists, interested in Byron, Rupert Brooke and the like. They come and look at the river and stare at the houses. Japs mainly, nowadays.'

'It wasn't the Japs,' said Sinclair drily.

Godfrey saw the tall figure of Mark Somerset running up the drive. He left the policemen and met him, putting his arm round Mark's shoulders. 'I'm sorry, Mark. I'm so very sorry.'

Mark looked at Godfrey. His eyes were wild and his face very pale. He made a gesture as if to brush aside Godfrey's sympathy. 'Where's Teresa?'

'They've taken her to hospital. I've asked Angela to come. She's on her way.' Godfrey turned to the three policemen. 'This is Mark Somerset, from MI6,' he said. 'Edmund Hamilton was his half-brother.'

'I'm very sorry, sir,' said Lacey. 'I was on his protection team until it was withdrawn. He was a good man.'

'Why was the protection withdrawn? Who the hell withdrew it?' said Mark. None of the policemen answered him.

Sinclair then said, 'Is C on his way?'

'No,' Mark replied. Sinclair raised an eyebrow. All three looked at Mark and then at Godfrey.

Godfrey took Mark's arm. 'Let's go to the hospital. There's nothing you can do here.'

The superintendent said, 'We'll have to let the press and the cameras come up soon. What shall we say?'

'It has all the hallmarks of an IRA bomb, the kind they use,' replied Sinclair.

'Well, tell them that,' said Mark. 'You needn't tell them that he was under police protection until some bastard took it away. They'll find that out soon enough. I'll make sure of that.' He turned, and Godfrey led him away.

At the hospital, Mark went into Teresa's room and sat with her, holding her hand until Angela arrived, when he was sent out of the room. Angela stayed while Teresa's dead child was delivered.

When it was over, Teresa said, 'It was a boy.'

'Yes,' said Angela. 'It was a boy.'

'It should have been me,' said Teresa. 'He was going to leave me the car, but he knew it was difficult for me to get into it in the garage.' Angela took her hand. 'Oh, Edmund, my darling Edmund!' Teresa whispered – and then was silent, the image of the mangled body of her murdered husband floating again and again before her eyes.

Godfrey made Mark come in his car back to London, and the MI6 driver was dismissed.

For a long time they drove in silence. Finally Mark said, 'I can't believe I shall never see him again.' He had his head turned away from Godfrey towards the flat countryside through which they were driving. 'Poor Teresa. Poor, bloody Teresa!' After another long silence, he asked, 'Did you know protection had been withdrawn?'

Godfrey told him what Kent had said the night before. 'He thought there was no danger.'

'The bastard!' said Mark. There was another pause, then he went on, 'Kent hated him, you know. He hated him because of what he was. Like he hates me.'

'It was an error of judgement,' Godfrey said. 'The protection people came to him.'

'A word from Kent, and they would have left it as it was.'

He was right. A word from Kent, and Edmund would be alive today.

Mark began again. 'He'll try to cover it up in order to save his own skin. And he won't try and find the murderers. Well, I'm going to force him to.'

Godfrey drove on in silence. Mark said, 'What about that friend of yours in the House of Commons, Harvey Thompson? Could he help?'

'In what way?'

'By making them say something in Parliament.'

'Perhaps.'

Sir Harvey Thompson was an old friend of Godfrey, a former minister who took a particular interest in security and the Intelligence Services.

Mark went on, 'Kent'll just go through the motions, sending signals to the overseas stations, and Interpol, and the Embassies abroad. He won't want them traced.'

Neither spoke again until they had reached the end of the M11 and the ouskirts of London. Then Mark said, 'Well, I'll do it for him – even if they kick me out of the service.'

'You'll do better by staying.'

Mark glared at Godfrey. 'I'm going to get them, Godfrey! Whatever Kent does or doesn't do, I'm going to get them.'

He means it, Godfrey thought. He means it now. But time will pass. There's nothing he can do on his own. He dropped Mark at Vauxhall Cross and then drove to the House of Commons.

FIVE

'Is he in?' Mark asked the girl in Kent's outer office.

'Yes, he is.'

'Alone?'

'Yes, but . . .'

Mark strode to the inner door, knocked and entered without waiting for an answer.

'Somerset!' Kent looked up from the papers on his desk.

'She said you were alone.' He sank into a chair facing Kent. 'You've heard the details?'

Kent looked at Mark's drawn face, and his wild eyes.

'I cannot express how shocked I am at what has happened. I know what you must be feeling . . .'

Mark interrupted him. 'It was a trembler device under the driver's seat held by a magnet. It exploded when he was moving off after talking to their cleaning lady and her child. All three were killed. Teresa witnessed it. She's had a miscarriage.'

Kent took off his glasses and began to polish the lenses. 'It is terrible, quite terrible. I can only repeat, Somerset, how distressed I am, how very distressed and shocked we all are, and how much we feel for his wife – and for you.' He studied the figure in the chair opposite. 'It is a terrible blow for all of us who knew him, let alone for his family. I know how much you must be going through. If you would like to get away for a time, Somerset, please take some leave immediately.'

He would like that, Mark thought. He would like me out of the way. 'No,' he said. 'Not immediately. Perhaps later.'

'As you wish. But I think you should. It is a terrible tragedy for

39

you and your family – and, as I said, for all of us.' Kent was still polishing his glasses.

'Yes, and one which some are saying could have been avoided.'

Kent looked up at the lanky figure now leaning forward in the chair, his elbows on his knees and his hands cupped under his chin, his eyes fixed on Kent. 'What do you mean?'

'Godfrey Burne drove me back to London.'

'Burne? Burne was at Grantchester? What was he doing there?'

'He went there as soon as he heard the news on his car radio. He said Edmund had been one of his people, so it was right he should go.'

Kent folded his hands on the desk, 'I know what the loss of your brother must mean to you,' he said quietly, 'so I can understand how deeply distressed you are. But as I tried to explain, if I had gone to Grantchester, my presence would have been noted and . . .'

'And you also had important business. I have a message from Burne. After he'd dropped me, he said he was going on to the House.'

'The House?'

'The House of Commons. He was going to see Harvey Thompson.'

'What does Burne want with Thompson?'

'I don't know. He just asked me to tell you.'

Kent again began to polish his glasses agitatedly. 'Burne has no right to speak to anyone about matters which might affect the service, not even to Thompson. He is still bound by the Official Secrets Acts.'

'That didn't seem to be worrying him. He just said he wanted to talk with Thompson and asked me to tell you.'

In the silence that followed, Kent replaced his glasses and fiddled with the papers on the desk in front of him.

At last he said, 'Thank you, Somerset. I'm sure you will want to get away now. I can only repeat my deepest condolences. Please, if you want any leave, take it.'

When the door closed behind Mark, Kent rose and began to pace around the room. He had known that Somerset would blame him. So would others. But it had been Turnbull from the Protection Unit who had begun it. Turnbull had come to him to request the removal of Hamilton's protection. And the station chief in Bogota had reported no sign of activity from the Colombian drug cartel. Minutes recording this were on file.

Then he sat down again. But if the murder had nothing to do with the South Americans, that would put a different complexion on the matter. For it was against the South Americans that Hamilton was being guarded. If they had nothing to do with the killing of Edmund Hamilton and it had been the work of others from whom no threat could reasonably have been anticipated, who could be blamed?

He sent for Morgan, his Deputy. Morgan had been well promoted under James Kent's regime.

'This terrible business over Hamilton,' he said when Morgan had joined him. 'I've been told that the bomb and the technique employed have all the hallmarks of the IRA.'

'There's been no statement from them.'

'No, but there are other Irish factions. We should look into Edmund Hamilton's background. I seem to remember some family connection with Ireland. I know he never served in Northern Ireland, but I'd like you to check out the family. I shall want a preliminary report, and by tonight.' As the Deputy turned to leave, Kent called him back. 'Somerset is, naturally, very shocked and distressed. As you know, he's capable of acting rather wildly, indeed irrationally. Of course I've told him to take leave, but I'd like an eye kept on him. See to it, will you?'

When Morgan had gone, Kent picked up the telephone. As Harvey Thompson had been alerted by Burne, he would not delay in making his own political dispositions. 'Get me the Secretary of State's Private Office.'

The team of watchers who had planned the bombing had

melted away and only Andreas and Manolis stayed on in their discreet hotel off Warwick Way in Pimlico.

Donal had flown to Dublin. As he sat in the snug at Murphy's on the Quays on the night he had returned to Ireland, he began to brood about the girl he had raped in the back of the car. He put his hand to his cheek and felt the scabs of the scratches.

In the past, both in England and in Belfast, he had been on operations with women, and he had always obeyed the rules against getting involved. But none of those women had attracted him. This girl, with her small, trim figure and dark, mysterious face, had. During the two days they had spent practising in Kilburn and the two nights alone together in the caravan parked in the building-lot, he had never once touched her. He tried to excuse himself for what he had done, telling himself that it had been the relief from tension after the danger was over. But he knew it had been because he had wanted her – and the opportunity had presented itself when he knew she could neither stop him nor complain when it had been done. Now he could not get her out of his mind. He wanted her again.

When the men had paid him – in £50 notes sterling – they had said that after it was over he could go anywhere, anywhere in the world. He had replied that no one knew about him. He had no reason to go abroad. But McGiven, who had brought the men to Donal, had insisted. So he had chosen Dublin.

The girl, he knew, had come from Marseilles, but when they'd handed her a ticket he had seen her hand it back to them.

'I'm not going there,' she'd said.

That evening he asked, 'Why would you not be going home?'

'I'm joining a friend.'

'Where?' he had asked. But she had not replied.

Later, he had seen her bag on the bunk in the caravan and had searched through it. The new ticket they had given her was for Rome. That was all he knew. The only way he would ever find her would be through the men who had hired her.

The first time he had met them was when Dermot McGiven had brought them to the Bricklayers Arms in Kilburn, and all four had drunk together. McGiven was the man who had given the orders in all the operations Donal had done. Donal was one of the foot-soldiers. He was not important. McGiven was. He was a senior officer, and he made sure everyone knew it. But on this occasion he had acted differently, not like a superior giving orders but more friendly.

'This job,' McGiven had said, 'is not one of ours. Some friends want our help, and I've told them I'd see what we could do.'

'Who are they, Dermot?'

'Business associates. They're foreigners, and it's important to keep them friendly.'

'Why?' Donal had asked.

'They help over supply.' Of Semtex, Donal had presumed. 'You can ask for your own money and they'll pay well. It'll be extra to what we get. But what they want you to do and why is nothing to do with us. And nothing to do with you. Understand?'

The men McGiven had brought were certainly foreigners. Turks or Arabs, Donal had thought. The one who did the talking was older, short and fat. They had not told him their names and he had not asked. On that first meeting they had been sizing him up. Two evenings later, McGiven had brought them back to the Bricklayers and they had told him what they wanted. It won't be easy, Donal had said, and it won't be cheap. He had demanded and got his price so quickly that he wished he had asked for more. But by then it was too late. McGiven had been there, saying nothing, but listening.

A few days later they had taken him to their hotel in Pimlico, to Room 32, and produced sketches and photographs. They would need a girl, he told them, someone slim enough to get in; and later they said they had a girl who would be coming from Marseilles. McGiven had found for them the building where they practised, and the girl had been taught to place and prime the device. He had also got them the caravan in which they lived, and on the night before the operation, he had brought round the car. The girl was to take the car to Heathrow and post the car-park ticket to McGiven, who would have the car collected, checked and cleaned of fingerprints and then abandoned.

'Burn it,' said Donal. 'That's what they do in Belfast.'

'That's not so easy here,' McGiven had replied.

So Donal knew the hotel where the foreigners were staying. But would they still be there? They might, if he got back quick enough. There would be little risk if he did go back. There was no reason to link him to the bombing in Grantchester. But he would need to keep well clear of McGiven, for McGiven would not understand about wanting to find a woman.

On the next day, he returned to London.

SIX

Kent had been summoned to breakfast at the minister's official residence in Carlton House Terrace, and at half-past seven on the following morning he was shown into the dining-room where the minister, a portly, bespectacled man, was standing before the sideboard. He was wearing a silk flowered dressing-gown in place of a jacket; otherwise he was fully dressed. He did not turn when his visitor was announced. He suspected he knew why Kent wanted to see him.

'Good morning, C, good morning,' he said over his shoulder. 'Have some kedgeree. Coffee? Tea? China or Indian? Help yourself.' He bore a plate piled with steaming kedgeree and an outsize cup of coffee to the table, sat down and began to eat. He had still not looked at Kent.

'I don't know about you, but I have a terrible day ahead of me. A Cabinet committee, the French ambassador with a complaint, lunch with Randall Crauford, the newspaper magnate, Questions in the House, a reception for the Poles and, to cap it all, the Royal Academy dinner when I have to make a witty yet meaningful speech about Art.' He buttered his toast while Kent helped himself to a modest spoonful of kedgeree. 'Are you good on Art, C?' Before Kent could reply, he went on, 'Not one of your strengths, I should imagine.' He looked at Kent's plate. 'Off your oats?'

'I eat very little in the morning, Foreign Secretary.'

'A mistake, C, a mistake. You should always eat well at breakfast. It's the time to pump in the fuel.' The Foreign Secretary laughed jovially but there was no humour in the small eyes behind the spectacles. He pushed aside his empty plate. 'Well, now, what do you want to see me about?'

'The Hamilton bombing.'

'I thought as much. A shocking business. Wasn't he one of your people?'

'One of Burne's.'

'Oh yes, I'm beginning to remember.' The Foreign Secretary remembered very well. He had remembered as soon as he had heard the news. 'He was the man Burne sent to Colombia on what you thought was something of a wild-goose chase?'

'He was.'

The Minister drank from his cup. 'I seem to recollect your telling me that Hamilton's South American escapade wasn't significant, that it was one of Burne's "hunches"? Or am I being, as I so often am, obtuse?' Although his eyes had narrowed behind his spectacles, his smile as he said this was genuine. The thought of his being thought obtuse amused him.

'I think I said, Foreign Secretary, that in my assessment the importance of this cartel in Colombia was being exaggerated, but . . .'

'I thought so. I seem to remember you scoffed about Burne's obsession with the drug barons bringing their civil war into Europe.' He wiped his lips with his napkin.

Kent forked up some of his kedgeree. 'There is no evidence that they have.'

'If the South Americans were responsible, Burne's "hunch" was not so fanciful.'

'At the moment it seems probable that it was one of the Irish factions. The bomb was of the kind they use, and the method one they commonly employ. The Hamilton family had connections in Northern Ireland; they had an estate in Armagh which was sold by Edmund Hamilton's father. His grandfather had been a minister in the Stormont government in the thirties.'

'That's a long time ago.'

'The Irish have long memories, Foreign Secretary.'

'I am well aware of that, C,' said the minister sharply. He brushed some crumbs from the lapels of his silk dressing-gown. 'I understood that Burne had insisted Hamilton should be given police protection. So how did they, whoever they were, get at him?'

'Turnbull came to see me and said that the Special Protection people were under great pressure and he wanted all cases reviewed. He enquired if it was necessary to retain Hamilton's protection. Based on my information, I decided it was not.'

The eyes behind the minister's spectacles were now glinting even more sharply. 'And you were wrong.' Before Kent could say anything, he went on, 'I hear that Harvey Thompson is demanding a government statement in the House. What story is being prepared?'

'You must say very little, Foreign Secretary, because . . .'

The Minister threw his napkin down on to his empty plate and leaned across the table.

'What on earth do you mean – "You must say very little"? What is it to do with me?'

'By you, I meant the government, Foreign Secretary . . .'

'I don't mind what you meant. You said – "you". Let us be perfectly plain, C. Any explanation to Parliament about this affair will be for the Home Secretary to make, not for me.'

'All I meant, Foreign Secretary, was to caution against saying much and . . .'

'If that's your advice, see that it's given to the proper quarter. This is a matter for MI5 and the police, both of whom come under the Home Secretary.'

'I only came to you, Foreign Secretary, in order to brief you so that your colleague . . .'

The Minister interrupted him. 'You came to see me to involve me in your own troubles. Well, let me make it plain. The matter does not concern me. This – this terrible occurrence has come about because you consented to the withdrawal of protection from this unfortunate man, and you did so because you never believed in the seriousness of the threat to him. And you were wrong.'

Kent rose and took his cup back to the sideboard. 'I came to you, Foreign Secretary, as the minister to whom I answer. Of course I appreciate that it'll be your colleague, the Home Secretary, who will have to make the statement in the House and I am on my way to the Home Office to discuss it. But I wanted to warn you . . .'

His host swung round. 'Warn me! Aren't you presuming? Whatever your theories about the Irish, you are in a scrape, C, and how you get out of it is a matter for you and you alone. There's no point in your running to me. You give whatever explanation you can to the Home Office. As I explained earlier, I am extremely busy.'

The Foreign Secretary pulled his dressing-gown tightly round his ample frame and swept out of the room. Kent followed him into the hall, but the Foreign Secretary had disappeared.

Randall Crauford awaited his luncheon guest. Meanwhile he was at work in an armchair in the sitting-room of his suite in the Connaught Hotel. He was a small, rotund little man, with tufts of grey hair encircling the shiny bald dome of his head. It was a large head, out of proportion to his small body with its little feet and white, feminine hands. The mouth above his double chin was sensitive, but any good humour which the mouth might have conveyed was belied by the hard blue eyes behind the rimless spectacles. He was fifty-three, but looked twenty years older.

Balanced on his knee was a bundle of documents. When he had read one page, he let it drop so that his little feet in their highly polished shoes were surrounded by a carpet of white paper. On a table beside him was a telephone, and periodically he would lift the receiver and press a single button. Because the only number he ever called was to the office of the Editor-in-Chief, he was immediately connected.

When Randall Crauford paid a visit to the United Kingdom, visits which were as rare as he possibly could manage, he stayed in an hotel, for he took pains to avoid ever contributing a cent to the British Exchequer. Although he had been born and spent

48

his early years in England, he disliked the country, its people and especially its institutions. As, however, his British interests were, at present, the main profit-making centre in his financial empire, he was milking them as hard as he could. This did not deter him from his opinion, frequently expressed: 'Britain and the British are finished.'

As a young man scarcely out of his teens, he had crossed the Atlantic, made a fortune in the computer software industry, acquired US citizenship and multiplied that fortune many times by speculation on Wall Street based upon judicious insider information which had, so far, remained undetected by the US Securities Commission. But recently he had almost jeopardised his whole fortune through a build-up of massive debt incurred from investment in real estate in recession-hit Texas. As a result, the Crauford empire was now almost wholly dependent on the flourishing profits from his newspaper interests in the United Kingdom, whose people and institutions Randall Crauford so heartily despised.

He had purchased these newspaper interests almost by chance, and certainly for a song, from the family of the former proprietors who had been squabbling among themselves. The principal title, the *Daily Echo*, a hitherto middle-market, middle-of-the-road daily with a middling circulation, he drove firmly down market with the well-tried format of sex and sensation. When it began to put on circulation, he had launched an equally down-market sister, the *Sunday Echo*, and the profits began to roll. On one thing the proprietor insisted. That was an above-average coverage of British public affairs, which he orchestrated by daily telephone calls from his penthouse on East 62nd Street overlooking Central Park in New York City. From there he originated political campaigns, and used his newspapers to pay off imaginary old scores which he imagined he had suffered at the hands of the British Establishment.

He had only one friend in England, a boy who had been at school with him in Nottingham, Rex Weston, now Her

Majesty's Principal Secretary of State for Foreign Affairs. It had been Rex's aunt, a Miss Primrose Weston, who had made possible Randall's success in life. When they were boys and later students at Nottingham University, Rex had often brought his friend to visit his aunt, who for some reason had been touched by the solitariness and vulnerability of her nephew's ungainly little friend. He had a monstrous chip on his shoulder, she told Rex. He must be very unhappy at home.

Miss Primrose Weston had been right. The only child of a solicitor who had been widowed when Randall was twelve, he had been neglected and ignored. So when his father died, penniless and under investigation for raiding his clients' accounts, Randall at the age of twenty decided to emigrate. It was Miss Primrose who had made this possible by the loan of £500. With this, he had made his start, and he had repaid her by shares in his flagship company. When she died, Randall attended her funeral, arriving and leaving by Concorde within twenty-four hours so that he could pass as short a time as possible in the country he disliked so much. The shares she had received in discharge of Randall's debt were sold, and the money swelled the capital of the Priory Trust which Miss Weston had established in her will for the benefit of her nephew, Rex. However, when the newspapers acquired such importance in sustaining the Crauford empire, he was obliged to visit more often, although he limited these visits to a few days each quarter, when he would bully his journalists and select and appoint new editors, who came and went with great regularity.

It was during one of these quarterly visits that he was in his suite, reading through the reports which fluttered to the floor around him like giant snowflakes as he worked through the bundle and awaited his luncheon guest. When the door opened and Rex Weston was announced by his Hong Kong Chinese manservant (who, it was said, was his master's sole confidant), he rose and advanced over the sea of white paper to greet his old friend. 'Welcome, Rex,' he said, shaking hands. 'We're both busy men, so let's go straight in to lunch.'

Weston would have liked, and needed, an aperitif and knew he would get only water for luncheon. But he followed his host into the dining-room without demur.

'Nasty business, that bomb yesterday,' Randall said, shaking out his napkin. 'What's behind it?'

'It's a bit of a mystery. The man killed was of no significance, but I'm told he had Irish connections.'

'It seems to have been a smart piece of work.'

'I'm not conversant with the background,' Weston said uncomfortably, gloomily regarding the tumbler which his host now filled with water. 'It's a matter for the Home Office and the police.'

'I've never thought much of your police. Scotland Yard was always over-rated. The police in this country ought to be organised and armed like ours in the States.'

Like the Los Angeles Police Department, Weston thought, but he said nothing.

Randall went on, 'This country's so small you should create a national force. As it is, your police forces are inefficient – and, like everything else in this country, riddled with upper-class twits.'

You could accuse the police of much, thought Weston, but hardly that. But again he said nothing.

Randall now moved on to subjects that Weston found more agreeable. 'But I haven't asked you round to talk about the police. What I wanted to discuss was politics. I think it's time you made your move.'

The Foreign Secretary laughed genially. 'Oh, come, Randall. I've not been long in my present office – and I'm enjoying it.'

'You may be, but I think you should step up the pressure. Don't you want the leadership?'

'Certainly, in good time.'

'That's the trouble with all of you in this country. You always put off to tomorrow what ought to be done today – and then it's too late. The present man is too old. He's lost his grip.' Randall re-filled Rex's glass with water. 'And he's a monumental snob.'

Two years earlier at a reception, the Prime Minister in his absent-minded way had ignored Randall Crauford – not deliberately, but because he had forgotten who the odd little man was with the enormous head surrounded by tufts of grey hair. Randall had never forgotten or forgiven – just as he had never forgotten or forgiven when on an earlier occasion a minor Royalty had not paid what he considered was sufficient attention to the anecdote he had been telling. Both incidents had strengthened his opinion that the United Kingdom, its constitution, its monarchy and its system of Cabinet government were all bunk.

'He ought to be got rid of. He's too old.'

'He's having – we're all having – a rough time of it just at present. All governments go through a rough patch from time to time. Look at the President.'

'The President has a fixed term. He's there for four years certain, not like your absurd system. And then there's always Congress to keep an eye on him. No, you ought to get rid of that fellow. When are you thinking of making your move and taking over? You know that the *Echo* will be behind you.'

Rex Weston tried to avoid looking too pleased. It was true that the PM had been there a long time and he was certainly getting frail, but Randall's directness was unexpected. In fact, Rex Weston had for some time past begun to make his move. He was already chatting up the backbenchers, seeking to gather support, for when the PM retired, the choice of a successor lay solely with them.

'I'm most grateful for the advice, Randall. And I agree. I don't think it can be very long now before the PM hands in his cards.'

'Well, don't miss the bus. Over the next week or two we're coming out with some pretty tough criticism of him. You know I've always wanted to see you in No.10, Rex – not that the place is of any importance nowadays. But your Aunt Primrose would have liked it.'

The House and the Parliamentary Lobby in the Press gallery

were impressed by the performance of the Foreign Secretary at Question Time that afternoon. Rex Weston had been delighted and stimulated by what Randall Crauford had said at lunch and was, accordingly, at the top of his form. The Lobby agreed that he had been at his most adroit and jovial best. Humming to himself under his breath, he bustled out of the Chamber just as the Home Secretary rose to answer Harvey Thompson's Private Notice Question about the bombing the previous day at Grantchester.

The Home Secretary stuck strictly to the brief that had been prepared for him. He described the scene in detail, expressing shock and horror and deep sympathy for the bereaved. None of the victims, he assured the House, had anything to do with anti-terrorist activity in Northern Ireland.

Harvey Thompson confined himself to a single supplementary question and expressed sympathy with the victims. Then Crichton Smith, an Opposition member, asked whether Edmund Hamilton was a member of the British secret service.

The Home Secretary emphatically – and truthfully – denied that he was, but when another Opposition member asked if Edmund Hamilton had ever been connected with intelligence, the Home Secretary had to admit that some years ago, after leaving Cambridge, Hamilton as a very young man had been for a short time in government service. He had then left Whitehall to take up an academic career. The Home Secretary said that it was not in the public interest for him to say more.

Other MPs began to press for more details, but the minister declined to elaborate. Crichton Smith told an uneasy House that he was not satisfied and that he would seek the earliest opportunity to bring the matter up for debate on the Adjournment of the House.

The Home Secretary then left the Front Bench, stopping beside the Speaker's chair to speak to the Chief Whip, who warned him that he would now have to face a difficult short debate and it would be sensible to bring it on as quickly as possible. Unlike his colleague, the Home Secretary was not humming to himself as he returned to his office.

SEVEN

When he returned to Kilburn, Donal stayed away from the Bricklayers Arms, even though he had heard from friends that McGiven was in Belfast. At half-past seven, he went to the Pimlico hotel where he had been taken by the foreigners when they were planning the murder of Edmund Hamilton. He was carrying a white envelope. At the desk, a woman in her forties with dyed blonde hair scraped back and tied at the back of her neck was writing in the ledger.

'Hullo, there,' he said smiling at her. 'I have a personal delivery for the fella in Room 32. Is he in?'

'What name?' she asked.

Donal looked at the envelope. 'It doesn't give a name, darling. Just Room 32. Personal delivery. By hand.' He held out the envelope to show her.

The woman looked at it but did not return his smile. 'Then leave it here. I'll see he gets it.'

'I was told to get a signature.'

'What name were you to ask for?'

'I wasn't given a name.'

'I'm not giving out the names of guests. What's yours?'

'McGiven,' he said. He thought that if he gave that name, that might bring them to him. But the woman did nothing. He went on, 'What about his friend, the fella in Room 33? Can you get one or other on the house phone?'

'I can, but I won't.'

He saw her glance down at the register. So they were still in the hotel. 'Well, if I can't deliver it in person, my darling, I'd better take it back. Bloody waste of time. Tell them I called. See you.'

He walked out of the front door and down the steps. It was a warm evening, and people in the pub on the corner were sitting at tables on the pavement. He bought himself a drink and sat where he could watch the entrance to the hotel. It was growing dark when he saw the two men come down the steps and turn up the street.

He got up and followed them. 'Hullo,' he said, and they swung round to face him.

'You! You're meant to be in Dublin,' said Andreas.

'I wanted to have a talk, like.'

'Not here,' said Manolis, looking over his shoulder.

'Where are you living?' asked Andreas.

'15 Temple Lane, Kilburn.'

'We'll be there at eleven. Now leave us.'

Donal walked on. At the corner, he turned and saw that they had gone, and he went back on the underground to Kilburn to await them.

The door of the small house in Erskine Mews, Kensington, was opened by a small young woman with a cheerful expression and long tawny hair. She wore no make-up and was dressed in jeans and a smock: she stood in the entrance wiping her hands on a rag. A small black poodle darted out onto the step. Mark's Australian, Godfrey thought and bent and patted the dog. 'I'm a friend of Mark,' he said. 'I've come to see how he is.'

'He's not here.' She stood in the doorway, looking him up and down. 'Do you want to wait?'

He followed her into the front room which was fitted up as a small studio. From the back, a circular flight of iron stairs led to the upper floor. A young man, naked except for a loincloth and a black hat tilted over his eyes, was reclining on one elbow on a sofa a few feet from the easel. Behind him hung a bright scarlet back-cloth.

'I'm Jakes,' the girl said. 'That thing there is Tabbitt,' and she went back to her easel. 'As you can see, I'm painting the little horror.' Tabbitt grinned. The dog settled on a cushion.

'I'm interrupting your work,' said Godfrey.

'Wait upstairs. I'll join you when I've finished his bloody hat. Help yourself to Mark's booze.'

Godfrey threaded his way between the tables towards the stairs. As he passed the easel, he looked at the painting. 'That's very good,' he said.

'It's bloody awful,' she replied. 'But he's a foul subject.'

Tabbitt had lain back and closed his eyes. Jakes switched on the radio beside her and went back to work.

Godfrey wandered round the room upstairs. On the walls were landscapes and a drawing in crayon of Mark, all presumably by her. Books were scattered on the floor; on the desk stood a computer. A door leading to a small kitchen was open. Two other doors, one on each side of the room, were shut. He could hear the music from the radio and sat down to wait.

The telephone rang. From the studio below, the music was still blaring. After a time he went halfway down the stairs and shouted, 'The telephone's ringing!'

'Then answer it,' she shouted back.

'No,' he shouted in reply.

Jakes cursed and, laying down her palette and brushes, switched off the radio. 'This place is bloody Piccadilly Circus,' she said.

Godfrey heard her say, 'There's a man here to see you – an old bloke in a suit. All right.' She rang off. 'You're to wait,' she called up to Godfrey. 'Mark's on his way.'

Godfrey went back to his chair. A little later the music ceased and he heard voices. After an interval the front door banged. A moment later, Jakes appeared up the stairs. 'Are you a mate of Mark's?' She was wiping the paint off her hands with a rag. Godfrey nodded. 'Funny we haven't met.'

'I live in the country.'

She flung herself into a chair. 'God, that was awful about Edmund. And poor darling Teresa. Mark's in a bad way. Only to be expected, and I'm no good for him at the moment. We're having a bit of a fight. We would be, just when this has

56

happened.' Godfrey said nothing. 'He won't talk about it, at least not to me. Just shuts himself up in his room. I wish I could help him.'

'I'm sorry,' said Godfrey.

'Why should you be? It's our problem.' She got up and walked to one of the doors. 'At the moment I'm only in the way. I'll be going out when I've changed. No need to tell him. He won't be interested.' She disappeared.

Two minutes later Godfrey heard the front door, and Mark came up the stairs. He looks dreadful, Godfrey thought.

Mark went straight to the table and poured two glasses of whisky. 'You've met Jakes?'

'She let me in.'

Mark flung himself down in a chair.

'How are you?' said Godfrey.

'Pretty suicidal. I hear Teresa's with you.'

'Yes, Angela has taken her home.'

'I'll come down and see her tomorrow.' He got up and paced up and down the room. 'I've been with Lacey. Do you remember him?'

'Yes. Have they come up with anything?'

'Nothing. To get through that window one of them must have been very small, so they're checking the ports and passenger lists for flights out of the country for women, especially those to Belfast or Dublin.'

'It's not the Irish,' said Godfrey.

'Kent's putting it around that it is. He says it's one of the Irish factions. That's what he's suggesting to MI5 and the police.'

Jakes's door opened and she came out. 'Can I do anything for anybody?'

Mark shook his head. She stood for a moment looking at him and then went down the stairs. The poodle followed. Godfrey heard the front door slam.

'Kent suggested I take some leave,' Mark went on.

'You should.' Godfrey stood up. 'I've come to take you to dinner. You look as if you need to eat.'

'No,' said Mark, getting up. 'I don't feel like eating.'

He helped himself to more whisky.

'Not too much of that.' Godfrey started down the stairs.

Mark followed. In the hall, he said, 'Kent didn't like it when I told him you were with Thompson. He'll suspect you and I might get up to something.'

'I'm sure he will. But we're not.'

'Not yet.'

Godfrey looked at him. 'I'll be down tomorrow to see Teresa,' Mark said, opening the door.

Godfrey walked away down the cobbled, unlit mews. Before he got to the corner, he turned and looked back. Mark was still standing where he had left him in the doorway. Further down the mews, standing in the shadows of one of the garages, Morgan's man watched as Godfrey disappeared and Mark went back into the house.

Donal stayed in a pub where he was not known, drinking alone and thinking about the girl. Back at his lodgings in Temple Lane in Kilburn, he let himself in with his own key. He was carrying a bottle of Jameson's whiskey wrapped in brown paper, and before going upstairs he knocked on the landlady's door. He had heard about her in Dublin. Old Bridgit's place, a friend had told him, was not generally used by the lads in London. Tell her the tale; she'll look after you, the friend had said.

'I know it's late, but I'm expecting a few of the boys, my old beauty,' he said, giving her a peck on her cheek and handing her a £20 note. She smelt the whiskey on his breath. 'Send 'em up when they come, there's a darlin'.'

In his room on the first floor he shut the door, unwrapped the bottle and put it with the toothmug on the table in the centre of the room and helped himself to a drink. It was after eleven when he heard the front-door bell. He opened his door and stood leaning in the doorway, smiling and listening to the footsteps as they mounted the stairs. But it was not whom he expected. It was McGiven – and he was alone.

Although the night was warm, McGiven was wearing a long navy-blue raincoat fastened by a belt. He was a short, thick-set man with broad shoulders and dark red hair flecked with grey. He pushed past Donal and entered the room without a word. Then he said, 'What are you doing here?'

Donal closed the door. 'I just got back, Dermot. I got back this afternoon.'

'You were to stay away. That's why you were given the ticket.'

'Ah well, there didn't seem any real point in staying over there. Will you have a little drink, Dermot?' Donal spoke jauntily, but he was frightened. He had been told McGiven was in Belfast. He poured himself another stiff glass. '*Slainte*,' he said as he drank. McGiven was still standing, staring at him. 'It's all right, you know, Dermot, me coming back,' Donal went on. 'I'm not known. I'm better back here.'

'Are you?'

'Sure I am. And sure it's all right me not staying on over there. As you told me yourself, Dermot, the job I did was special. It was not one of our jobs. There's nothing to connect any of us to this job.'

'The car was never collected. The girl never sent on the car-park ticket.'

Donal drank more whiskey. Why hadn't she? he wondered. 'The poor creature must have forgot. She was very shook up by the time we'd finished. She's a little thing, and I wouldn't've left her with the car, but that was their plan.'

'The police will have the car, with your prints all over it.'

'But the police don't have mine, or the girl's. There's no need to worry yourself, Dermot.'

'Why have you been to their hotel?'

Donal was trying to think fast, but the alcohol was having its effect. 'To see them, Dermot, just to see them,' he said thickly. Then, as if confessing, 'Well, it's like this. I met up with some of the lads in Murphy's and we started betting on the races at Lepardstown. I'd had a few too many jars. You know how it is, Dermot.'

He laughed, not very convincingly. 'When we'd done, I'd lost every cent I got for the job I'd just done. Would you believe that? Lost the lot, and I hadn't a penny left. I had promised my mam some, and now I hadn't any. So then I thought to meself that I'd slip back and have a word with them foreign fellas to see if they'd let me have a wee bit more – a kind of little loan, Dermot.'

'A kind of blackmail.'

'Certainly not, Dermot. Certainly not.' He tried to sound offended. 'Jasus, Dermot, I'd done a fine job for them! A great job, and it did what they wanted. I read all about it. And it wasn't easy. I can tell you, it wasn't easy.' He shook his head. 'So when I lost on the nags, I just wanted a bit more cash, that's all. Just a few quid to help me along, and I knew those foreign fellas wouldn't miss it. There's plenty there, Dermot, plenty there.' He winked and tried to smile.

'Why did you give my name at the hotel?'

'Ah, your name, now. Your name at the hotel. Yes, well I shouldn't've done that. That was a joke, Dermot, just a joke.' He again tried to laugh as he poured himself more whiskey.

'Why was it a joke?'

'The bitch at the desk wouldn't let me in and kept asking me name and I thought to meself . . .

'So you gave her my name.'

Donal pulled out a pack of Sweet Afton cigarettes. He offered one to McGiven, who took no notice, his hands still deep in the pockets of his coat. Donal rose and, staggering slightly, went to the side table and brought back a saucer for an ashtray. The shakiness of his hand as he lit his cigarette was more pronounced. 'I'm sorry about that, Dermot. I'm truly sorry if you're offended. I didn't expect the bitch to ask for a name. It just came into me head, sudden like.'

'What were you doing there?'

'I told you, I needed cash. I'd lost all I had. They wouldn't've missed a little more.'

'You never met the lads at Murphy's and you never bet on the races and you never lost your money. You were alone at Murphy's, and you went from there to your mam at Dun Laoghaire – for one night. Now, tell me. Why did you go to the hotel?'

Donal stubbed out his cigarette in the saucer. McGiven was still standing, feet wide apart, hands still in the pockets of his trench-coat. At last Donal said, 'Well, if you want the truth, Dermot . . .'

'Yes, Donal, I want the truth.'

'Well, God's truth now, mind you, God's truth. It was the girl, the little girl I did the job with. I fancied her, Dermot – and she fancied me. I wanted to see her again. So I went to those fellas to find out where she was.' There was silence while he drank again.

Then McGiven said, 'You disobeyed orders.'

'But it wasn't an Army job, Dermot. You said that yourself. They weren't orders. Not real orders, not like a real job. I only went away to please the foreign fellas.'

'You came back from Dublin. You went to the hotel. You gave my name. You spoke to my friends in broad daylight in the street. All because you wanted to find the girl.'

'I know, I know, Dermot. But, you see, she and I had planned we'd meet in Rome. But I couldn't remember where. I told you I'd had a few too many jars in Dublin. So I went to them to find where she was.'

Donal had started drinking that night when he had been at the pub in Pimlico. He had drunk more when he had returned to Kilburn. Now the whiskey was making him queasy. 'Jasus, it's hot in here,' he said. He got up and walked towards the window to raise the blind and let in the summer air. As he reached for it, he heard from behind him, very loud, 'Leave it alone.'

Donal turned. 'Dermot,' he began, then he put his hand to his mouth. 'Christ, I'm going to spew!'

He lurched over to the basin in the corner and began to vomit. He heard footsteps behind him and when he paused in his retching, his head still in the basin, he felt an arm over his shoulder turning on the tap.

'Wash yourself,' McGiven said.

Donal cupped his hands under the running water and threw it over his mouth and eyes.

'Take this,' McGiven said as Donal turned, and with his eyes still shut and full of water, a towel was thrust into his hands. He put the cloth to his face and began to wipe the water from his eyes and the vomit from his mouth. Suddenly he dropped the towel.

'Jasus,' he said, bending forward and clasping his hands to his belly, seeing the blood seeping through his fingers. 'Jasus!' he repeated, looking up now, staring at the blood-stained knife in McGiven's hand. 'What have you done? In Christ's name,' he screamed, 'what have you done?'

McGiven leaned forward and grabbed Donal's hair, forcing him onto his knees. When Donal was kneeling, McGiven jerked back his head. Then with a sweep of the knife, he drew it across Donal's throat from ear to ear. The last thing Donal saw before he slipped to the floor was the man with the dark red hair in the raincoat standing above him.

McGiven watched as Donal writhed beside his feet, and he stepped back as Donal's blood poured out like a torrent over the shabby carpet. When at last the body was quite still, he picked up the towel and wiped the knife. Then he rinsed his hands at the basin, and dabbed with the towel at the blood on his raincoat until it was clean. Skirting the body and the great pool of blood, he left the room, closing the door.

In the doorway of the room on the left of the front door, the old woman was standing in her dressing-gown, her white hair in curlers. She had heard the scream from the room above.

'You know who I am?' McGiven said.

The woman stared at him as he waited for her reply. Then she backed into the room, and he followed. 'I do so,' she said.

'You haven't seen me. I have not been here.'

'No, sir, that you have not.'

'The man upstairs came in after you'd gone to bed. Later, you heard voices in the room above and then the sound of the front door closing. Nothing more, do you understand?' The woman nodded. 'Go upstairs in the morning. His room is unlocked. When you find him, call the police.' He threw a bundle of banknotes on the table beside her. 'You wouldn't want to get yourself into any trouble, now, would you, Bridgit?'

'That I would not, sir,' she said, looking at the money.

'When I leave, lock the front door and your own, and get into your bed.' Then he was gone.

The landlady did what McGiven had told her. It was ten o'clock on the following morning before the police came. They got nothing out of her – only the story McGiven had told her to tell. But they got Donal's body, and from Donal's body they got his fingerprints. Two days later they matched them with the prints on the abandoned car. The Garda in Dublin helped them over Bridgit's house. It was rumoured to be a safe house, but not well known.

Bridgit was questioned for several hours, but she stuck to her story. She'd never seen the dead man before he came to her house and took the room. She had no idea who he'd been with.

When this was reported to Kent, he said to Morgan, 'First, an Irish-type bomb, fired by an often used Irish technique; second, Hamilton's Irish connections; third an abandoned car with the prints of an Irishman murdered in an Irish safe house.'

'But still no statement from the IRA,' said Morgan.

'As I said, it could be one of the factions. On any analysis of the facts so far known, the evidence points conclusively to the Irish.'

That's what you want to think, thought Morgan. And that's what you want others to think. But he said nothing.

EIGHT

Angela brought Teresa from the hospital to Wiltshire and installed her in a sunny room overlooking the lawn, which was framed by herbaceous borders that led down to the beechwood at the end of the garden. At this time of year the grass and the leaves were at their greenest and the borders ablaze with the colour of lupins, petunias and hollyhocks – all the English country flowers that Angela loved.

But Teresa did not see them. She had the blinds drawn. When sleep came, she dreamt only of Edmund. When she woke next morning, she put out her hand to touch him – and when she felt nothing she lay with the tears streaming down her face. But when Angela brought her tea and told her Mark was coming to see her, she said she would see him.

Mark spent two hours with her, sitting on her bed, talking about his and Edmund's childhood. When he came downstairs, Godfrey took him into the library and gave him the sandwich which was all he said he would eat. His face was still very pale, the skin taut over his forehead and round his mouth. 'I don't know what she'd have done without you and Angela,' he said.

'She can stay here as long as she likes. And you must come down often to see her.'

'I will – if I'm here.'

'What do you mean?'

Mark did not reply directly. 'Lacey told me they have a car that was left by a girl in the car-park at Heathrow on Monday. It had been stolen two days earlier in Kilburn.'

'That's odd. To have abandoned the car at the airport was not very professional – and these people were certainly professionals.'

'Perhaps. As I told you yesterday, they've also been checking the women who left the country that day because it had to be someone small to get through that fanlight. And it was a girl who left that car.'

'Have they come up with any girls who left that morning?'

'A few. I have a note of some of them.' He took out an envelope. 'One was travelling alone on a Cypriot passport to Cyprus; another, a Maltese, flew with a boyfriend to Malta. The first has connections with Lebanon, and the second with Libya.'

'This was not a political murder.'

'Kent is still insisting it was the Irish.'

'That would suit him, for the protection which was withdrawn was protection from the South Americans, not the Irish. But he should be looking for the Colombians – and the people they work with.'

'Who are they?'

'Is there any record of a girl flying to Italy?'

Mark looked again at the envelope. 'There was one, on the 7.55 BA on that morning. Nothing's known about her, and they haven't much description.'

'The flight to Rome?'

'Yes.'

Godfrey got up and walked to the french windows. 'However much Kent doesn't want to believe it, the South Americans killed Edmund, and in Europe it is in Italy where the cartels have their agents.'

'The Mafia?'

Godfrey sat down again. 'The Mafia are the South Americans' main clients, importing into Sicily and running the raw drugs up into northern Europe. They have, or they had in my time, depots as far north as Mannheim and along the Rhine in Germany. By now they must have many more. The Contrera brothers, the treasurers of the Mafia international drug-trafficking operation, were arrested in Venezuela. Riina, the so-called "il Capo di tutti Capi", the Boss of Bosses, is known to have been in South America. Kent knows all this perfectly well.'

'So?'

'So he's no need to look in Ireland, or in Libya or Beirut, and not even in South America. He needs to look in Italy.' Then he smiled at Mark. 'But James Kent would say that's just one of Burne's hunches, and that his computer tells him that a Maltese, with a link with Gaddaffi, is the one to follow. And he may be right.' He got up. 'Come on, let's walk in the garden. You need fresh air.'

They walked down the lawn to the beechwood. At the gate, Mark said, 'You think the girl who went to Rome might be involved?'

'If it was up to me, she'd be the first I'd try to trace. I wouldn't go hunting in Dublin or Belfast. You can tell Kent that, but if he knew it came from me, he wouldn't listen.'

They were now on the grass path in the shade of the trees. Mark took off his jacket and slung it over his shoulder. He bent and picked up a stick and threw it into the trees. 'Then I'm going to Rome,' he said.

Godfrey stopped. 'What did you say?'

'I said, I'm going to Rome. That's where I'll start.'

'Start what? Be serious, Mark.'

Mark swung round. 'I've never been more serious in my life. Kent'll put in hand routine enquiries and he'll see they check with Interpol, but he won't make any serious effort to find them. So I'm going to.'

'What do you mean?'

'I'll go after them myself. And I'll follow your hunch. I'll start with Rome.'

'That was only a hunch, Mark, based on no information. The girl who went to Rome, if she's still there and if you ever find her, may have nothing to do with it. I only said Italy because of the Mafia link with the South Americans.'

'Perhaps this girl won't be the right one, and if she isn't, I'll go on – to Cyprus or Malta, or wherever there's a trail. I'm not going to sit here, Godfrey, doing nothing. I'll go on until I've found them.'

They were now in the middle of the woods, and Godfrey turned. 'Let's go back,' he said. 'It's too warm to walk.' They returned in silence. 'You can't do anything on your own,' he said quietly. 'It would be mad to try.'

'I could, if you would help. You know everyone in every MI6 station in the world.'

'Two years ago.'

'And you know the head of every overseas agency. They'd help you. So will you help me?'

'How?'

'Kent has offered me leave. Well, I'll use it, and I'll start with your hunch – in Rome.'

'It's madness, Mark!'

'I shall do it, with or without your help.'

At the garden gate, Godfrey stopped and faced him. He means it, he thought. He really means it. He'll do it on his own. 'You're determined?'

'I am.'

They walked on. When they reached the centre of the long lawn, Godfrey looked up at Teresa's window and the drawn curtains. 'In Rome,' he said at last, 'I do have a special friend.'

'Can you get in contact today?'

'I'd have to go personally and ask.'

'You're a free man. You can go where you like.'

Godfrey smiled. 'Yes,' he said, 'I'm a free man.'

'If you went on ahead, I'll take my leave and join you there. I'll bring Jakes, so that it looks like a holiday. I'll tell her I need to get away, and I need her to be with me.'

'Oughtn't you to tell her the truth?'

'I shall – later on.'

'Is that fair?'

'To hell with being fair!' he said savagely.

No one and nothing will stop him, Godfrey thought. He said, 'Very well, I'll go tomorrow.'

Mark thought for a moment. 'Kent may be curious, so I won't go direct.'

'Neither shall I.'

'I'll get to Rome on Saturday night. Where'll I find you?'

'Stay at the Hotel Raphael. It's near where I'll be. I'll leave a message.'

In the evening, Godfrey told Angela. 'You're too old,' she said. 'You're quite mad.'

'That's what I told Mark he was,' he replied wearily. 'But he's obsessed, and nothing I can do will stop him. All I can do is see he doesn't get into too much trouble. Rome will probably prove a wild-goose chase. Then I'll get him home.'

Late that afternoon, Mark went to Kent's office. 'I've changed my mind. I've decided I ought to get away.'

'I think you're very wise, Somerset. You should. Arrange it with Morgan.' Then he added, 'Where will you go?'

'To France. Somewhere in the south. We haven't decided exactly where.'

Kent made a note on the pad in front of him. So Somerset would be with his Australian. He would get Morgan to check.

Godfrey booked on the LOT flight to Warsaw. He knew they would pick up his name when he went through Immigration. In Warsaw, he took a cab to a a block of flats overlooking the Vistula. A tall, stooped man with close-cropped iron-grey hair opened the door.

'It is not necessary now to use so old-fashioned a method of passing me a message,' he said as he took Godfrey's bag.

'I can't get out of the habit. Can I stay until tomorrow?'

'Then where?'

'Away . . . and while I'm away, I want you to arrange for me to have been visiting the Siemienskis in Crakow.'

In the evening Godfrey sat with a sandy-haired man at a café by the church in the square in front of the Royal Palace, destroyed in the fighting in the war and rebuilt exactly as it had been. The next day he flew to Rome.

Kent had duly received a note from Immigration that Sir Godfrey Burne had boarded a flight to Warsaw, and he sent a signal to the Embassy. He was advised that Sir Godfrey on his arrival had made contact and was on his way to Crakow to stay with friends, but would be returning in a few days. Kent said he was to be informed when Sir Godfrey left Poland; the Embassy undertook to report.

Mark drove the hired Renault out of the car-park at Nice airport and took the road towards Cannes. As he drove, through the mirror he watched the black Citroën which, keeping a discreet distance, had followed them from the airport. As he expected, Kent was checking where he had gone.

Jakes stretched her arms above her head and turned to look at the huts and topless bathers on the *plage*. 'It's always the old bags,' she said. Mark grunted, and she looked beyond them at the blue sea and the white hulls of the yachts with their coloured spinnakers.

It had been very sudden. The night before, Mark had come to her room. 'I'm taking some leave and going to France tomorrow. Will you come?' She had looked up, surprised. 'I'd like you to – very much,' he had added.

They had scarcely exchanged a word since the start of their quarrel, now six weeks ago – not even when she had tried to comfort him after Edmund's death. He had gone straight to his room and lain there in the dark. That had been on Monday. Now, on Wednesday evening, he suddenly asked her to come away with him.

They had first met two years earlier in Spain. After Sydney University, she and a girlfriend, Janet, were on the conventional, almost mandatory, tour of Europe, and one evening when the two girls had been sitting at a café in the Ramblas in Barcelona, Mark had come over to them. A few days later, instead of going on to Italy with Janet, Jakes had left for London and had been with Mark ever since.

She had moved into Erskine Mews straight away. Mark told

her nothing of what he did, except that it was do with the civil service, and she had not been curious. He was often away – where, he never told her. He would just come home and announce he had to go. They had got on well, but it was a casual relationship. She liked London, and she had liked Edmund and Teresa whom she and Mark used to visit in the country. They had had a few fights, but nothing serious – until the Bank Holiday weekend six weeks back in May when they had gone to Venice and quarrelled.

It had begun when Mark had insisted on finding the Palazzo Mocenigo where Byron's mistress, La Fornarina, had thrown herself into the Grand Canal. It had been hot, and Jakes had been tired and said she wasn't interested; she said she'd never liked Byron, or his poetry. He was the worst kind of Pom, she said – a snob. Mark had got mad. That was how it had all begun, as silly as that. But it had ruined the weekend, and it had gone on even after they had got home, when she had moved into the other bedroom, Edmund's old room. Then, just over a month before the news about Edmund, Tabbitt had come on the scene.

Tabbitt was small, with neat little features and a skin as soft as a girl's. He always wore jeans and T-shirts, and, invariably, a hat – a Digger hat or a baseball cap. His latest was a black Western-type sombrero with a silver badge on the front. 'You look bloody silly in that,' she had told him. But he had laughed – and saluted, like a trooper from the US cavalry. He had been sent round by a painter friend of Jakes to see if she needed a model. He hoped she did, he had said. He was skint. He needed the money. It wasn't long before she learnt he always wanted money – as well as something more. But he was good, holding the pose and never complaining, standing well or lying still on the couch, his brown spaniel eyes never off her, chewing gum, talking in monosyllables. At the end of the first session, he drank tea with her, took his money and left.

That went on for a week. Then one afternoon, when she had walked up to where he was posing half-naked on the couch in order to shift the position of one his knees, he stretched up, pulled her down on top of him and then rolled her over until she was underneath. For a moment she had struggled, shouting at him, but for one so small he was surprisingly strong. He began to touch her, and she stopped struggling. He was still wearing his absurd hat, and she swept it off. He was still chewing gum, and she slapped his cheek to make him spit it out. Then she grabbed his hair as he moved on top of her and had yelled, a great Aussie yell. Tabbitt himself had remained quite silent, imperturbable; and when they had finished he climbed off her and lay with a hand on his head and elbow on the couch, watching as she pulled on her clothes. Then he had asked for a beer.

It had gone on for three weeks, even though she didn't really like him – and she certainly didn't like doing what they were doing under Mark's roof. But she did like what Tabbitt did to her, and each time Tabbitt reached out for her, she went to him; each time, when he had gone, she felt grubby. If it hadn't been for the quarrel with Mark, it wouldn't have happened.

So when Mark suddenly asked her to come away with him, at first she had been uncertain. But he had pressed, saying that he needed to get away and he wanted her with him. 'Like the old days,' he had said. 'We could go to the South of France and drive inland. You've always wanted to paint in the hill towns and I'll read and walk. I must get away, and I'd like you to be with me.'

When she rang Tabbitt to tell him not to come, as she was going away, all he said was, 'I'll have to find someone else. I need the cash – and I'll miss the extra.'

She had slammed down the receiver. That, she swore, would be the last she'd see of Tabbitt.

'How long do you need to paint at Gourdon?' he asked.

'As long as it takes,' she said. 'Why?'

'I thought we might move on after a couple of days.'

'Restless bloody Pom!' she said.

As they approached the underpass before Cagnes-sur-Mer where they would turn away from the coast towards the mountains, he had to brake hard. At the time he was watching the black Citroën and involuntarily he put his hand on her bare knee. She had travelled in red leather shorts, and her legs were stretched out like stalks in front of her.

'Christ,' she said, 'be careful!' Then, 'Have you booked a pub?'

'There's nothing in Gourdon, only a restaurant. We'll try Valbonne.'

'I'm hungry,' she said.

They saw a sign to a restaurant, a grand restaurant in a garden. As he was pulling into the car-park, he had to stop and reverse to allow a large white Mercedes to come slowly out of the car-park. It was driven by a chauffeur, with a man in the passenger seat beside him. Alone in the back sat a black woman, dressed in white, with a white turban. She looked at them as the Mercedes drove away.

They ate chicken, the skin crisp and the meat juicy, and *frites* and a salad, then they drove on up the steep, winding road to the little medieval town of Gourdon, poised on a peak which jutted out from the main mountain range towering above it. The town itself was dominated by a twelfth-century château with a garden and yew hedges. The church and the shops, stocked with pots of jams and honey and trinkets and coloured lavender bags strung together, huddled around its foot. The lanes were narrow and cobbled, and from the outer wall the cliffs fell sheer for scores of metres down to the shrubs and rocks beside the River Loup which wound through the valley far below. In the distance at the other side of the valley rose another but lower crest, thickly wooded; beyond it, in the far distance, the deep blue of the Mediterranean.

Mark carried Jakes' painting kit up the steep path from the car-park and sat on a bench while she chose her position. He's being very friendly, she thought as he helped her set up her easel. When she was established, he left her, ambling off down one of the cobbled passages.

He bought some local honey, and then walked to the wall which circled the town. On it was mounted a large telescope, with a slot to take francs. He inserted a coin and, focusing, idly swept the horizon, picking out Cannes in the far distance to the south. Across the valley, but still many kilometres away, on the ridge lower than Gourdon and heavily wooded, he could make out a large château, isolated and buried deep in the forest. He could just pick out the towers at either end. Then he lowered the lens to look at the fields at the foot of the crest. That, he thought, would make the devil of a climb. Suddenly he saw what he first thought was an enormous coloured kite in the sky above. It was a hang-glider, and he watched as it circled and dropped out of sight. Then he left the telescope and wandered away to a café.

As he sat, he saw a tall, fair-haired man in a flowered shirt take a seat at a table behind him and order beer. Kent's man, Mark thought, so he got up and walked down the road and sat this time looking at the mountains which rose above and behind the little village, watching where the hang-gliders took off for their flight and descent into the valley below the château he had had seen through the telescope. He knew that Kent's man would be watching him.

In the evening, as the light began to fade, he returned to Jakes. 'That's a good start,' he said.

'It's bloody awful,' she grumbled.

The auberge in Valbonne overlooked the square and it could be approached only on foot through an arch, so they had to carry their luggage. He booked two rooms. Not quite like the old days, she thought. At least, not yet.

The tall man Mark had seen at Gourdon took a seat at the café opposite from where he could watch the entrance to the inn and the tables under the cloister already laid for dinner. When Mark and Jakes appeared, the man left the café and walked to a shabby hotel on the outskirts of the town. Next morning he was back at the café when they came down for breakfast. He returned to his car and drove to Cannes. At the Carlton Hotel he telephoned London and advised Morgan that Mark Somerset and his friend were indeed holidaying a few miles inland from the Côte d'Azur.

73

NINE

In London, it had been Cabinet day, and ministers were assembling in the ante-room outside the Cabinet Room at No.10. Under their arms they carried their stiff crimson folders embossed with the Royal Coat of Arms. The Foreign Secretary shouldered his way through the throng to the Home Secretary. 'I hear you had a pretty rough time in the House yesterday, Dick.'

The Home Secretary stared at him frostily. It had been more than rough; it had been very unpleasant, trying to explain, or rather disguise, how the Cambridge don had come to be assassinated and two bystanders killed. 'Why ever did C consent to Hamilton's protection being removed?' he asked.

'He says your Protection Squad wanted to free some of their men for more urgent duties.'

'If C knew the danger to Hamilton, he should have refused.'

The door of the Cabinet Room opened and ministers were summoned inside. 'I know. It was very wrong of him.' The Foreign Secretary took his colleague by the arm as the ministers filed into the room. 'Let's lunch together after Cabinet. There's something I want to discuss.' In the seating arrangements for Cabinet, the Foreign Secretary's place was in the centre on the far side of the long curved table with his back to the windows which overlooked the garden and the Horse Guards, directly opposite that of the Prime Minister who sat with his back to the fireplace, flanked on his right by the Cabinet Secretary and on his left by the Home Secretary.

Each week, nowadays, Rex Weston noted, the PM looked a little more frail. He wondered how he would stand up to their trip together to the conference in Rome. For several months, well before the lunch on Tuesday with Randall Crauford, Weston had been holding court with his cronies and any who cared to join their circle at their usual table in the corner of the smoking-room in the House of Commons. He knew that his only serious rival to the succession was Dick Burnett, the Home Secretary, and at some stage in these sessions over whisky and soda, Weston made a point of bringing up his name.

'Dick,' he would say, 'is one of the great successes of this government. He's doing a splendid job at the Home Office. He is, of course, one of my oldest political friends.' Then a troubled look would fall like a shadow across the Foreign Secretary's frank and open face. 'The only thing that troubles me about old Dick is his lack of grasp of finance and economics which, as you all know, is so important nowadays. Poor old Dick is quite at sea in that field, whereas he's an absolute master over crime and prisons and the fire brigade and broadcasting and fox-hunting and all the rest of the rag-bag of Home Office oddities.' Here he would chuckle and then, suddenly serious again, shake his head sadly. 'But he has absolutely no interest in economics or finance. Do any of you fellows remember Alec, the PM for a short time in the sixties, and his matchsticks?'

Alec, when he had succeeded to the leadership, had once by way of a pleasantry remarked that he used matchsticks when making financial calculations, and had been lampooned about it ever after. 'Well, in my opinion,' the Foreign Secretary would go on happily, 'Alec was a financial genius compared to poor old Dick.'

And the cronies would smile and nod. By now Rex Weston was pretty confident who would be the choice when the party came to vote for a successor to the ailing PM.

As he was opening his folder, he heard the Prime Minister say, 'Before I ask the Chief Whip to give us the Parliamentary business for the week ahead, I'd like to congratulate the Home Secretary and the Attorney on the handling of last night's debate on the Cambridge bombing.' The Attorney, a jolly, fat

75

man with sleeked back grey hair, was attending this Cabinet and was seated at the end of the table well over to the Foreign Secretary's left. He was one of the cronies, and at the mention of himself, he smiled across the table at his patron. 'It might have led to much greater public criticism of the government, however unfair, but thanks to them, that has been avoided.'

In the chorus of growls of 'Hear, hear' which greeted the PM's statement, the loudest came from the Foreign Secretary, who added, 'I agree, Prime Minister. They did splendidly. Quite splendidly.'

The Home Secretary looked stonily across the table. The Foreign Secretary, unlike other colleagues, had not troubled to be present to demonstrate his support. He had only arrived in time for the division when the debate was over. 'But may I enquire,' the Foreign Secretary went on, 'what likelihood there is that the perpetrators will soon be apprehended?'

'Very little,' the Home Secretary replied shortly. Weston shook his head, as though saddened by this confession of failure which indicated, his gesture seemed to convey, some lack of grip at the Home Office. 'They had probably left the country by the time the bomb exploded,' the Home Secretary added.

'It was unfortunate that the protection . . .' the Foreign Secretary began, but the Prime Minister intervened.

'The subject is not on our agenda. We must move on.' He glanced to his left to the far end of the oval table and said, 'Chief Whip.' And the Chief Whip read out the timetable for the Parliamentary business for the week ahead. When the Cabinet moved to the main item for discussion, the Foreign Secretary noticed with satisfaction that the eyes of the Prime Minister were closed. But the Prime Minister was not dozing. He was thinking how little he was looking forward to the Rome conference next week in the company of his devious Foreign Secretary.

When the meeting broke up and ministers were in the ante-room preparing to leave, Weston again took the Home

Secretary's arm. 'A very well deserved tribute, Dick. Now, what do you say to a spot of luncheon at my club, Blakes?'

The Home Secretary, who would have preferred to have lunched with almost anyone other than the Foreign Secretary but who knew that it would be unwise to neglect any opportunity of discovering what that crafty man had in mind, had nothing to say against the invitation and a few minutes later the two men were in the first-floor dining-room of Blakes' Club in St James's, seated at a table directly under a portrait of the young Benjamin Disraeli.

'C made a gross error of judgement,' said the Foreign Secretary as he pierced a lemon with the point of a fork and squeezed the juice over his potted shrimps. 'Either he was ignorant, or he was disgracefully indifferent.'

'Kent was your choice for C.'

'I know. And I have been greatly disappointed by him. We must do something about it, Dick.'

'Another change? It's under two years since Burne went.'

'Why not, if the public interest demands it?'

'Harvey Thompson might have something to say about it.'

'I don't care a fig about Thompson. The day of Sir Harvey Thompson has gone. He's the last of a dying breed, the Knights of the Shires. The younger fellows no longer pay attention to him. I know the modern party.'

You certainly do, thought Dick as he spooned up his soup. Most of the merchant bankers and journalists who predominated in the present Parliamentary party had been selected as candidates when the Foreign Secretary had been the Chairman of the party.

The Foreign Secretary watched as his guest's spoon rose and fell. Then he made a mistake. 'General de Gaulle always said every true Frenchman takes soup with his luncheon – whereas my predecessor at the Foreign Office, the great Marquess of Curzon, used to say that no English gentleman ever took soup at luncheon.' As soon as he had uttered the words, he regretted them. So he added hastily, 'But no one could say that of you,

Dick.' He laughed genially. 'But to return to Kent. He's not turned out to be the man I thought he was. He's too narrow, too provincial, if you know what I mean.'

That, too, was a slip and the Home Secretary saw his chance. He had not been amused by his host's pleasantries about soup. 'You started life in the provinces, Rex.'

The Foreign Secretary did not care to be reminded of his beginnings. He had served his articles in accountancy in Nottingham before migrating to London and employment in a prestigious finance house. It was the income from the Priory Trust established on her death by Randall's benefactor, Aunt Primrose, which had allowed him to enter politics.

'A long time ago, Dick, a long time ago. But, as I said, Kent has proved a great disappointment. He's too petty to be a successful head of an Intelligence Service.'

But Dick Burnett was not to be mollified. He returned to the subject of the provinces. 'The Marquess of Curzon, to whom you've just referred, had a provincial accent. He always used short a's. He pronounced brass to rhyme with crass.'

The waiter put their next course before them. As he helped himself to mustard, Dick went on, 'He had, I presume, no strictures over an Englishman eating liver and bacon at luncheon?'

'Of course not, Dick. Of course not. As I was saying, James Kent has proved himself to be a failure. I hear, he's even got up against his own people, and he overreacts to what he imagines are slights or reflections upon himself.'

'Don't we all?'

'Nonsense! Of course we don't. No, Kent's not up to the job. So I've concluded we must get rid of him – and soon.'

'Bring back Burne?'

'Good God, no! Burne's retired, growing roses or something in Devonshire, I believe. No, I've been thinking about whom we ought to have, but I'd like your support before I put up a name to the PM. I believe we ought to go outside MI6 and get someone from the Foreign Service, a trained diplomat.' Whoever it is going to be, thought the Home Secretary, it will be someone useful to him. 'What would you say to Piers Grenwich?'

The Home Secretary considered the name of Grenwich. He could not, for the moment, place him, but the name struck some chord in his memory.

'I think he'd do the job excellently,' his host went on. 'He finishes as Ambassador to NATO next week and plans to retire after the Rome conference. But if we offered him MI6, he'd jump at it.'

No, thought the Home Secretary, that wasn't the reason the name was familiar. 'I'll think about it, Rex, and let you know.'

'Do that. Now tell me, how do you think the PM was looking? He seemed to me rather tired. I hope he'll stand up to this tiresome trip to Italy. Do you think he might be seriously ill?'

In the car on his way back to Whitehall, the Home Secretary remembered why he had recognised Grenwich's name. Some weeks before, at a dinner for the President of the European Commission, he had heard talk about Grenwich Industries and their expansion in Europe. What exactly had been said, he could not now recall. In his room he told his Private Secretary to make enquiries about Grenwich Industries. Later, when discussing the previous day's debate over a cup of tea with the Permanent Secretary, Tom Blakely, he mentioned that the Foreign Secretary had expressed dissatisfaction with James Kent.

'I'm surprised,' said Blakely. 'I thought he was a great favourite.'

'Not any more,' the Home Secretary replied, and went on to ask Blakely what he knew about Sir Piers Grenwich. The Foreign Secretary, he said, had been speaking about him with a view to some important public office. The connection was not lost on the Permanent Secretary, and not long thereafter, as so frequently occurs on the Whitehall grapevine, all this came to the notice of Jame Kent himself.

TEN

A porter in shirt-sleeves let Godfrey in through a tall oak door in the Via Giulia, a narrow street of old houses in the ancient part of Rome, and led him across the inner courtyard to the rickety, creaking lift.

On the second floor Carla Marreo was standing at the open door of an apartment. 'You look as if you had just stepped in from your garden,' she said.

He leaned forward and kissed her on both cheeks. To do so he had to stretch, for she was taller than he, with green eyes and very short white hair but the soft, unlined skin of a much younger woman. She was dressed in black with a diamond brooch above her left breast. He held her shoulders with both his arms, examining her and smiling. 'And you as if you'd come straight from a reception at a palazzo – which you probably have.'

She turned and, his arm in hers, led him upstairs into the small drawing-room.

Thirty years ago they had been lovers. They had met in London at the Italian Institute where he was learning Italian and she English. That summer they had gone to Capri, sharing a creaking brass bedstead in a room in a small pensione at the edge of the town overlooking what had then been meadows. During the day they walked among the wild flowers on the hills and swam from the rocks; then took a boat around the island, lying on the bottom and paddling it under the rocks of the Blue Grotto. At night they danced at a night-club where a trumpeter played a tune, 'Volare', over and over again. At the end of the holiday they had separated, he to England and she to Milan, and they had not seen each other for two years – until he was married to Angela, and she to Paolo who had been posted to London in the Embassy. Later, Paolo had been the head of the Italian Intelligence Service, SIMI, at the time when Godfrey was C.

'You haven't been here since Paolo died.'

'No. Not since then.' Paolo had died, slowly, painfully, a year ago.

'How long will you stay?'

'Three or four nights.'

She got to her feet. 'Come,' she said. 'It's too hot in here.'

The apartment was on two floors with two rooms on each, and outside the drawing-room an iron staircase led to a roof-terrace decorated with pots of roses and clematis growing along a trellis. Around and below them were the roofs of old Rome.

'Why are you here?' she asked as they sat.

'To seek your help.'

She listened, her hand under her chin, while he told her. Then she said, 'There is a man Paolo used, but I haven't seen him for a long time. He is not very admirable and he's greedy, but he'd be the one who might find the girl you are looking for – if he's paid enough.'

'It is always expensive to find someone who doesn't want to be found.'

She went to telephone.

At ten o'clock, a short, stout man in a bronze silk suit entered the restaurant. It was still very hot and, mopping his face with a red handkerchief, he walked to the table where Carla and Godfrey were sitting. 'It is a pleasure to see you again, Signora.' He raised Carla's hand to his lips and, unbidden, sat.

She turned to Godfrey. 'This is Giorgio Rosetti.'

He bowed to Godfrey across the table and, without being invited, poured himself some wine. They ordered their food.

'My friend,' said Carla in English, 'wants to trace a young French girl who came to Rome from London on the morning of 9 July. Her name on the passenger list was Françoise Poincet.'

'If she's using that name in Rome,' said Godfrey, 'she'll not be the one I'm looking for.'

Rosetti looked at Godfrey. 'Can you describe her?'

'No, except that she's probably young and small.'

'That is not much. Are you in a hurry to find her?'

'I am. I myself leave Rome on Monday, but a friend will be coming. Carla will know where to find him.'

Rosetti said, 'There are many young foreign girls in Rome.'

'Not many who may have been involved in murder in England on the day they came to Rome.'

The fat man looked up from his bowl of pasta. 'Your police are not looking for her?'

'They are, after a fashion.'

Rosetti tucked his napkin under his double chin and began to twirl the pasta round his fork. He did not ask Godfrey why it was only after a fashion that the English police were looking for her.

Carla broke the silence. 'My husband used to say that, in Rome, Giorgio Rosetti can discover everything.'

The fat man paused in his eating, and bowed. 'Given time,' he said, as he drank some wine. Then he went on, 'Many enquiries will have to be made, not only with immigration and the police – that, if expensive, is easy. But more importantly, around the boarding-houses and clubs and other places where young people are likely to go. Many will have to be accommodated.'

Godfrey took out a roll of lira and placed it on the table. 'You can ask the Signora should you need more.'

Rosetti took the money and placed it in his breast pocket. 'I shall do what I can.' It was midnight when he left.

'He has many informants, but you cannot trust him,' Carla said as she and Godfrey walked back to her apartment. 'But if anyone can find her, he will. I warned you about the money.'

At the door of Godfrey's room Carla kissed him on the cheek and put a hand to his face. 'Do you remember the tune the trumpeter played?' she said. Before he could reply, she turned and left him.

Godfrey threw himself on the bed, remembering the tune, and the trumpeter who appeared to know no other.

In Valbonne, when Mark and Jakes were drinking their coffee and eating croissants, he said, 'Today's Bastille Day. Everywhere'll be crowded.'

After he had left her to work at Gourdon, he drove through Grasse to Mougins, where he wandered round the galleries and sat and read. There was no sign of the man who had been following them. On the way back to Gourdon, he drew into a small garage to fill up and saw again the large white Mercedes which had been pulling out of the car-park at the restaurant the day before. There was only one pump, and the garage man was filling the Mercedes. It took quite a time, and Mark had to wait. The man who sat beside the chauffeur paid; the black woman was again in the back seat. As the Mercedes pulled away, he saw her plainly. She had an oval face and a small aquiline nose, like an Abyssinian, he thought. This time her turban was turquoise, and Mark caught the glint of diamonds in her ear.

'That's a wonderful-looking woman in that car,' he said to the attendant as the man filled up his tank. 'I saw her near here yesterday. Does she come from around here?'

'A château. Somewhere near,' the man growled.

Mark drove back to Gourdon to collect Jakes.

'It's still bloody awful,' she said, showing him what she'd done.

'It's not. It's good.'

During the day a dais covered with a tricolor had been set up in a corner of the square in Valbonne, with a microphone and loud-speakers and a disco apparatus. Crowds were gathering as Mark and Jakes took their seats for dinner and the canned music began. Over the microphone the MC started cajoling people to come and dance, and soon the square was packed with dancers, mainly old people and pairs of women waltzing together and grandfathers dancing with very small girls in white frocks. Then the music became noisier and young men in jeans

83

and coloured shirts and their partners in tight-fitting pants drove the children and old men to the safety of the tables outside the cafés. Dinner took a long time and, while they waited, they drank pitchers of iced white wine.

'Come on,' Mark said suddenly and pulled her into the square. After they had danced, he led her to where fireworks were being set off from a field behind the church. Then they went back to the café opposite the auberge and drank cognac.

'You're trying to get me drunk!' she said. 'Where are we going tomorrow?'

'Where there will be much more for you to paint.'

'Where's that?'

'Rome.'

She stared at him. 'Rome! But that's miles away!'

'I know. I have to meet someone there.'

'We're going all the way to Rome – just for you to meet someone? Why didn't we go straight there?'

'Because I couldn't. I only want to get there tomorrow night.'

She banged her glass down on the table. 'You want to go all that way just to meet someone!'

'Yes. I have had to take precautions.'

'Precautions!'

'It's about Edmund.'

The last time she had seen Edmund had been before the quarrel. Edmund and Teresa had dined with them, and Teresa had talked to Jakes about the baby she was expecting. She remembered the look on Mark's face when he told her Edmund was dead and that Teresa had lost the child.

'I believe there's someone in Rome who may know something about his death – and I'm going to find out.'

'Someone who knows about the bomb?'

'Yes. Edmund had once worked for the government and that's why he was killed. Some in London aren't anxious to find the people who did it.'

'Why?'

'Because it was the fault of one of the high-ups. In Rome

I'm meeting the man, Godfrey, whom you met when he came to the studio.'

'I thought you wanted me to come on this trip because you needed to get away and wanted me to be with you.'

'I do need you, Jakes. The people in London who are to blame for Edmund's death are watching me, to see what I'm up to. They shadowed us from Nice, and now they know I'm on holiday with you, they won't follow to Rome.'

She looked at him steadily. 'I thought you needed me because you wanted us to be together again, as we used to be. But you really asked me to use me as cover for what you're planning to do.'

'I asked you because I need your help. As well as wanting you to be with me.'

'Well, why didn't you say so? Why didn't you tell me?'

He was silent for a minute. Then he said, 'Because I wasn't certain you'd come.'

'Too bloody right! I wouldn't have. Now, when you've got me here, you tell me. Well, I'm off back to London. You can do what you have to by yourself.'

'If you do, London will know, and they'll come looking for me. Come to Rome, Jakes, so that we arrive there together. That's all, and then, if you must, you can go back from there.'

He stretched across the table and took her hand, but she snatched it away. 'You take a damn sight too much for granted!'

He shrugged. 'It was such a damn silly quarrel. Let's do this together, Jakes. Even if it's the last thing that we ever do together.'

'Is that what you want? The last thing we ever do together?'

'No, of course not. But what I'm doing, I have to do. I'm going to find Edmund's murderers. I've got to.' He took her hand, and this time she let him hold it.

'What you'll be doing in Rome, will it be dangerous?'

'Not for you, not in the slightest for you. It may all be a waste of time.'

'And your friend, Godfrey. Is he in Rome now?'

'Yes.'

'Why is he doing this with you, and not with the official people?'

'Because he knows they'll do nothing unless we make them.'

She sat with her hands in her lap, looking at him. Then she took up her glass. 'Christ, I've had too much to drink! But, all right, I'll come with you. For a day or two – no longer.' She drank again. 'You're a proper bastard, Mr Bloody Somerset!'

'And you're a proper sheila,' he said. 'Come and dance.'

ELEVEN

At the doctor's room in the Via Cavour in Rome, the girl came from behind the screen dressed only in a white wrap, and mounted the couch. When the doctor had greeted her and told her to undress, she had spoken with an accent and with her olive-skin and dark hair he thought she might be South American or even an Arab. It was his last appointment before the clinic closed at noon.

He drew back the wrap and felt her small breasts. Her build was so narrow, with hips like those of a boy, that he thought she would have a hard time if she were to bear a baby. Her only large features were her eyes set wide apart on her oval face – eyes so black that the pupil ran into the iris. He was impressed by the trimness of her muscles. An athlete, he thought. He noted the scar on the top of her left thigh which looked like a knife-wound, but he said nothing.

'Turn on your side and bring your knees up.' When he pressed her stomach, he asked, 'Any pain?'

'No.'

He took a swab and then examined her for any signs of tearing. He pulled the wrap down and stood looking down at her. 'There's no damage. You were not torn. Were you a virgin?'

The girl shook her head, her great eyes looking into his.

'You may sit up.' She sat on the edge of the couch, her legs dangling over the side, her eyes following him as he returned to his desk.

'You were not on the pill?' She shook her head again.

'You say you were raped?'

'Yes.'

'As I said, there is no sign of tearing. When was this?'

'Last Sunday.'

'As it is only six days ago, I shall need to take a blood sample.' While he was preparing the syringe and dabbing her arm with the spirit, he said. 'Where did this happen?'

'In England.'

'Did you report it?' She shook her head. He drew the blood and went back to his desk. He sat and made a note.

'Why not?' he asked.

'It happened the night before I had to come away.'

He looked up, but did not enquire why that should have prevented her complaining. 'Did you know the man?'

'I had only just met him.'

'Where did it happen?'

'In a car, at night.'

'Had he forced you into the car?'

'No.'

'So you'd gone in the car voluntarily?'

'Yes. The rape was later.'

She was still sitting on the edge of the couch. 'There are no physical wounds.'

'My head was bruised.'

He got up and parted her hair and examined it. 'It is not serious.' He returned to his desk. 'You told my nurse that at the time of the rape you were expecting your period, and it has not come?' She nodded. 'These are early days. Is it so important for you to know?'

She looked at him, an expression of contempt on her face. 'Have you ever been raped?' she said.

'No,' he replied, 'neither have I ever been pregnant. In view of what I presume you want me to do, I have to ask these questions.'

'I wish to know as soon as possible if I'm pregnant.'

'The blood test will tell us if you are pregnant. That will take a few days.'

'And the other?'

88

'There is no point in the HIV test so early. You must come back in, say, six months. Have you any reason to suspect the man?'

'I did not know him well enough. I had only met him a few days before.'

'Did he appear the high-risk type? Bisexual? Drugs? From Africa?' She shook her head. 'Then let's hope he was not infected. If the pregnancy test is positive, what then?'

'I told you. I want it removed.'

He wrote on the pad. Then he said, reciting automatically as he had so often before, 'The law in this country permits abortion for social, socio-medical or socio-economic reasons up to the first ninety days of pregnancy. But to establish such reasons, enquiries have to be made. Do such conditions apply to you?'

'It was rape,' she said.

'Where there has been rape, the law requires the woman to receive counselling.'

'I don't need counselling.'

He looked at her steadily. 'You made no complaint at the time in England, or any when you first arrived in Italy. There is no evidence of any injuries, save for a bump on the back of the head.' He began to write again. Then he said, 'All this may be quite unnecessary. It will be best to wait for the result of the blood test. Give my receptionist your particulars so that we can contact you.' She nodded. 'Do you live in Rome?'

'I am visiting. I will stay in Rome until . . .' She paused.

'Until we have the result?' he said.

'Yes.'

He put down his pen. 'As I said, let us wait for the results of the test. You may get dressed now.'

When she appeared from behind the screen in her expensive clothes, designer jeans and a pink silk shirt, she walked out of the room straight past him. She had not offered to shake his hand. She wants no enquiries, he thought, so she has to claim she was raped. But she had paid, and in cash.

He rang the bell, and his nurse came in. She was small and blonde and a foreigner. He enjoyed teasing her. 'Make sure we have that patient's address before she leaves,' he said in English. When there were no patients present he always spoke English with her. It was good practice for him, he said.

'She is giving her particulars to Anna now. She's French.'

'I thought she was a foreigner. But she's not a divine blonde foreigner, like my Elena.' He was writing as he spoke.

She disliked his calling her Elena. Her name was Helen. 'I thought she might be an Arab.'

He handed Helen the file. 'There is a specimen of blood here. She claims she was raped,' he said. 'In your country.'

'In my country?'

'Yes, in England.'

'England is not my country,' she said.

He knew perfectly well that she was not English. She had been working for him for two months and he had given her a job when he shouldn't, for she was Australian and not allowed to work in Italy. So he paid her half what he would have to pay an Italian or other European. But for her it meant she could stay on in Rome with the man she had met; so she put up with his teasing and pinching.

'Of course. I forget. You're not English, and she's not an Arab.' He smiled at her. He had a thin, dark moustache which she particularly disliked. 'She claims she was raped a week ago in the back of a motor-car in England at the end of an evening when she'd consented to go for a drive in the moonlight with a man she hardly knew. It happened, apparently, the night before she had to come urgently to Rome – so urgently that she had no time to make any complaint. Now, if she's pregnant, she demands an abortion and, to encourage us, has already paid – in cash.' He handed the nurse his notes. 'She is the last?' She nodded. 'Very well, I shall be going now.' As he passed her on his way out, he fondled her buttocks.

In the outer office Helen read the doctor's notes. Anna, the receptionist, a pale and plump young woman whose skin sweated sourly in the heat, came from her desk and looked at the notes over Helen's shoulder. 'The French girl?' Helen nodded. 'The usual, I suppose,' Anna said.

'She may not even be pregnant,' Helen replied, handing over the file. The smell of Anna's skin was so strong and sharp that she hated being in the office with her.

Anna took the file and read as she walked to the steel filing cabinet. 'Rape!' she snorted. 'And no time to complain in England because she was in such a great hurry to come to Rome! But he'll do what she wants. She's paid already.' She closed the filing cabinet and went back to her desk. 'I'll lock up.' She waited until Helen had changed from her white overall and left, then she picked up the telephone.

Quite often in the course of his business, usually on behalf of men, Giorgio Rosetti had cause to make enquiries, of those who kept the records in the doctors' rooms in the Via Cavour, the street in which many Roman gynaecologists practised. Among them were the particular doctors to whom Roman ladies resorted when anxious to get rid of their embarrassments, and Rosetti paid the receptionists well.

On the Saturday morning after he had met Godfrey and Carla, and before setting off on his round of visits to the offices of the police and Immigration and the likely hotels, boarding-houses and night-clubs which he thought a young woman might frequent, he also telephoned those receptionists of the doctors in the Via Cavour who were on his list. He asked to be informed if any young Frenchwoman visited the doctor seeking medical advice – on, of course, the usual generous terms. It was just one of the sources of information which, in the past, Giorgio Rosetti had found to prove useful. He took care to ring early when the receptionists were alone. Anna was one of these who received his call, and this was why, when the doctor and Helen had left, she telephoned Giorgio Rosetti and gave to him the address of Nadine Arletti, No.18, Via Marco Aurelio.

*

When Nadine left the doctor's rooms, she walked to a shop in the Via Veneto where she tried on and bought two pairs of shoes. That done, she walked down the street, glancing in the windows. Since her arrival, she had spent much of the money she had earned in England, and this morning she spent more, not only on shoes but also on ear-rings and a silk blouse.

It must have been one o'clock in the afternoon when she hailed a taxi and told him to take her to the corner where the Via Marco Aurelio joined the Via Claudia. She lay back against the imitation brown leather her eyes closed. The smell of the leather brought back memories of the back seat of the car in England, and she began to feel queasy. I must be pregnant, she thought. It was only six days but she needed to know, because if she were, she would not return to Marseilles until the doctor had dealt with it. She wasn't going to tell Michel about the rape.

There was also the money. Before she had left for England she had boasted about what she was to be paid. Michel had said that she was his woman and he wanted his share. But she was to be paid only when she had arrived in London, so she had been able to tell him she hadn't got it yet. But when she was back, she knew he'd get it out of her. So she might as well spend some now.

The taxi jerked to a halt, wedged in among the traffic, and the driver cursed. 'It gets worse every day,' he said over his shoulder. 'You live in Rome?'

'Visiting,' she said.

'Where do you come from?'

'Paris,' she said.

'The French, they're mean over money. Are you mean?'

'No,' she said.

He laughed. 'Not with tips, I hope.'

She thought of the Irishman who had raped her. When they had been together in the caravan, she had known he had been attracted; but during those days, he had been so professional – although once she had seen him drinking from a flask, but he hadn't drunk anything on the night they had gone down the river. There had been no smell of drink on him when they had been in the car before they had set out for the river – or when he had attacked her. During the preparations, he had seemed so serious. And, God knows, what they were to do was serious enough – to kill a man, to blow him into small pieces. When she had arrived in England, she thought it was to be a job like those she had done so often at home, when her part was to climb and let in the others. So when they had told her what she had to do, she had thought of refusing.

But the Irishman had seen the look on her face and taken her aside. 'There's no going back,' he had warned her. 'These fellows are pros. So keep your mouth shut, and do what they say.'

The taxi jerked to a halt again and the driver swore. The journey was taking an age.

A wave of hatred for the Irishman passed over her. She remembered tearing up the car-park ticket at Heathrow in her fury so that his friends would be unable to collect the car which might lead the police to him. She now began to worry about that. In England they would be looking for the bombers, and if they traced the Irishman, they might trace her. She began to think about the men who had hired her. She had never enquired why they wanted to kill the man in the house. It was a grudge, Donal had said. A contract. Revenge for what the man had done to them. The older of the two, who had hired her in Marseilles, the fat one with the greasy face, had been the more friendly of the two, patting her shoulder, telling her it would be all right. It was the younger one, the silent one, whom she had most disliked. He had frightened her.

The traffic began to flow again, but it took another half hour to reach her corner. As she paid off the taxi, something made her look up and down the street. When she had first come to Tina's, she hadn't thought about danger – she had not thought about danger since she and the Irishman had left the river and they were back at the car and before the man had attacked her. Now, for some reason, she was frightened, and as she walked

93

down the narrow, curving street she became convinced she was being followed. When Tina's front door closed behind her, she ran up the stairs and into the room, calling out to her friend.

Tina, a square, sturdy young woman with broad shoulders and hips and brown, almost red, hair cut in a fringe above skin as dark as that of a Tunisian, as indeed she was, came from their bed in the alcove. 'What's wrong, Nadine?'

Nadine sank into a chair. 'I don't know. I thought I was being followed.'

'From the doctor's?'

'No, in the street. Then I thought someone might be in the house.'

'There's no one here except me.'

Tina leaned down and stroked her forehead, pushing back the hair. 'No one was following you. It's just part of what's happening to you. It'll be over soon – when the doctor takes it away.'

Nadine's shopping and the taxi ride had taken long enough for Rosetti, when he had received Anna's call, to be able to arrive before her. From No. 18, there was no window which overlooked the street, so neither Nadine nor Tina saw the short, stout figure of a man in a shiny bronze silk suit walk slowly past their door and disappear round the bend in the Via Marco Aurelio.

TWELVE

By six o'clock in the morning, Mark and Jakes were in the car. Several kilometres down the double carriageway along the main road from Grasse, where the road curved at the bottom of a steep hill, a large white Mercedes saloon swept out of a side turn to their left, pulled alongside and cut in front of them, forcing them on to the verge.

'For Christ's sake!' Jakes cried as her body was flung forward against her seat-belt when Mark slammed on the brakes.

'You bloody maniac!' Mark shouted as the Mercedes pulled away and disappeared round the bend ahead. 'What the hell did he think he was doing?'

By the time they reached the corner, the white car was out of sight. Shaken, they drove on, through Nice to Monte Carlo; then to the frontier and through the tunnels to Genoa on the road south to Florence and Rome.

The white Mercedes that was being driven in such a hurry had come from the château in the oak forest and was on its way to the airport to collect a passenger. As the name of the passenger was Vincente Consuero, the driver was anxious not to keep his master waiting.

Vincente Consuero mounted the inner stone staircase of the château and entered his bedroom.

'Run me a bath, Philippe,' he told the servant who had carried up his bag. 'And tell Orianna that first I shall sleep.'

He had a long soak in the hot water and then, in the bedroom, drew the curtains and slept for four hours. When he woke, he put on a bath-robe and went across the landing to the room opposite.

Orianna was seated by the open window looking across the valley to Gourdon and the mountains of the Gorges-du-Loup. She had been warned that he was expected home that morning and had sat in her room listening for the sound of the car with her usual feelings of fear and loathing. When he was away, she was at least free from his never ceasing demands – although whether he was home or not, she was not allowed from the house, even for a walk, without Frederik, the escort Consuero had appointed to guard and watch her.

She was wearing a scarlet peignoir, nothing else, and as he entered the room, she threw it off and climbed naked on to the bed where she lay with her legs bent and apart and her hands stretched above her head, the sunshine from the window falling on her ebony skin.

Without a word, he climbed on top of her. But the hot afternoon sun was on his back as he sat astride her and the sweat began to pour from him. Before he had finished, he abruptly broke off and went over to the window to draw the blind. She remained on her back, her breasts rising and falling, her eyes following him across the room. He would not have liked the look of hatred on her face. He returned to the bed in the now darkened room, and wiped the sweat from his face with the edge of the bedspread. He turned her over and she raised herself on her knees, resting her head on her arms in front of her. When he had finished, he rolled over and lay on his back beside her. He motioned, and she cradled his head on her breast, putting the nipple to his mouth. When his eyes were shut, she looked down on him with the same expression on her face as when he had left her to shut out the sunlight. After a half an hour, he got up and went to her bathroom, beckoning her to follow. All this time, not a word had been spoken by either.

While he was under the shower, she stood by the glass door of the cubicle, still naked, with a towel in her hands. He stepped out, and she knelt and dried him. Then she handed him his robe.

'I'm expecting a visitor,' he said. He returned to his bedroom and she followed, handing him a white silk shirt, a pair of black trousers and white canvas shoes.

She returned to her room, still naked, while he went down the stairs and out on to the flagged terrace on the south side of the house overlooking the garden and the olive grove. A small table had been laid, and he poured himself a glass of white wine and rang the silver hand-bell which stood beside the decanter. The manservant appeared with fruit and a pot of coffee on a silver tray. He ate a little of the fruit and drank the coffee with his wine.

He was still sitting there when a car came down the drive and drew up at the main door. He did not look round as the stout figure in a crumpled grey suit walked on to the terrace.

'Welcome back, Andreas,' said Consuero, pointing to a chair. Andreas seated himself. 'How was your trip?'

'Useful.' Neither Andreas's Spanish nor Consuero's Turkish were sufficient, so they spoke English. 'I went to the ports in Sicily to see some cargo landed, but most of the business was in Naples and Salerno.'

'Who was with you?'

'Genaro and the others from what they call in Naples the Camorra family – the local Mafia. He is the young man who succeeded the uncle who died last winter – died in his bed, I may add. Genaro is very young.'

'In Palermo, they say too young and too headstrong – the vices of youth, Andreas, which you and I have long since left behind us. But he has charm and we have become firm friends, as well as partners. I tell him that my name is, in origin, Italian and that my ancestors came from Naples.'

'Does he believe you?'

'I doubt it. But he finds it a pleasant conceit.'

'Do you trust him?'

'Does anyone? Does he trust us? But he and the Sicilians control the bulk of the imports into Europe. Genaro now occupies the uncle's house in Scario which goes with the headship of the family. What the English call a tied house, and

97

in it he has installed not one but two of his women. Which has confirmed the anxieties of the Sicilians.' Consuero smiled, then added, 'He has invited me to visit next week. I shall want you to join me.' He examined Andreas across the table. 'But you look hot and uncomfortable. You have come because you have trouble.' Andreas nodded. 'Then before we talk, we shall swim.'

Consuero rang the bell for Philippe. 'Tell Orianna to bring my robe to the pool.'

He led Andreas up the path through the garden to the swimming-pool. The two men stripped under a wattle awning where towels were laid out on chairs. Consuero, his body lean and bronzed, plunged in stark naked. Andreas, conscious of his white, fleshy figure, undressed more slowly and then walked to the shallow end where he stepped in carefully and swam slowly breaststroke across the width of the pool.

Consuero was swimming strongly up and down, turning rapidly at each end, obliging the other to keep clear. When he had completed a dozen lengths, he put both hands on the edge of the pool and levered himself athletically out of the water. He stood on the tiles like a statue, his arms akimbo, staring out over the garden, waiting for Orianna, who appeared up the path with a white bath-robe and slippers which she held while Consuero briskly dried himself with a towel. Then he put on the robe and without a word walked back down the path to the house, followed by the black girl carrying his clothes. There was no robe for Andreas, who dried himself and dressed again in his crumpled suit, stuffing his tie into the pocket of his jacket.

Consuero was sitting in a cane armchair on the lawn beside the east tower facing the low parapet that bordered the lawn, watching a blue and yellow hang-glider circle over the valley. In the far distance the faint outline of Gourdon could be seen on the peak opposite. He had lit a cigar, and gestured to Andreas to sit on the parapet beside his chair. 'Now tell me about your trouble.'

'The Irishman has been killed.'

'By whom?'

'His own people. In London.'

'Is there anything to link him to us?'

'Not on the face of it.'

'And beneath the face?' Consuero drew on his cigar. 'Come, Andreas, London will know well enough who planned what happened to Hamilton. Or Godfrey Burne would, if he were still in charge. But they have got rid of him. We saw to that.'

'It is the girl who troubles me. Contrary to his orders, the Irishman returned to London from Dublin, where he'd been sent after the bombing. He came to find me and approached me openly in the street. He wanted to find out where the girl was.'

'Do you know?'

'All I know is that she flew to Rome. The Irishman claimed they'd arranged to meet. He said she'd given him her address, but he'd lost it. So he came to me.'

Consuero gazed over the valley behind Andreas as another hang-glider drifted down and disappeared below the tops of the trees on its way to land in the meadow in the valley. Then he said, 'Where did you find the girl?'

'She was with professional thieves in Marseilles who work the coast and the large houses inland. She was needed to get into the garage. Afterwards she refused to return there and flew to Rome – to visit a friend, she said.'

'And she knows you and Manolis?'

'Yes.'

Consuero was about to toss his cigar over the wall, but he checked and stubbed it out before throwing it away. 'Then you'd better find her,' he said. 'And quickly.'

'All I know is that she is somewhere in Rome.'

'My Italian friends must help you. I will arrange it.' He got to his feet. 'Tell Philippe that you will be spending the night here. We dine at eight.'

They walked back into the house, Consuero to the telephone in the library, while the manservant led Andreas to a room on the first floor. From the cupboard he took a silk dressing-gown and a pair of pyjamas, waited while Andreas undressed and took away with him the discarded clothes.

Andreas climbed on the bed and slept. At seven, his clothes were returned, the underclothing freshly laundered and the suit brushed and pressed. He went down to the drawing-room and waited. At a quarter to eight Orianna and Consuero appeared, she in a white evening dress cut low over the shoulders and breasts, the back bare to the waist, the white fabric setting off the black of her skin. She had diamonds at her ears and round her neck. Consuero wore a yellow jacket with brass buttons above a white shirt with ruffles and black trousers. Philippe served champagne.

At dinner Consuero, at the head of the table, with Andreas on his left and the girl on his right, talked about ivory poaching in East Africa and the ivory sculptors in Hong Kong. Andreas said little and ate greedily, his eyes furtively on the girl. Orianna said nothing. After dessert, she rose and without a word left them alone. When she had gone, Consuero said, 'Is she not beautiful?'

'She is,' Andreas replied.

'You like her?' Andreas nodded. Consuero laughed. 'I found her in Rio, a child of the slums, the *favelas*. I bought her from her mercenary old father. I'm glad you approve. You are a man of taste, Andreas.' He smiled as he examined his guest's greasy face. 'Now to business. What was your original plan after the Irishman and the French girl had completed their work?'

'Get them out of the country, he to Dublin and she to her friends in Marseilles. They were well paid.'

'The man is dead because, presumably, his own people mistrusted him?'

'Yes.'

Consuero helped himself to brandy and pushed the decanter across the table. 'London will come looking for her. So you must deal with her.'

'First we have to find her.'

Consuero finished his brandy. 'Go to Rome tomorrow morning and find the girl. When you have done what is necessary, come to the Excelsior in Naples, where Genaro will meet you. I shall travel by sea in the *Phydra*. From Capri we shall sail to Scario in Calabria. Be in Naples by Tuesday night at the latest.'

'If I can find the girl,' Andreas repeated.

'You will. I have arranged for you to be given help.' Consuero rose and turned towards the door. Then he came back to the table and pressed the bell. 'I am going to my bedroom,' he told Philippe. He looked at Andreas, and smiled. 'Send Orianna to me.' Andreas picked up his glass and drank. When the servant had left, Consuero said, 'There will be a message for you at the Hotel Plaza from the man who will help you. He will find the girl. His name is Rosetti, Giorgio Rosetti.'

It was growing dark when Jakes and Mark turned off the motorway and entered the outskirts of Rome. On the long drive from Nice, they had stopped only once for petrol and a sandwich, outside Florence. During the many hours on the motorway, Jakes sat mostly in silence and brooded.

He should have told her the real reason why he had asked to come – to help him disguise what he had come to do. But then, as he had said, perhaps she might not have come. So why had she? She knew why. It was because what she wanted, in her heart, was for them to be back together, as they had been. All she wanted was him. That was the reason why she'd agreed to come with him to Rome. But she would not stay. She knew from what he had told her that she'd only be in the way, sitting in the hotel while he and his friend did what they had come to do. So she would stay one day, and then go back home to wait for him.

'Not too long now,' he said. He took his hand off the wheel and held it out, and she took it. 'Friends?'

'As they say in the newspapers – just good friends.'

'We let that bloody silly quarrel go on too long.'

'We did.'

'Has it buggered everything up?'

'What do you think?'

'I hope not. I really hope not.'

After another silence, she asked, 'When we get to Rome, could it be dangerous?'

'You asked that last night.'

'I'm asking again.'

'If we find the girl, and she's the right girl, that might only give us a lead to the real people. If we find them, they could be dangerous.'

She thought of Teresa. 'The girl was prepared to kill. She did kill.'

'Yes,' he said. 'She did.'

'Bitch,' she said. 'Murdering bitch.'

After a silence, she said, 'Tomorrow I'll try and find Janet. She's somewhere in Rome. She married an Italian. Do you remember her?'

'Of course.'

At the hotel, before they had registered, Mark was handed a message. When he had read it, he said, 'I have to go out.' At the door of her room, he held her and kissed her forehead.

She looked up at him. 'I'm a good sport, ain't I?' she said, exaggerating her Australian accent. He kissed her cheek, turned and left her and made his way to the Via Giulia.

Lying on her bed, she thought about the café on the Ramblas in Barcelona where she and Mark had met two years back. The day after, he had taken her and Janet to a bullfight, but when the picadors began to plunge their lances into the neck of the bull, she had turned and buried her head against him, and he had led them away. Later he had driven her alone down the coast to an open-air night-club with a stone dance floor surrounded by tamarisks perched on rocks high above the sea. Two days later she had gone to London with him. Before she drifted off to sleep, she swore she'd not see Tabbitt again. That was over. All she wanted was Mark. She hoped what he was going to do would not be dangerous.

THIRTEEN

Godfrey had not left the apartment in the Via Giulia during either Friday or Saturday. He had one visitor on Saturday, a small man with a broken nose which contrasted oddly with his neat business-like appearance. He stayed for two hours before slipping away as quietly as he had come.

When he had gone, Godfrey told Carla, 'That was Brereton, the MI6 man here. He's what Kent would call "one of Burne's".'

At eleven on Sunday night Mark arrived at the Via Giulia. On the terrace, he went to the hedge of roses that grew along the trellis on the walls and looked at the surrounding roofs of the city. It was a fine, cloudless night and he could see the floodlit Borromini dome of the church in the Piazza Navona and, to his left, the fortress of the Castel Sant'Angelo.

'I leave tomorrow,' said Godfrey. 'When I'm back, I shall stay at the SOE Club in Hans Place until you return. It will be safer there.'

'From prying eyes and telephone taps?'

'Just a precaution. As you said, Kent will be curious to know if we're up to anything, and he'll notice if I'm away too long. I'll be in London by noon on Tuesday and you must keep in touch.'

'I will.'

'I don't want you haring off into the blue without consulting me. Telephone me every day. 489 5000 is the number at the club.'

'I know.'

'You can get me there at any time of the day or night. The man Carla found for us, Rosetti, will contact you through Carla. Do you know Brereton?'

'We've met.'

'He came to see me today, but he's leaving Rome tomorrow for a short trip. I shall see him in London.'

'What did he have to say about London?'

'An Irishman whose prints were on the car has been found dead in an IRA safe house. Kent claims it confirms that it was the Irish, but the police are still checking on the women who left on the Monday morning.'

'Then the authorities here will have been approached. It would be helpful to know exactly what London is asking the Italians.' Mark looked at Carla. 'Is there any way we could find out?'

'I've few contacts now, but I know someone who has.'

'Can I meet this someone?'

'I'll try and arrange it.'

'Now?' said Mark.

Carla looked at him. 'It's very late.'

'Now,' he repeated. 'Please?'

She got to her feet, looked at Godfrey and disappeared down the stairs.

'Gently, Mark,' said Godfrey. 'Gently.'

Mark went and stood by the terrace rail. 'I know. But if you're right, that girl is somewhere out there.'

'If I'm right.'

Carla reappeared. 'Tomorrow, at noon. Here.'

As Mark left the Via Giulia, Godfrey reminded him, 'Do nothing without checking with me. And keep in touch.'

When Mark walked back to the hotel, he was followed. So this, Rosetti was thinking, is the second Englishman. He would wait a little before he provided the English with the information about the girl at the Via Marco Aurelio, for earlier that day he had received another commission. Now the same information would be worth double. He slipped into the hotel lobby and saw Mark take his key and go to the lift. When the night porter was alone, Rosetti handed him a 10,000 lira note. It took another before Rosetti got the name of Mark Somerset, who had arrived that night from France with a Miss Hunter.

Early next morning, Godfrey flew back to Poland. At eight o'clock on the following day, the man from the Warsaw Embassy saw him off to London. His flight was due to land at Heathrow at nine-thirty am. A signal went to Kent. Burne was on his way home.

On Monday, at the Hotel Raphael, Jakes awoke late. When she had telephoned room service for coffee, Mark knocked and came in. 'Were you late last night?'

'Fairly.'

'And today?'

'I've a meeting at noon. Want to look around before then?'

'To show we're on holiday? Sure, but first I'll find Janet. I'll be down at eleven.' She looked up Janet's married name in the phone book. There were at least a dozen Ridolfis, and she tried six before she heard Janet's voice. '*Pronto. Chi è?*'

'You sound as if you'd never left North Shore, Sydney!'

'Who the hell is that?'

'Jakes Hunter.'

'Jakes Hunter! Good God! Where are you speaking from?'

'Rome.'

'What are you doing in Rome?'

'I'm visiting, and I thought I'd call you.' They arranged for Jakes to come for lunch.

At eleven she joined Mark in the lobby and they walked to the Trevi fountain, to the Spanish Steps, past the Pantheon and back to the hotel. They did not notice a stout man in a bronze-coloured silk suit, sitting in the café opposite the hotel when Mark summoned a taxi to take Jakes to her lunch.

When she had gone, Mark walked to the Via Giulia. Andrina, the maid, showed him in. Carla was waiting at the top of the stairs. 'Come on up,' she called.

As he climbed the stairs, the first he saw of the person whom

Carla had arranged for him to meet was a pair of very long, very bronzed, legs in very high-heeled shoes.

Andreas had arrived in Rome from Nice airport in the morning. At the Plaza Hotel he was handed a note from Giorgio Rosetti. He got a map of the city and in the early afternoon set out for his rendezvous. He picked his way down the Spanish Steps between the bushes of azaleas long past their bloom, stepping between the empty bottles and over the sprawling bodies of the tourists squatting in the sunshine.

At the bottom of the steps, as he paused by the fountain, he was suddenly surrounded by a gang of children with their hands out, begging, clutching at his sleeve and fluttering around him like a flock of birds. Two carabinieri in their dark blue uniforms with the red stripe down their trousers approached. As quickly as they had come, the children were gone, and Andreas, map in hand, turned and walked quickly down the Via Condotti, across the Corso.

The note had instructed him not to ask for directions but to use a map, and walk to a small café directly opposite the Pantheon. He took a seat and watched the passers-by. The first he heard of the other's approach was the scraping of a chair being pulled back. He looked round and saw a plump figure in a bronze silk suit taking a place beside him at the table.

'I was told we were rather alike – at least in shape.' Rosetti was smiling.

'And I was told you are to help me,' Andreas replied, but he did not smile. When the waiter came, Rosetti ordered Campari, Andreas lemonade.

'I have been instructed that you wish to find a young French girl, calling herself either Nadine Arletti or Françoise Poincet who arrived in Rome a week ago today?'

'That is correct. And I have to be in Naples by tomorrow night.'

Rosetti stirred the ice in his glass. 'That does not give us much time. Can you describe her?'

'Slim, short, very dark hair and olive skin. Pretty features. About twenty-two. She comes from Marseilles. I don't know if she speaks Italian. She will be staying with friends.'

Rosetti drank before he replied. 'She is popular, this young woman.'

'What do you mean?'

'I mean that others are looking for her, too.'

'The police?'

'I don't think so.'

'Who are they?'

'How should I know? It's just what I'm told.'

'Are they here, in Rome?'

'Yes.'

'Then I must be the first to find her.' Andreas had taken his wallet from his inside pocket.

Rosetti smiled. 'So you didn't lose your purse? I saw the gipsies around you.'

Andreas took some notes from the wallet and held them out. Rosetti looked at them and shook his head. Andreas took out more, and Rosetti stretched across the table and pocketed them.

'Go back to the hotel and wait. I'll get in touch. It should not be long. We'll meet later.' The plump figure strolled away and disappeared into the crowd in the Piazza della Minerva.

Just before lunch, two taxis, one behind the other, turned off the Appian Way immediately before the Porta San Sebastiano, mounted a steep drive and drew up in front of the low white house. Jakes was in the second. She only noticed the blonde head in the car ahead when her taxi braked sharply and followed the other into the drive.

So she was not to be alone with Janet, as she had hoped. When she was fumbling for money, she saw the blonde walk to the house, noting the girls's plain summer dress and ordinary shoes. A maidservant was holding the front door open; the dumpy figure of the blonde had disappeared.

'The signorina said, please, go to the garden.'

Jakes followed into the drawing-room, her heels clacking on the black-and-white tiles of the hall. My friend, she thought, lives in some style! Through the french windows she saw the pool, and went into the garden where the blonde was now standing by some chairs and a glass-topped table under a yellow-and-white striped umbrella.

'You must be Jakes Hunter. Janet told me you were coming. I'm from Sydney, too. I'm Helen Page.'

Her voice was even more Sydneyside than Janet's as she launched into her life-story – or at least that part of it which began when she had set out for Europe. She had been in Rome for a year and was now working for a doctor. Today was her day off. 'It's not allowed, but I need the money.'

'Why do you stay?' Jakes asked.

Helen coloured. 'I've made a friend here.'

Obviously a man, Jakes thought, and then turned as she heard a shout from behind her. 'Jakes Hunter, you old bitch!'

Janet came from the house, a tall, young woman of Jakes' age, with short dark hair and a prominent nose. She put her arms round Jakes and hugged her. 'It's two bloody years since you ran off with that bloody Pom!' She flopped into a chair. 'You still with him?'

Jakes told her they'd come to Rome together but she was going home almost immediately, alone.

'Why?'

'It's a long story.'

Janet said, 'Helen, be a dear and tell Maria that we'll have lunch out here.' When Helen had gone into the house, she asked, 'What's wrong?'

'Just sorting it out.'

Janet poured herself a tumbler of white wine and lit a cigarette. 'Are you still in love with him?'

Jakes looked at the pool. 'Yes.' Then she said briskly, 'But tell me about you.'

'Me? Oh, I'm in hell of a lot of trouble.'

'What do you mean?'

'Pregnant, and not by my bloody husband, who, when he finds out, will not be very pleased. That's not done in the best Roman society.'

'Is he here now?'

'Thank God, no. He's in Porto Ercole with one of his little tarts. *Mariage à la mode romaine*. What isn't *à la mode* is me being pregnant, and not by him.'

'When's he back?'

'He's usually away a month, and this time the longer the better. It'll give me time to deal with this.' She patted her stomach as she drank from her glass. 'That's where Nurse Page comes in.'

'Nurse Page?'

'Helen. She works for a quack who'll do it – provided he's paid enough.'

Helen joined them. 'Maria's bringing the lunch,' she said.

'I've been telling Jakes that you're going to fix my little problem, Nurse Page.'

'It's not so easy in Italy, Janet.'

'Oh yes, it is, and it's got to be done soon.'

Maria appeared with a dish of antipasto, a salad and bread. She laid places before Jakes and Helen, but Janet waved hers away and poured herself more wine.

'They ask questions and there have to be reasons,' Helen said when Maria had gone.

'Not if it's rape. You tell them it was rape. It certainly felt like it.'

'They ask questions even if it is rape. We had a girl only last week. She's French – said she'd been raped in England the night before she flew to Rome, but she hadn't reported it. She just came here and said nothing.'

Poor little bitch, thought Jakes. She knew what she'd have done if she'd got pregnant by Tabbitt.

'And this one certainly didn't want any questions asked.'

'Who does!' Janet interrupted, pouring herself more wine.

'Well, I'm just explaining. She just came along and put down her cash and said she wanted an abortion. Didn't say anything about herself, why she'd been in England or why she came away so quickly and never reported what had happened. It sounded as if she'd thought up the rape story only when she got here.'

Janet lit another cigarette. 'The girl said she'd been raped.'

'Well, why didn't she stay in England, where she could get an abortion just by asking for it? I'm just trying to explain, Janet, it's not so easy as you think.'

'Bollocks,' said Janet. 'I'll pay.'

As Janet and Helen went on arguing, Jakes stared over the blue water of the pool to the lawn and the rose-beds and the line of cyprus trees and umbrella pines in the garden beyond. Not even her old friend's trouble really interested her. All she could think of were her own problems. She helped herself to some wine. She had done what Mark wanted by arriving here with him, but wouldn't be any use to him now. She'd be better at home, waiting for him. Provided he came back.

Gabriella Fontini had taken Mark to a small restaurant near the Palazzo Spada for the lunch to which he had so unexpectedly invited her. She drew out a chair from an outside table beneath the canopy, bordered from the street by tubs of bushes, but he took her by the elbow and steered her inside. He chose a table and sat her with her back to the door, seating himself so that he could see outside.

'You have to be so careful?' she enquired.

'Perhaps.'

'Your wife? Your mistress?' She was smiling at him, and he smiled back.

'No,' he said, 'neither.'

'Who, then?'

'People who might be curious.'

The waiter came, and she ordered – mozzarella and tomato and Pellegrino water. Mark studied her over the menu. She was very beautiful, tall and slim, perhaps in her early forties, her skin alabaster white, and her nose slightly tilted above a soft, full mouth. She had black hair which fell to the shoulders of her expensive floral silk dress. She wore no wedding-ring.

'I'll have the same,' he said, putting down the menu. 'And a bottle of Frascati.'

At the Via Giulia, all that Carla had said was that Mark needed to trace a young girl who had recently come to Rome. He thought official enquiries might have been made about her from London, and Carla asked if Gabriella, through her connections, would be able to confirm it.

'I have a friend who might know,' she had said.

'Could you ask him?' said Mark.

'Him?' She smiled. 'Yes, you're right, it's a him, and he's in a position to know about such matters – if the enquiries are official.'

'How soon could you find out?' He had spoken very abruptly, and she raised her eyebrows. 'I'm sorry. I didn't mean to be rude. But it is very urgent.'

'If it is so urgent, perhaps I might be able to find out by tonight. I happen to be seeing my friend this evening.'

It was then, to Carla's surprise, that Mark had asked Gabriella to lunch and she had at once accepted. Carla watched them as they went down the stairs from the terrace. They look good together, she thought. But Gabriella was a figure in Roman society, a beauty with a powerful lover. It would be unwise of Mark to become involved.

At the restaurant, when their food had come and Mark had poured some wine, Gabriella asked, 'Why is it so important for you to find this girl? Is it a love affair?'

He shook his head. 'No, it has nothing to do with love. It has to do with murder.'

'Murder!'

'Yes. The murder of my brother in England.'

She stared at him, and then said, 'I'm sorry.' He shrugged, and she went on, 'But what has this girl to do with the murder?'

'My brother was killed by a car-bomb. She could have been one of the people involved in planting it.'

'Isn't that a matter for your police?'

'It is. But I don't think they're trying very hard – or not hard enough for me.'

'Why not?'

'There are reasons.'

She waited for him to say more, but he did not elaborate. She went on, 'So you are doing their job for them?'

'In a way.'

'You are not working for the government?'

'No.'

'Are the people who might be curious to see who you are with, the government?'

'Perhaps.'

She studied him across the table, her dark eyes moving from his face to his hands and the long fingers round his wine-glass, with the gold signet ring on the small finger of his left hand. 'For you, then, it is a family matter?'

'Yes. It is personal.'

'This is Italy,' she said. 'Looking for people who might have been involved in murder can be dangerous.' He shrugged again, and after a pause, she asked, 'Do you know this country?'

'I have been here once or twice. Umbria and Tuscany.'

'Never to the south?'

'No,' he lied. He had been to Naples over the affair of the naval spy three years back.

'Italy is divided into two. The south is very different. I come originally from the south, from near Naples. I still have a house there, in the hills behind the city, overlooking the bay. It is very beautiful, but I go there very rarely. I have lived for many years in Rome.' She was watching the set of his mouth and his eyes, and the unruly lock of black hair which every now and then he swept from his forehead. 'So it would help, if you could discover what London has officially asked about this girl from the Italian authorities.'

'Yes. Could your friend do that?'

'He probably could.' She looked again into his eyes. He is obsessed, she thought. But he is very handsome. 'Where do you live?'

'In London.'

'I like London. My cousin used to be the ambassador there, and I often used to visit. Do you play cricket?'

He laughed. 'No, I don't.'

'I thought all Englishmen played cricket.'

'Not now. My hobby, or rather sport, is rock-climbing.'

'That is a dangerous sport. But then, you are a man who obviously enjoys danger. What do you do when you are not doing the work of your police?'

'I work in an office.' He had his eyes on her soft, full mouth.

They had finished eating, and she asked suddenly, 'Do you know this city?'

'Not well.'

'Then you should see a little of it while you are here. There are two Romes – Renaissance and Classical Rome, pagan Rome, which is the Rome I prefer. In the Colosseum, some say you can still smell the blood.' He was paying the bill as she spoke, and he looked up, surprised. 'If you like, I will show it to you,' she said, getting to her feet.

'I would like it very much.'

She put her arm through his as they left. In the taxi, she leaned against him. The scent she was wearing was heavy and exotic, almost overbearing in the back of the car.

They went first to the Vatican, then to the French church, to see the Caravaggios; then up the hill to the Gianicolo gardens where they leaned over the wall, looking at the panorama of the city below, her arm again through his.

'Now pagan Rome,' she said. At the Colosseum, she led him through the arches up the stairs to one of the tiers overlooking the floor of the whole amphitheatre. 'Can't you smell the blood?' she asked, taking him by the hand.

He looked at her, surprised again. 'No,' he said. 'I can only think of the wretches who died here in such agony so many centuries ago.'

'You are very English,' she said. She took him back to the Palazzo Borghese, where she had an apartment in the entresol – a long, low set of inter-connecting rooms each with the ceiling decorated with a fresco.

'This is magnificent,' he said. On a small table he noticed a photograph in a silver frame of a distinguished-looking man with white hair, dressed in some kind of uniform with a sash; the friend, he presumed.

A manservant in a white coat brought them tea. As he drank he could feel her studying him. Then she said, 'You must go now.'

She led him to the front door and as he was leaving kissed him lightly on each cheek. 'Come back at half-past ten. I may then have news for you.'

Outside he waited, standing behind one of the pillars at the entrance. At six o'clock precisely two black limousines drew up at the barrier leading into the courtyard of the Palazzo Borghese, the first obviously a police car. In the back of the second, looking even more distinguished than he did in the photograph, sat Gabriella's friend.

FOURTEEN

Jakes rang Mark's room. It was eight o'clock in the evening.

'Had a good day?' she asked.

'Interesting.'

'Let's have dinner.'

At the restaurant, they sat at a table under the awning. She told him at once, 'I'm going home, Mark. Tomorrow. I can't be of any help to you here, and I can't sit around in the hotel all day.'

'What about painting?'

'No. I don't feel like painting, not in the city. If anyone wants to know, you can say I've been called home.'

'Won't you stay another day?'

'No, I've no part in what you're doing. I'm only in the way.'

'I'll miss you.' He put out his hand and she let it rest on hers. 'I'm very fond of you, Jakes.'

She looked at him and smiled. 'What a lovely Pommy word! And I am very fond of you, mate. So let's see what happens when you get back. Unless you want me to move out?'

'No, of course I don't. I'll be back in ten days at the latest. If I have no luck here, I may move on.'

'Where to?'

'Malta, Cyprus.'

She looked at his face. There was nothing to be done until all this was over. 'Let's get out of here,' she said. 'It's too hot.'

When they had reached Piazza Navona, he said, 'What about a nightcap?' and they sat down at a café.

Gorgio Rosetti had followed them from the hotel to the restaurant. Now he sat at a table behind them, trying to listen.

'How was Janet?'

'In trouble.'

'I'm sorry.'

'Not so sorry as Janet. She's pregnant – and not by her husband. There was a nurse there, and Janet was getting her to fix it. She's an Australian who works for a doctor in the Via Cavour and was telling Janet about a French girl who had come from London.'

A noisy group of Germans came and took the table next to Rosetti, who now could hear nothing of what the girl and the tall Englishman were saying.

'The girl said she'd been raped.'

'Man's inhumanity . . .'

'Yes, to women.'

He paid the bill. 'Have you booked a seat?' She nodded. 'Have you any money?' She shook her head. 'I'll pay the hall porter for the ticket and leave some pounds with him for you to collect in the morning – and a cheque for London. What about lire?' Again Jakes shook her head. 'Then I'll leave some lire. You'll need that for the taxi. And when you're back, will you do something for me? Will you phone my friend Godfrey for me? He went home this morning.'

'Sure. Where do I find him? He told me he lived in the country.'

'He'll be in London, but not until fairly late tomorrow. His number is 489 5000. Shall I write it down?'

'No, I can remember that. 489 is the same as ours. 5000 is easy. What'll I tell him?'

'That I'll be in touch in a day or two.'

'Let's go,' she said.

At the desk, while Jakes waited for her key, Mark said, 'Will I see you in the morning?'

'No. Next time it'll be in London.'

At they walked to the lift he bent forward and she let him kiss her on both cheeks. Then she took his hand in her two hands and kissed him on the lips.

'Good-bye, Pom.' She put her hand on his cheek. 'And watch yourself. Don't get into trouble.'

'Be there when I get back,' he said. 'And don't forget Godfrey.'

'I know, I know. 489 5000. I can't forget that.' She blew him a kiss as the lift door closed on her.

It was too early for his rendezvous at the Palazzo Borghese so Mark walked back to the café in the Piazza Navona and sat drinking, watching the crowd around the Bellini fountains.

Rosetti had seen them walk across the square to the hotel. I shall call on you a little later, Mr Somerset, he thought, when I have dealt with the other and collected a little more money. And then the two of you, the Englishman and the Turk, can fight it out over the girl whom you are both so keen to find. The Turk, however, would have a head start. He had, after all, paid most. Then he, too, got up and left.

At the corner of the Piazza della Minerva, Giorgio Rosetti stopped to check if the Turk had arrived. When he saw the back of the bulky figure sitting in the shadows at the front of the café, he threaded his way through the tables and, as he had at their earlier meeting, pulled back a chair and sat before the other had seen him.

'You are finding your way around Rome very well,' Rosetti said as he beckoned to the waiter and ordered Strega. 'We must celebrate, for I have news.'

'What does that mean?'

'It means that I may have located a person who could be the girl you want. But only you can tell if it is.' He looked at Andreas, and sipped from his glass. Andreas took out his wallet and pushed across the table a bundle of banknotes pinned together. Rosetti took it and tucked it into the inside pocket of his bronze jacket. Then he said, 'It has not been easy finding her – if it is her.'

'That's why you've been paid so much.'

Rosetti looked at him. He'd teach him some manners! 'Since we last met,' he said, 'I've learnt that this girl is more important than I thought.'

'From whom?'

'From others, who are also interested in finding her. So perhaps I should speak to those who sent you.'

'Your orders were to deal with me.'

'I was told you needed help and that I was to give it. Now that I have some information, I think it'd be best if I were to speak directly to those most interested.'

Andreas played with the spoon in his coffee-cup. He understood well enough what this was about. 'My chief would not be pleased if you were to do that. And, anyway, he's on a boat, at sea.'

'There'll be a radio link. Telephone him.'

'Even if I could, I wouldn't – merely because you ask.'

'Where is he sailing to?'

'That's his business.'

'You said you had to be in Naples tomorrow?'

'Yes, to meet someone you've heard of.'

Rosetti looked down at his glass. Then he drank. 'Genaro?'

'Yes. So, you see, I'm in excellent company – and my friends won't be pleased if, because of you, I don't get there tomorrow. Now, tell me who are the others looking for the girl.'

'They are English. From London.' Rosetti had his eyes on Andreas' wallet on the table in front of him.

'And you are getting paid by them also.' It was a statement, not a question. Then Andreas took from the wallet two slim bundles of 100,000 lira notes, pinned like the one he had already handed over. He put the wallet back in his pocket and placed the two bundles on the table side by side, with a hand on each. 'When you give me the information, you may have one. When I have confirmed that it is accurate, you shall have the other.'

Rosetti looked down at the soft, brown hands covering the bundles of notes and then up into the other's dark eyes. 'So you and I must meet again tonight.'

'Where?'

'There's a club at the corner of the Campo dei Fiori called

Gianni's,' Rosetti said. 'Meet me there after midnight. I won't be there before that. Ask inside for me.' He took from his pocket a slip of paper and passed it across the table. At the same time he gently prised Andreas' left hand from one of the bundles and pocketed it.

Andreas read from the paper. 'Is it a house or an apartment?'

'It is an address.'

Andreas put the paper and the second bundle of notes into his pocket. 'Show me on the map.'

Rosetti showed him. 'You'll need a taxi,' he said.

Andreas rose. 'I shall be at Gianni's at half-past midnight.' Then he walked away towards the Corso.

Now, thought Rosetti, for the English. The same night porter was on duty in the Hotel Raphael. Once again he handed him money. 'I wish to speak with the Englishman, Signor Somerset. It is urgent.'

'He's gone out.'

'Where can I find him?'

The porter shrugged. Rosetti thought for a moment. 'I wish to telephone.'

The man pointed to the booth by the corner of the desk.

Andrina, Carla's maid, answered. Carla too was out, and not expected home until late.

'I shall come to the Via Giulia with a note for the Signora. It is very important that she gets it as soon as she returns. I shall ring the bell in five minutes.'

At a table in the lobby, he wrote:

I must speak with the Englishman, but he is not at his hotel. If you can contact him, tell him I have left a message for him. He is to come to Gianni's in the Campo dei Fiori and ask for Rosetti. He must be there before midnight. Not a moment later or I shall be gone. Warn him that certain people from the south are also very interested in the task you gave me.

He underlined the words 'before midnight'. To the porter, he said, 'If Signor Somerset returns, tell him Giorgio has been to see him and that he's to come to Gianni's in Campo dei Fiori immediately.'

At the Via Giulia he handed over the note to Andrina. She placed the envelope on the pillow of Carla's bed.

Andreas paid off the taxi at the corner and walked slowly down the dark, narrow street. When he came to No. 18, he paused for a moment, sufficient for him to check that there was no window in the front of the house, only the studded wooden front door set in a shallow alcove. He walked on and stopped at a point where the Via Marco Aurelio curved and he was able to see its whole length. He stood in the shadows, looking up and down. There was only one light showing, and that was ahead of him, in the ground-floor window of a house at the far end. He retraced his steps to No.18, where he stood listening, with his back to the shallow entrance.

The street remained silent and deserted, so he turned and examined the dim light that shone faintly above the plate of an entryphone with a single bell. He pressed it and waited. When there was no reply, he pressed it again, then a third time, keeping his finger on the button.

Over the entryphone came a voice, harsh and angry. It was a woman's voice, but not that of the girl he knew. 'Who is that?'

'I have come to see Nadine,' he said in French. 'It is very urgent.'

'Who are you?'

Andreas put his lips closer to the entryphone. 'I am a friend. Tell Nadine I've come from London. She knows me. Tell her I was with her in England and I must talk to her.' There was no answer. He went on, 'It is very important that I speak with her. She's in danger.'

Still silence; then, 'Wait.' So Nadine is not alone, he thought; but it had been the voice of a woman. 'What is your name?' It was the same voice.

'Nadine doesn't know my name, but she knows me. Tell her it was I who brought her from Marseilles to Kilburn where she shared the caravan with the Irishman. She's in great danger. I must talk to her.'

'Wait there.'

From beyond the bend in the street, he heard the voices of a man and a girl, laughing. A door slammed; then came the roar as the engine of a motorbike was kicked into life. He pressed himself into the alcove with his back to the street as the machine swept past. He turned and could just make out the shape of a girl on the pillion clinging to the back of the rider, before the rear light disappeared and the noise of the engine faded. Then he heard bolts being withdrawn and the lock turning. The door slowly swung back, but only for a few inches, held by a chain. A beam of light shone on his face, and he raised his hand in front of his eyes.

'Move back,' said the voice he had heard over the entry-phone. 'And take your hand from your face.'

He stepped back a yard into the street, turning his head away as the beam from the torch moved up and down. Then it went out. Behind the door he could hear voices, the chain was unhooked and the door swung open. He stepped quickly into a small hall, dimly lit by a lamp standing high up on a ledge at a corner of a flight of stairs directly facing him. Behind him he heard the front door closing and the noise of the bolts and the lock.

At the foot of the stairs, a torch in her hand, stood Nadine. She raised it and shone it on him again, and again he put his hand to his face, shading his eyes from the light. 'What are you doing here?' she said. 'What do you want?'

'I have come to warn you,' he said. The light was still in his eyes. 'You're in great danger.'

'What do you mean?'

'You're in great danger,' he repeated. 'We must talk.'

The torch was extinguished and he could see her silhouetted against the lamp on the staircase. At his back he could hear the breathing of the other woman.

'Come up. Tina is behind you,' she said at last, and turned and walked up the stairs. As he followed, he heard the other behind him. Halfway up, when he was under the lamp on the ledge, he turned and saw that on the stairs behind him was a square, broad-shouldered young woman holding a long kitchen knife.

He smiled at her ingratiatingly. 'I've come as a friend. You'll not need that,' he said, and continued up the stairs.

At the top Nadine was waiting, and when he was two steps below her, she turned and he followed her from the landing into a large half-furnished room, dimly lit by a single lamp on a wooden table. In the far left corner, behind a half-drawn white net curtain, he could see a large double bed, the bedclothes turned back and tumbled. To his right, unlit, stood an old-fashioned stove with a tall pipe disappearing into the ceiling; to his left, an open french window, through which he could see a balcony with an iron rail and beyond it the tops of small trees. In the centre, beside the table nearer him, was an armchair; on the other side of the table where Nadine was standing, a sofa.

She was dressed in a long white shirt hanging loose over dark slacks, her hair tousled and her feet bare. Behind her, to his right as he faced her, were a pair of doors. The kitchen, he thought. A bathroom? Or another bedroom?

'How did you find me?'

'Does that matter?'

'It does. How did you know I was here?' The long, heavy torch was still in her hand by her side. He heard Tina close the door behind him.

'Others found you. I learned where you were from them, although they do not know I know. I came straight away to warn you.'

'What do you mean?'

He went over to the balcony and looked out. As he had thought, it overlooked an inner courtyard. There was no light in any of the surrounding buildings. Without a word he drew the curtain. Then he turned to face Tina, who was by the door. 'When you let me in, did you see anyone?' She did not reply. She was still holding the knife. He said to Nadine, 'They know you're here.'

'Who? The police?'

'No, the people you worked with in England. They're looking for you.'

'Why?'

'Something has gone wrong in London. We discovered that they know you're here and they are coming for you.'

'Who is we? And who are they?'

'My friends; and the others are the Irish.'

'How did you discover the Irish knew where I was?'

'From one of them.'

'I don't believe you.'

'You must.' He sat in the armchair. He was still facing Nadine and he heard Tina come and stand behind him. 'You never sent the ticket from the car-park. The police traced the car to Kilburn. You should've done what you were told.' Nadine did not reply. 'The man you worked with,' he said, 'is dead.' The girl put her hand to her throat. 'Yes,' he said. 'His throat was cut. He was found in his lodgings in Kilburn about a week ago, killed by his own people. They think you and he have betrayed them. Now they're looking for you.'

'How do you know all this?'

'I told you we have an informant, one of them. We didn't know where you were in Rome, but they managed to trace you. How, I don't know. When we discovered this, I came immediately.' He raised his hand to his top pocket and he heard Tina take a step forward. He pulled out a red handkerchief and mopped his face.

'You've been following me since I've been here?'

'Not I. I only found you because they traced you.'

'How did they find me?'

'I do not know. They sent people to Rome.'

'Why should they want to kill me?'

'Why did they kill the man? You did not do as you were told and, as a result, you set the police on to them. The man came back from Dublin when he'd been told to stay away. So they didn't trust him. He told them he was going to meet you.'

'He did not know where I was.'

'Maybe not, but they thought he had betrayed them, so they killed him. And they think he will have told you too much about them.' He looked around the dimly-lit room. 'It's very hot. I would like a drink.' He wanted one of the women to fetch it. Then he would know what was behind the two doors.

'You can have water,' Nadine said. She turned and went through the left of the two doors, leaving it open. It was a small kitchen. So the other door must be the bathroom. She brought him the glass, and he drank greedily.

'I have been travelling all day.'

'From where?' she asked.

'From France.' Tina was still standing behind the armchair where he was sitting. He half-turned and said to her, 'There's no need.' He was smiling, and she could see the gold in his teeth. 'I've come here to help.'

But she remained where she was, directly behind him with the knife still in her hand. Nadine now sat on the sofa opposite him. He wanted Tina to move and sit beside her. He needed both of them in front of him. It would be easier then. 'Why is your friend behind me?' he asked.

'It does not matter. You've been following me since I have been in Rome.'

'I arrived in Rome only today, about an hour ago. If anyone has been following you, it was not me. It would have been the others.'

'I'm glad about the man,' she said suddenly.

'Why?' he asked, surprised. 'Don't you understand? Now they'll come for you. That's why I came to warn you. I've come a long way to try and help you.'

'Why have you?'

'Because we owe it to you. If they needed to kill him, that's their affair. He was one of theirs. You are not.' He put the glass of water on the floor beside him and began to remove his jacket. 'It's very hot.' He sensed Tina move nearer to him. 'It's all right,' he said over his shoulder. He had his jacket on his lap and he picked up the glass and drank again. 'If you choose to stay,

124

that's your business. I have done what I can. I'm leaving Rome tonight.' He looked at his watch. 'Or, rather, this morning. If you're wise, you'll do the same. Where you go, I don't want to know. I've done what I was asked to do. Do your people in Marseilles know you're in Rome?' She shook her head. 'Then it must have been the Irish who have been following you.'

Nadine looked at Tina behind him, and then down at her hands folded in her lap. She drew up her legs beside her on the sofa. Now, he thought, Tina will never seat herself in front of him.

'I may have been imagining.'

He put the empty glass down again on the floor. 'I've done what I can. I'll go now.' He rose, his jacket in his hand. Tina stood aside and he walked towards the door which led to the stairs. Then he turned. 'Have you a lavatory?' he said.

Nadine again looked towards Tina. 'In there,' she said, pointing at the other door.

He went into the bathroom and closed the door. Inside, he took the Beretta from the inner pocket of his jacket and the silencer from his trouser pocket and screwed it into place. He flushed the pan and ran the water in the basin. When he stepped out he had the pistol hidden under the jacket over his right hand. Both the women were now standing together by the sofa.

He walked straight past them towards the door to the stairs. As he went, he said without looking at them, 'It's up to you now.'

He put his left hand on the door-knob as though to open it, at the same time saying, 'If I were you, I'd get away – as soon as you can.' Then turning very slowly, he looked at them. They were only half a dozen paces away. 'Leave tomorrow. Go back to Marseilles. You'll be safer with your own people.'

He let the jacket on his right hand slip to the floor and they saw the pistol. He fired twice, very quickly, the noise of each explosion making little more than a muffled crack, less noise than the sound of their two bodies as they fell to the floor. As they lay there, he fired twice again, to make sure. When he was satisfied that they were dead, he carried the bodies and laid them side by side on the bed.

He ransacked the apartment and found money, some still in £50 notes, a part of what he had paid Nadine in England. There was more money in lire. He pocketed it, together with some trinkets from the dressing-table, emptied the drawers of their clothes and threw them on the floor, scattering a few coins and lire notes beside them. With his handkerchief he wiped the glass from which he had drunk and the handles of the doors. From the pocket of Tina's jeans he took the front-door key, and from a drawer, Nadine's passport in the name of Françoise Poincet. Then he went down the stairs and let himself out, locking the door behind him.

It was just past midnight when he arrived at Gianni's. Rosetti was sitting alone at a table in a corner, waiting for him.

FIFTEEN

Mark left the café in the Piazza Navona shortly before half-past ten. In the doorway of the apartment in the Palazzo Borghese, Gabriella greeted him. She put her hand to his face and then kissed him on the lips. She was wearing a long white wrap, gathered at the neck by a gold brooch and at the waist by a gold sash. Her scent was even heavier than it had been during the day.

'Leave your jacket here,' she said as she closed the door. 'And your tie – unless, as an Englishman, that will make you uncomfortable.' He threw them off and followed her into the inner room. She was bending over a cabinet in a corner of the room. 'Whisky?' she asked. He could see her gold slippers of soft leather beneath the folds of her wrap. 'I have done what you asked,' she said over her shoulder, 'although what I have to tell you may not be of much use.' She turned and handed him the glass. 'Come and sit over here.'

As she led the way to the other side of the room, she said, 'An official enquiry has come from London about a French girl, Françoise Poincet, who is one of several young women they wish to trace following the bombing of an English professor in Cambridge. They have also contacted the French Intelligence service, the DSGE, in Paris. Rome has warned them that they keep no register of EEC citizens.'

'Did London give Rome a description?'

'No more than you gave me.' She pointed to a sofa against the wall beneath a fresco of two cherubs holding the train of a smiling woman. She sat down directly in front of him in a tall armchair covered in red brocade. He noticed that the photograph in the silver frame had gone.

'They are checking with the French Embassy to see if there's any record of Frenchwomen residing in Rome, and the carabinieri are making enquiries among the French community. But they have said there is little else they can do.'

'It's what I expected. Is the enquiry being treated as priority?'

'Reasonably. The girl is not known to either the French or the Italian police.'

'I knew that.'

'What will you do now?'

'Wait to hear from my other informant. I am told he knows everything that goes on in Rome.'

'That is very improbable.'

'Everything, that is, in his world – which is certainly not the official world.'

'So you have two spies: I, in the great world, and the other in the underworld. But I warn you, the underworld in Italy can be dangerous. It is very hot,' she added, and she unfastened the brooch holding her wrap. It fell off her shoulders and lay on her lap, leaving her breasts naked. She sat in the tall chair very still and upright, like a statue, save for the rise and fall of her breasts. He put his glass on the table beside him.

'Carla told me you have a companion at the hotel,' she said.

'She's a friend,' he said shortly. 'She is returning to London tomorrow.'

She was about to ask more, but checked, and then asked, 'Does she know why you have come to Rome?'

'She knows I'm searching for a girl.'

She saw his eyes were on her breasts, rising and falling as she breathed. 'There is a fan on that table over there. Will you bring it to me?'

He went to the table and brought it to her. It was of black lace with a mother-of-pearl handle and she took it and began to fan herself, stirring the sides of the black hair which framed her face. He sat again on the sofa opposite, lounging, his hands deep in his pockets, his long legs spread out in front of him, watching the fan moving to and fro.

Suddenly she stood, looking down at him, one hand holding the wrap to her waist, the other at her side, the fan folded. With her naked torso and the folds of the wrap gathered low around her hips, she looked more than ever like some classical statue.

He got to his feet, and she turned and walked ahead of him from the salon, through a small ante-chamber into a large inner room, its low ceiling painted like the other rooms with frescos, cherubs surrounding a nymph. In the centre of the room was a great four-poster bed with bedposts reaching to the painted ceiling and hung with crimson drapes. She stopped beside it and turned to face him, letting the wrap fall to her feet. Her briefs, which were all that she now wore, were gold, matching the slippers.

He came and stood close in front of her and she began to undo the buttons on his shirt, but when he bent to kiss her she turned her face away. She began to stroke the skin and play with the dark hair of his chest, and she pressed herself against his belly. She bent her head and unbuckled his trousers, letting them slip to the floor, pushing down his underclothes. She took hold of him and led him to the bed.

Once more he bent to kiss her, but she shook her head and climbed up on the bed, pulling him down on top of her. He tried again to kiss her lips, but again she turned her head away. Suddenly she twisted and pushed him onto his back and mounted him. Only then, bending forward, did she press her mouth and tongue on his before leaning back, arching her back with her hands on either side of him, staring down. Then she took his wrists and pulled them over his head. She lowered her head again. 'Do as I say.' She straightened once more and began to move.

The telephone by the bed began to ring. It went on, insistently, on and on. With a curse, she leaned across, lifted the receiver and flung it down on the bed, where it fell close to his head, so near that he could heard the voice at the other end. It was Carla.

'Gabriella, Gabriella! Is Mark Somerset with you? It's urgent. He is wanted. Please answer! Gabriella, is Mark there?'

He twisted and picked it up. As he did so, Gabriella slapped his face and he warded her off with his other arm. She flung herself off him, rolling to one side, moaning, her head on the pillow.

It was half-past midnight.

'Signor Rosetti?'

'*Si*, Signor Rosetti *sta dentro*,' said the doorman.

Mark looked at his watch. It was a quarter to one. He pushed open an inner door and from the top of a small flight of steps carpeted in frayed crimson, he looked down on a strip of dance-floor between tables lining each side wall of a narrow, rectangular-shaped room, lit only by the lights above the band and small table-lamps with frilly red shades. On a small stage, a three-piece band was playing dance music. Half a dozen couples were dancing. Many of the tables were unoccupied. As Mark leaned over the rail, peering down at the dancers and the people at the tables, the music stopped and the dancers drifted back to their seats. A waiter in a grubby white coat came up to him.

'Signor Rosetti?' Mark enquired, but a roll of drums and the clash of a cymbal drowned his voice. The waiter beckoned him to follow and led him to a small table near the foot of the steps.

'Good table,' the waiter said in English, brushing the cloth with a rag he took from his pocket.

'Signor Rosetti?' Mark asked again.

The waiter put his finger to his lips. 'Cabaret,' he said, beaming. 'Good cabaret. I bring whisky.'

The table lights had gone out and a spotlight shone on a curtain over an entrance on the dance-floor to the right of the band. A man in a spangled jacket carrying a large doll, dressed like a policeman in carabinieri uniform, pushed through the curtain and ran up the three steps on to the stage. He sat, and for ten minutes he and the doll talked together. Now and then some of the audience laughed. But not often.

Mark looked around the room. Carla had described Rosetti –

fat, with a round face, probably wearing a bronze silk suit. There was no one who fitted that description. The ventriloquist now descended from the stage and, carrying the doll, took it among the audience, inviting them to ask questions which the doll answered. This made the audience laugh more. The spotlight that accompanied him gave Mark a better chance of looking round the room, but there was no fat man in a bronze suit.

The ventriloquist had come to a table near the stage where a group of four men, dressed in dark suits, were smoking and talking to each other, ignoring the performer. He stopped at their table, and one of the men looked up and nodded. The ventriloquist bowed, a respectful, deferential bow before he turned abruptly, waved to the audience and disappeared through the curtain. The drums began a roll and again the spotlight fell on the curtains which parted as a blonde girl in a long silver evening dress appeared and climbed on to the stage where she began to sing in a husky voice into a microphone. When she tossed her hair, Mark could see the dark patches at the roots where the hair had grown.

The arm of the waiter suddenly appeared over his shoulder and put a bottle of whisky and a glass in front of him. Before Mark could ask again for Rosetti, he had gone. He poured himself some of the whisky but after he had tasted it, he put the glass down and did not touch it again. Whatever it was, it was not Scotch whisky.

The girl now handed over the microphone and, followed by the spotlight, strutted down the steps from the stage and began to parade down the dance-floor. When she was near Mark's table at the end of the room, she put her hand behind her and pulled at the zip of her dress. Stepping out of it, she flung it over her shoulder. For a second Mark caught her eye. There was a look of ineffable contempt on her face. She winked at him and, in bra and briefs, marched back. At the stage, she swung her dress deliberately above the heads of the men in dark suits, making them stop their chat and look at her. One made a gesture with his fingers, and she laughed before she flung her dress into the wings. She sang again before she started another strut down the room to the rhythm of the music. At the table next to Mark's, she unhooked her bra, flung this over her shoulder, leaned over the table, twisting her torso, making her breasts dance just above the glasses. As she straightened and started to parade back, wearing now only black lace briefs, Mark caught again the look of contempt. On the stage she stood, feet astride, singing into the mike. Then she passed it to the band-leader, snapped the catch on the side of her briefs and throwing her hands high above her head posed stark naked, swinging her hips, bending her knees, pirouetting until the spotlight went out. When it came on again, she had disappeared.

The music and the dancing started. Mark saw the waiter standing against the wall and beckoned to him. He came to the table, smiling. Mark tried again. 'Signor Rosetti?'

The man's smile became even broader. '*Si, si*. Signor Rosetti.'

'Yes, Signor Rosetti,' said Mark. 'Is he in the club?'

'*Si, si*. Signor Rosetti always in the club.'

'Tonight?'

'*Si, si*. He here tonight. With a friend.' This time the waiter laughed and rolled his hands around his belly. 'Big, very big friend. Big as Signor Rosetti.'

'Are they still here?'

'*Si, si*. Signor Rosetti with his girl, the cabaret girl. Very nice girl, very nice figure. You like her? Signor Rosetti like her very much.' A man at a near-by table called him away.

Mark got up, and threaded his way through the dancers to the side door with the curtain. He pushed through the curtain and, as he did so, almost collided with a figure which brushed past him on its way back to the dance-floor. Mark half-turned; he got the impression of someone square and broad before the figure had gone. Behind him he heard a voice. He turned, and saw the ventriloquist.

'*Bagno.*' The man pointed to a door on his right. '*Bagno.*'

'I've come to meet Signor Rosetti,' Mark said in English.

But the man had turned away. 'No, no,' he replied over his shoulder, also in English. 'No meetings here. Lavatory over there.'

'Signor Rosetti . . .' Mark said, but the ventriloquist was opening the other door.

'Not here. Signor Rosetti not here,' he repeated, and disappeared.

Mark heard the key turn in the lock. He knocked, but there was no reply. He knocked again, but no one came. He looked to his left and then walked to the lavatory. Perhaps there might be a way from there into the back of the club, but once inside he found it was small and cramped, with a single washbasin, two stalls and two cubicles. There was not even a window.

The door of one of the cubicles was open and Mark looked in. It was empty. The door to the other was shut, and he knocked and called, 'Signor Rosetti!'

As he did so, he saw that the door was not completely shut and when he put his hand on it, it moved. But only by a few inches. Something prevented it from opening further. He pushed harder. Then he saw what was stopping it – a shoe, and above the shoe a thin, fawn sock – above the sock, the shiny bronze of the cloth of the trouser-leg. Lying face upward in a pool of his own blood, with bullet-holes in the belly and another just above the heart, was the body of the man Mark knew must be Giorgio Rosetti.

He stepped over the body into the cubicle, and bent to feel the corpse's skin. It was warm. The man could not have been dead for more than a few minutes, killed perhaps when his girl had been stripping on the dance-floor a few yards from him, and Mark remembered the figure which had pushed past as he had gone through the curtain from the dance-floor. He bent over the body and went through the pockets of the bronze jacket and the trousers, with difficulty turning the heavy body to get at the hip pocket. But there was nothing – no letters, no card, no driving-licence, no keys, no money, except for a few coins. But he had no doubt that this was the man he had come too late to meet.

He stepped back across the corpse and out of the cubicle, closing the door behind him. He could hear the faint sound of the dance music, and glancing down at his hands, he saw blood on them. He rinsed them under the tap, and went out into the lobby. Here the music was louder and he walked to the door through which the ventriloquist had disappeared. He tried the handle. It was still locked, so he turned and pushed through the curtain on to the dance-floor and walked slowly past the dancers to his table. He threw a 100,000 lira note beside the whisky bottle, and left.

Outside, he strode quickly through the deserted Campo dei Fiori and into the Via Giulia. At the front door of the courtyard to Carla's apartment, he pressed her bell and kept his finger on it. She answered almost immediately. 'I must come up,' he said into the entryphone. While he waited, a pair of lovers passed along the street behind him as he stood in the shadow of the doorway.

Then the big door swung open and Carla, in a long dressing-robe and slippers, let him in. 'I tried to reach you at the hotel,' she said as she closed the door. 'When you were not there, I thought you might be with Gabriella.' He followed her into the lift. 'Rosetti's message said you had to be at the club before midnight.'

He nodded. In the apartment she handed him the note Rosetti had left for her. While he read it, she drew the curtains. 'Rosetti is dead,' he said, and then he told her what he had seen.

Carla stood motionless by the window. 'You understand what this means?' she said.

'It means,' he replied, 'that the people whom Rosetti called "the gentlemen from the south" have taken a hand.'

'It will be the Camorra, the Naples Mafia. Their capo, who controls the whole of the south from Naples, is new – a young man called Guido Genaro. It will have been his people who have become involved. Rosetti wanted to warn us.'

'Why should they have killed Rosetti?'

'Perhaps they discovered he had been hired by us and they thought he might double-cross them. Or, if Rosetti found the girl and had told them, they thought he knew too much.' She shrugged. 'They'd know what kind of man Rosetti was, that he'd have sold anything and anyone, so they probably thought they'd be safer if he were dead. Who can tell?'

'Before I arrived, Rosetti had been seen talking with someone in the club. The waiter described him to me – a fat man, as fat as Rosetti himself.'

'If the waiter described him, he was not one of Genaro's. No one volunteers a description of the Mafia.'

'Then he is one of the others?'

'Perhaps. But whoever he was, you can be sure that the girl also will be dead. When Rosetti was killed, either he or they must have found her and then they would have no more use for him. What matters now is whether Rosetti told them about you.'

'He did not know about me.'

'Godfrey told him a friend was coming. He'll have found out all about you: what you look like, where you were staying. Rosetti will have had money from them, as well as from Godfrey. When you didn't show up at the club, he would have told them about you – for a price.'

'There was no money on him.'

'They would have enjoyed taking it back. If Rosetti has told them about you,' she went on, 'they will come after you. You should go home now.'

'No,' he said. 'If the girl is dead, then I have to follow them.'

'Genaro will have gone back to the south, and the south is his kingdom. He owns everything there: business, the politicians, the police.'

'And runs the South American drugs into Europe. That's why I shall follow him.'

'Rosetti is dead; the girl, I'm certain, will be dead. You should go home and report.'

'No,' he repeated. 'Not yet. I must find out more.'

'What can you do on your own?'

'Find the man who was with Rosetti. He'll be somewhere in what you call Genaro's kingdom. He'll lead me to the South Americans.'

'They'll know all about you. Rosetti will have sold you to them.'

'Perhaps.'

She looked at him. 'You need so much to avenge your brother?'

'Yes,' he said, staring back at her, 'I do.'

She shrugged. She remembered that Godfrey had warned her that nothing and nobody would stop him.

'Will you do something for me later in the morning?' he asked. 'Will you get a message to Godfrey for me?'

'You should speak to him yourself. He told you to keep in touch.'

'I know, but if I speak, he will want me to go home. It will cause trouble between us. Just tell him, from me, what I'm doing.'

'Which is what?'

'That I'm going to the south. I have a friend in Naples. I've worked with him before.'

'What of the girl at the hotel who came to Rome with you? You must not take her with you.'

'No. She is leaving for London at noon.' He looked at his watch. 'I must get back to the hotel. I have to make some arrangements for her. Do you know Godfrey's number in London?'

'He gave it to me.' Carla went to the window and looked through the gap in the curtains. 'Soon it will be dawn.' She turned to him, and he could see her age on her tired face. 'I'm also leaving Rome today for my house in Umbria, but I'll speak to Godfrey before I go.'

'Where is your house, in case I need to make contact?'

'It's in Armenzano, a hamlet in the hills near Assisi. An old farm, next to the church. I've only just moved in. It's very primitive, no running water. And no telephone, so you won't be able to get in touch.'

As he went towards the stairs, she asked, 'Would anyone in the club be able to recognise you?'

He turned back. 'There was the doorman, and I spoke to two inside the club – a waiter, and a man from the cabaret.'

'The police might start looking for you.'

'How could they trace me?'

'A foreigner in the club.'

'Who's to connect me to the foreigner in the club?'

She shrugged, and remained standing at the top of the stairs as he went down to the front door. 'If they did,' she said, 'Gabriella could say you were with her.' He stopped and turned. If he had not been with Gabriella, he would have met Rosetti. 'It was not sensible,' Clara went on, 'to have got involved with her.'

He did not reply. Then, with his hand on the door, he said, 'Will you be safe?'

She pulled her robe round her. 'None of us is safe if Genaro knows about you.'

SIXTEEN

Mark made the arrangements for Jakes with the porter. Then, when it was still very early, he went to the Palazzo Borghese. The manservant, surprised, opened the door, and he asked for Gabriella. He had to wait for some time in the salon. Eventually she appeared in a white dressing-robe.

'You are brave to return. What do you want?' She sat down.

'I'm leaving Rome this morning,' he said, 'and I wanted to explain about last night.'

'Why you suddenly rushed away from my bed? Or why you ever got into it?' She settled the folds of her wrap about her.

'The telephone call . . .'

'Oh, yes. Carla, checking on you.'

'As I told you last night, she had to find me. It was vitally important.'

'And she tracked you down to my bedroom.'

'It was very urgent. She knew we'd been together at lunch, and . . .'

'And thought we might breakfast together.'

'I didn't want to leave without seeing you and explaining. Carla had a message for me from the man I told you about, the man we'd hired to find the girl. When I turned up where he'd told me to meet him, he had been murdered.'

If he had expected to surprise her, he was mistaken. She just stared at him as coldly and evenly as when she had first entered the room. 'Is that why you're leaving Rome so hurriedly? Because of the police?'

'The police won't know about me.'

'Won't they? Or have you called to persuade me to provide

you with an alibi, so that you can tell the police you were with me – making love?'

'That won't happen,' he said angrily.

'Of course, I could tell them that we spent a very English evening – just talking. The Rome police would be amused.'

He stared at her angrily. Then he turned abruptly and walked to the door.

'Wait!' She jumped to her feet and ran to him and put her arms around his neck. 'I'm sorry. I'm sorry, but you left me last night so suddenly.' Surprised, he jerked his head back, but she pulled it to her and kissed him on the mouth. 'Does it mean I shan't see you again? Where are you going?'

'To Naples.'

'Searching for the girl?'

'She is probably dead.'

She was looking up into his face, serious now. He stood very stiff, wanting to get away. 'The man in the club, and now the girl. Both dead. Why are you going to Naples?'

'Because that is where I may find the people behind all this.'

She dropped her arms and turned away. 'Then let me help you. As I told you yesterday, the south is different from here. They don't like strangers asking questions. Where will you stay?'

'I don't know.'

She went to the writing-desk and wrote. 'This is the address of my house, the Villa Margherita. It's about a dozen kilometres south of Naples. Use it, if you like. Then no one will know you are there.' She handed him the paper. 'I'll telephone and warn the servants you're coming. They are very discreet.'

He took the slip of paper, and she again took his head in her hands and he let her kiss him.

'Phone me when you're there. Perhaps next time when we're in bed together, we won't be interrupted.'

He was glad to get away. As he drove through the outskirts of the city, he cursed himself for having become involved. Because he had been with Gabriella, he had failed to meet Rosetti. If he had not been with her, Rosetti might not have been killed. The girl too, if she was dead ... But he would stay at Gabriella's house. She was right. That way, no one would know he had come to Naples. He drove furiously, dangerously fast, making for the motorway to the south.

When Jakes appeared in the hotel foyer to get the taxi to take her to the airport, the hall porter handed her an envelope. In it was her ticket, the lire, a cheque and a letter.

> You were a darling to come. Please stay on at the mews. Please don't go. I know it'll come all right in the end. Thank you for everything you've done for me. All my love – and I mean it, all my love, from Pom.

For many years No.18 Via Marco Aurelio had been the pied-à-terre of a businessman who kept it to entertain his women on his frequent trips to Rome. For a few months, Tina had been his mistress. He had brought her from Tunis and installed her in the apartment, and it was in her arms that he had died of a heart attack eighteen months previously. To his widow, her son had described Tina as the daily maid, who, on arrival at the apartment in the morning, had found the dying man. In his will, the widow had been told that her husband had left the apartment to his son Mateo, and she was unaware that it had also provided for Tina to have the right to occupy it during her lifetime. That Tina now lived in the apartment was in recompense, the widow was told, for her loss of employment as well as the need to have a housekeeper to look after the property and attend to Mateo during his business trips to Rome.

When, the year before, Mateo had driven his mother from Caserta to join her daughter's family for their annual summer holiday in Porto Ercole, the Signora had insisted that, en route, they stop at Mateo's apartment and drink coffee with her son's housekeeper, the last person to have seen her husband alive. Tina had been warned that this year they would be coming again.

So at about ten o'clock on the morning after the murders, Mateo and his mother arrived at No.18 Via Marco Aurelio. When there was no answer to the bell, the Signora banged noisily on the door with the handle of her umbrella. Soon a small crowd had gathered to hear her complaining that the maid had no right to go out when she knew that her master was coming to visit. A neighbour volunteered that he had seen the young woman the previous evening with the girlfriend who was staying with her; the neighbour's wife said that she had been up early scrubbing her front doorstep and was sure that the girls had not gone out.

A patrol car from the carabinieri drew up, attracted by the small crowd. The Signora insisted on being taken to the police office, where she demanded that they force an entry into her son's house. After Mateo, prompted by his mother, had handed over money, a plain-clothes officer agreed to try to open the door with his bunch of skeleton keys. When this failed, the policeman forced the lock and broke in. The Signora angrily mounted the stairs. When she saw the dead bodies laid out on the bed, she fainted.

The radio and the midday papers carried the story of the murder of the two young women and gave the name of one, a Tunisian, Tina Makardi. The other was unknown. The police had been unable to identify her. The newspaper further reported that, from the appearance of the apartment, the young women had been the victims of robbers.

The midday papers also reported another killing – that of a stout middle-aged man whose body had been found in the lavatory of a seedy night-club in the Campo dei Fiori. It was much later that the police discovered that all three had been murdered by the same weapon, and not until the next day, when Helen and Anna at the Via Cavour had read of the murders and told the police, that the second girl was identified as Nadine Arletti. The only immediate consequence was that Helen's employment was investigated, and later she was required to leave the country and the doctor prosecuted. It was many days before Nadine Arletti was identified as the young woman who had flown to Rome from London on the morning of 9 July; using the name of Françoise Poincet.

At ten o'clock, Carla had rung Godfrey. He was out, and not expected until ten-thirty, eleven-thirty Rome time. She waited for him to return her call, fretting, wanting to be off to the country. It was midday when Godfrey telephoned. When she had told him what she knew, he was angry.

'I told that young man he was to do nothing without speaking with me! We must stop him and bring him home. I am seeing Brereton tonight. When he gets back to Italy, I'll send him after Mark.'

Carla set off for the country.

In the taxi to Leonardo da Vinci airport, Jakes read again the note Mark had left for her. Does he really love me? she asked herself.

She looked up. The taxi was racing down the motorway at a breakneck speed. She could not bear to look ahead so she stared at the flat countryside as it flashed past – and thought about Mark.

She was glad she had come, even though she now knew why he had asked her. But she also knew it was better to have left. It would give them both time, and she wouldn't have been any help to him in what he was doing. When he got back, and if he really loved her, perhaps this time it would be for ever. Suddenly she began to feel happy. The quarrel and Tabbitt were over; and Mark would soon be home.

She still had his note in her hand as the taxi drew up at the airport. She hauled her bag and painting-box out of the cab and just as she was paying off the driver, she noticed a large black limousine pulling up immediately behind her taxi. As Jakes picked up her bags to make her way to the check-in, a tall, dark woman jumped out.

'Excuse me,' the woman said in English, 'but are you the friend of Mark Somerset who was with him at the Hotel Raphael?'

Startled, Jakes replied, 'Yes. Why?'

'I've been sent to find you. I have some very bad news.' She spoke breathlessly, obviously very agitated.

'Bad news?'

'There's been a terrible accident. I've come straight from the hotel. They asked me to try and catch you before you left.'

'An accident?'

'Yes, earlier this morning when Mr Somerset was driving out of Rome. He's very badly hurt. The hotel was informed, and they sent me to find you.'

'Mark!'

'They've taken him to the hospital. He has asked for you and said you might still be at the hotel. He wants you to come. I know you're just leaving, but he keeps asking for you. I have the hotel car. We may be in time if we hurry.'

'Is he badly hurt?'

'It was a collision with a lorry, at about nine o'clock. I'm afraid Mr Somerset was badly crushed.'

A chauffeur came up to them, raising his cap. The woman spoke to him in Italian, and he took Jakes' suitcase and painting-box from her. The woman took Jakes by the arm. 'We must hurry. He kept repeating there was no one else.' Neither noticed the slip of paper which Jakes had let slip to the ground.

'The Embassy . . .' Jakes began.

'The hospital has informed the Embassy. Someone is on the way. I know this is a terrible shock, but we really must be quick.'

'How do you know all this?'

'I work in the Administration, and because I speak English, the manager asked me to come to see if I could catch you before you left. They've also left a message for the loudspeaker at the airport.'

'I've heard nothing.'

'No, it would be inside the building.'

The woman opened the back door of the car. By now the chauffeur was back behind the wheel. It was only then that Jakes noticed the smoked-glass windows. Suddenly a hand grabbed her from inside the car and pulled her in.

'What are you doing?' she began.

From behind her, the woman pushed her in the back and Jakes fell face down on the floor of the car, which by now had begun to move. She felt the woman scramble in, behind and on top of her and began to scream. A hand pushed her head down as the car gathered speed and she felt something hard and round and cold pressed against her temple.

'Be quiet, and do not struggle.' It was a man's voice, and she lay sprawled face downward as the car with the darkened windows sped out of the airport on the road south. Then she smelt the ether as her head was jerked up and the pad forced on to her face.

SEVENTEEN

When he had arrived at Heathrow the previous evening Brereton had taken a cab straight to Kent's home in Hampstead. A small woman with faded good looks and soft auburn hair answered the bell.

'Mrs Kent?'

'Dr Kent,' she replied firmly. She led him into the narrow hall. 'I expect you've eaten on the plane,' she said. He hadn't. 'So I'll get you coffee.'

'Thank you.'

She opened the door to the sitting-room. 'James is in the bathroom.'

Somehow he would be, Brereton thought. He had not often been in England since Kent had taken over, but he had heard about the atmosphere which had been building up among 'the friends' at Vauxhall Cross, and Godfrey had told him why the bombers had been able to get at Edmund Hamilton. While he waited, he wandered around the room. It was neat and tidy – like Kent himself, Brereton thought.

'I am glad to see you, Brereton. Please sit.' James Kent had bustled into the room, followed by Dr Kent with a tray with a pot of coffee and one cup. She left without a word. Brereton helped himself.

Kent stood, straightening one of the prints on the wall. When he had sat down he said, 'You know Piers Grenwich.' It was a statement, not a question.

'By sight. The last time I saw him was in Naples, when he came as ambassador to NATO on a visit to the naval base.'

'Do you know where Grenwich went after he'd left Naples at

the conclusion of that meeting?' Brereton shook his head. 'He went to Salerno. When he retires later this month, Piers Grenwich is planning to become Chairman of Grenwich Industries, an industrial and investment company which is managed by his brother George. Grenwich Industries is about to enter or just has entered into an association or joint venture with some interests in southern Italy. I wish to discover whom Sir Piers Grenwich was seeing in Salerno on his last trip, and with what interests Grenwich Industries is becoming involved.'

He has called me home, Brereton thought, about this!

Kent went on, 'It may not sound it, but the matter is important.' He was remembering that morning at the Foreign Secretary's breakfast table. And of what that minister was now putting around about the leadership, and the succession to the leadership, of MI6.

'Because the matter is so sensitive, I wished to speak to you personally as I want no written note or record made or kept about this enquiry. It must remain confidential to me and to you. Is that quite clear?'

Brereton nodded.

'I want you to go to Salerno to find out all you can about Grenwich Industries and their Italian connection. If you need to speak, call me here, never – and I repeat, never – in the office. I'll give you two days. A special courier will be waiting in Naples on Friday 20 July to bring me your report. This is where you contact him.' Kent handed Brereton a slip of paper. Then he went on, 'No hint of this matter is to leak out. I repeat, *nothing* must be said or recorded. It must remain confidential between you and me.'

'I understand.'

Kent rose. 'Keep away from the office tomorrow morning and spend it in the City, checking out Grenwich Industries. Then proceed to Naples and Salerno. Do not involve Jamieson or anybody else in Rome.' He looked steadily at Brereton. 'Now, doubtless, you will want to be off. I will call you a cab.'

Not, Brereton noted, his car. When he reached Hans Place,

Godfrey fed him on sandwiches and a drink. 'Rosetti is dead, and so is a girl who could be the girl concerned in the bombing.'

'I heard they're saying here it was the Irish.'

'It's not the Irish, although they may have had a hand in it. No, Carla and Mark believe this was the girl, and that she was murdered by the Mafia, the Camorra, as they're known in Naples, working for the South Americans. Mark left Rome this morning for Naples. I must get him to come home. Can you find him?'

'I'll try. I shall be there tomorrow night.'

'He's been to Naples once before, about three years ago when he worked with a man we employed called Alessandro.'

'I know him. I'll do what I can, but I have to go on to Salerno immediately.'

'See what you can do. And contact me here. Mark has deliberately avoided talking to me. He can't handle this alone. He's getting in far too deep.'

Mark arrived at the Villa Margherita shortly after midday. The drive, almost a track, led off the main road and wound through a belt of shrubs and umbrella pines up a steep hill to the villa, which stood on a plateau with a circle of gravel in front of the entrance. It was a two-storeyed house, its pale yellow-ochre walls covered in vines.

He turned the car on the circle of gravel and clambered out, glad to stretch his legs after three hours cramped behind the wheel. He had stopped only once, to telephone. Now he stood in the hot sunshine, arching his back and fanning himself with his map. Behind a clump of orange trees and oleanders, he could see a garden filled with yellow irises and white roses. A well-trimmed lawn led into a meadow which itself sloped down to what seemed to be a cliff-top, for, on the horizon, he caught a glimpse of the blue of the Bay of Naples. As he turned back to the car and bent to put the map beside his small field-glasses in the pocket in the dashboard, he heard footsteps on the gravel behind him.

He looked up and saw a middle-aged woman, with her grey hair drawn back and fastened in a bun, and large horn-rimmed glasses, walking towards him from the house.

'Donna Gabriella . . .' he began.

The woman nodded and beckoned. He took his grip from the car and followed her into a cool, dark hall, up a staircase, through a small book-lined sitting -room and a long drawing-room with white dustsheets over the furniture, into a corridor. The woman threw open a door and gestured for him to enter. The room was dark, for the blinds were drawn to keep out the heat of the sun. He walked over and let them fly up, flooding with light what he could now see was a bedroom which overlooked the circle of gravel where he had parked his car. From the window he could see the whole of the garden and meadow, the cliff-top and the sea.

'*No Inglese*,' the woman said, '*Mia figlia*, she speak.'

Mark drew down the blind, threw his grip on the bed and followed her back to the hall where a girl of about eighteen was waiting for them.

'I am Lucia,' she said, smiling at him. 'Donna Gabriella telephoned.'

She was small, very delicately-boned and dark, with large black eyes and a small straight nose. 'We have prepared something for you to eat,' she said in careful, precise English, her voice surprisingly deep. 'It is not much, but we were not expecting anyone before the Signora telephoned.'

In the dining-room, a large room filled with heavy furniture, a single place had been laid at the long oak table. Lucia signalled him to sit. From the matching sideboard, she brought a cheese-board, a basket of bread and a bowl of figs, and placed them before him.

'I hope this is enough. Tonight we shall do much better.' She began to pour him wine and, as he cut the cheese, she stayed, standing beside him. 'Goat cheese,' she said. 'Do you like it?'

'Very much.'

She watched him as he ate. 'How long will you be staying?'

'A day or so. I have to go to the city this afternoon. You speak English very well.'

'I learnt at school. Now I am at the university and soon I shall become a lawyer. My lover – at least he was my lover – is a lawyer, and he speaks English. Are you an English lawyer?'

'No,' he said.

'What are you?'

'I'm just on holiday.'

She still stood beside him. 'The lawyer is no longer my lover, not since May. But he is still my friend.'

He laughed. 'He must be sad.'

'I do not think so.'

Mark got to his feet. 'I must go now.'

Before he left, she gave him the telephone number. 'If we do not hear, we will expect you.' She came to the door and watched as he drove away.

In Naples, he drove along the Via Caracciolo and the Via Partenope with the bay on his right, past the causeway to the Castel dell'Ovo until he a found a garage in the Via Nazario Sauro. He parked and walked up the hill to the Palazzo Reale.

He bought a ticket and went up the Grand Staircase, and after wandering through some of the state rooms, he entered the small Court Theatre. He was early, so he sat in one of the red-plush seats in the back row of the small auditorium. In front of the stage, a group of tourists were huddled by the orchestra rails looking up at the proscenium arch while the guide lectured them. The group was English or American, for Mark could hear the guide speaking in English, telling the history of the theatre, describing the time of King Ferdinand IV, King of the Two Sicilies – 'known,' intoned the guide, 'as "Il Nazone" because of his great nose. His Habsburg queen, Maria Carolina, was the sister of the tragic Marie Antoinette.'

None of the tourists looked interested and the guide then led them round the side of the rows of seats to the rear, just behind where Mark was sitting. 'This,' the guide said, 'is the Royal Box.

In the year 1798, the English Ambassador, old Sir Hamilton, would sit beside them with his wife, the famous whore who seduced the Admiral Nelson. Later the Admiral took the King and Queen in his ship to Palermo to save them from the Revolutionary army of Bonaparte.'

Mark half-turned, listening. The tourists looked hot and bored. They're American, he thought.

'When the English Admiral returned,' the guide said, 'he hanged our Neapolitan Commodore Caracciolo from his yardarm for collaborating with Napoleon's army.'

The guide paused dramatically, to emphasise the enormity of the Englishman's crime. But there was no reaction from his audience. One or two leaned over the rail, fingering the hangings around the thrones in the Royal Box. The guide shrugged, and marched them out into the corridor.

'We now,' Mark heard him begin, 'enter the Throne Room.' Then his voice faded. Mark was alone in the small theatre. It was hot and silent and his eyelids began to droop. He neither heard nor saw the figure slip into the seat beside him until he felt the hand on his sleeve, and opened his eyes.

'I have kept you waiting,' said the newcomer. He was a small man dressed in a rusty black suit, middle-aged, with an iron-grey moustache and small, dark eyes the colour of raisins, which never kept still, darting to and fro, rarely resting on the person he was addressing.

'I only got your message at noon. I seem to have so much to do, although why I am not sure, for it is quiet here now. Not like the old days.'

'The good old days?' said Mark.

'I was useful then. Now I don't know how I shall live. So I was glad to hear from you. How long is it since we worked together during the time of the British naval officer and the Soviets?'

'Three years, Alessandro,' said Mark.

'Thanks to you, I got my money.' Alessandro loosened the button of his collar. 'There is very little to do now. Soon I shall be starving.'

Mark examined him, smiling. 'You appear to be in excellent health, Alessandro. And prosperous.'

'It is all show. I live off my savings. When I heard from you, my hopes soared. You have come to offer me much?'

'No, not much. It is a private commission – just you and me.'

'Not government work?'

'No. I want to buy something from you, and I want some information.'

'I haven't much to sell.'

'You will have what I need. A hand-gun with a silencer – and ammunition.'

Alessandro did not seem surprised, as though it were not unusual for a man seated in an eighteenth-century theatre on a hot afternoon to ask him for a hand-gun. 'It will cost much money.'

'Everything costs money with you, Alessandro.'

'What information do you want?'

'Information about two men. One you will know.'

'Who is he?'

'Guido Genaro.'

Alessandro stared at Mark. 'You want information about him?' he whispered.

'I want to see him. I want to see what he looks like. Most of all I want to see a man who is not one of Genaro's men but who, I believe, may be with Genaro.'

Another, noisier, group of tourists came into the theatre and stood by the Royal Box behind where the two were sitting, chattering loudly in Italian.

'Come,' said Mark, and they went out into the broad corridor and walked to one of the state rooms where they stood looking at the baroque furniture and the frescos on the ceiling above.

'The frescos,' said Alessandro loudly, looking about him, 'are by Francesco de Mura and Vincenzo Re.'

'As I said, the man who may be with Genaro,' said Mark, 'is not one of the Camorra. He is very large – very fat. That is all I know, and I want to find him.'

They wandered to the other side of the chamber and examined a pair of gilded candelabra on a chest. Mark turned when he heard footsteps behind him and saw the backs of a pair of sightseers, a man and a woman, standing in front of one of the tapestries. The woman was very elegantly dressed in a white linen suit; the man burly and tall. When the pair crossed the room, he saw that the woman was black. She was the woman in the white Mercedes he had seen driving out of the restaurant on the road to Valbonne and the next day at the garage near Mougins. The man with her was the one who had paid for the petrol and sat beside the chauffeur. You're a long way from home, Mark thought, as the couple wandered on.

Alessandro was tugging at his sleeve. 'It is not wise to show interest in Genaro or Genaro's companions.'

'I only want to see him, to see what he looks like.'

They walked on, through the Queen's bedroom into the chapel, the Oratory. 'Isn't he often in Naples?'

'Of course. But I have no wish to do anything about him.'

Mark handed him money. 'This is for the merchandise. As for seeing Genaro, try and arrange it for tomorrow. It cannot harm you to point him out to me.'

'With that one, everything and anything can lead to harm. It is foolish to have anything to do with him.'

They strolled out of the chapel back to the Grand Staircase. 'I will pay more,' said Mark as they descended the stairs, 'when you point him out to me.'

Alessandro said, 'If he's here.'

'I think he will be. If he's not, I'll go further south – and you will have to come with me.'

Alessandro stopped and turned, his dark, raisin-coloured eyes flickering over Mark's face. 'You are mad!'

'I shall telephone you tonight at nine o'clock,' Mark replied cheerfully.

Alessandro walked away towards the Piazza del Plebiscito, shaking his head.

*

Mark was halfway up the stairs on his way to his room in the Villa Margherita when he met Lucia coming down. She stopped and rested her hand on his arm and looked up at him. 'We have a good dinner for you.'

In the dining-room, she again poured his wine and stood beside him as he ate. 'You like the soup?'

'Very much.'

'What do you do when you are not on holiday?'

'I work in an office.'

'I think you are very clever.'

He smiled. 'No,' he said, 'I'm very ordinary. But you are clever. You speak English so well.'

'That was my lover,' she replied. 'The one I dismissed. He taught me.'

At nine o'clock, he went to the telephone. 'Tomorrow at ten o'clock,' said Alessandro, 'the trattoria at the end of the quay beneath the Castel dell'Ovo, facing the Excelsior.'

Lucia called to him. 'I will bring the coffee to the patio.'

When she had brought it with a bottle of Amaretto, she remained standing as she had at the dinner table. After he had finished his liqueur, she said, 'You should see the garden in the moonlight.' She strolled beside him through the scented garden to the lawn which led to the meadow. 'It is very beautiful,' she said. 'But I do not like it. There is something here I do not like.' Then she stretched up on her toes and kissed his cheek and ran back to the house.

EIGHTEEN

In Rome, the chauffeur lowered the window and handed out the large gold-embossed card. The policeman, especially smartly turned out for this special occasion, with his buttons and badges and toecaps of his shoes gleaming under the floodlight that lit up the gateway, took the card and called out the name. While his colleague behind him checked it on his clip-board against the guest-list the Embassy had provided, the first policeman looked through the side window into the back of the car. He took longer than he needed but, as he told his companion a moment later, it had been worth it. For there was light enough for him to see Gabriella alone on the back seat, magnificent in full evening dress, a gown of emerald green cut low in the front. Because the night was warm, her silver gauze wrap was on the seat beside her, leaving her shoulders bare. In her ears, around her neck, on her hands and on her head the policeman could see the sparkle of jewellery. Round her neck was a choker of five strands of pearls with a diamond at its centre; the ear-rings matched the choker and the white gloved fingers were encircled by rings, the most prominent an emerald. Her magnificent dark hair was crowned by a tiara.

She did not move during the policeman's examination but stared straight ahead and continued to do so when he stood back and saluted as the car moved on through the gates and up the drive to the Residence.

'The best so far,' the policeman said. 'Your turn next.'

But the next was a disappointment. It was a car with diplomatic plates and a cargo consisting of an elderly ambassador, his stiff shirt bulging untidily beneath his straggling white bow tie, beside him his stout consort in beaded, decorous black. They were waved quickly through. After them came a minister in a government saloon. He was known to them by sight, so he was sped on his way up the drive without even a check.

Outside the house, Gabriella climbed the broad stone steps from the drive. Ahead, guests were entering the main doors and she joined the queue in the hall as it wound its way slowly towards the grand staircase, at the head of which the Ambassador stood beside the guest of honour.

She felt a hand on her elbow. Her gloved hand was raised and held for a second beneath the man's lips. 'Giulio, I thought you would have been at the dinner,' she said.

'Oh no,' he replied, 'That was just for the two Prime Ministers, the Foreign Ministers and their interpreters.'

He was a tall man with a slim figure, olive-skinned with good features beneath his full head of silver hair. He was, she knew, in his early sixties, but if it were not for the colour of his hair, he would have been taken for much younger. He looked very handsome in his white tie, tail-coat and sash – as good as he looked in the photograph in her drawing-room.

Some of Gabriella's friends used to say, not to her face but among themselves behind her back, that there was something about his eyes, and the way the corner of his mouth turned down in repose, which made them uneasy. She knew he had many political enemies; that was to be expected of one who had been so long in government. But whether it was because colleagues shared the hesitation of Gabriella's friends, or because his political friendships were not strong enough, he had never risen beyond being a middle-ranking minister in the many coalition governments in which he had regularly featured over the past decade. He was never excluded because he had great influence in the party, especially in the south.

'My car was two behind yours. I jumped the queue to join you.' He had his arm on hers. 'Earlier this evening I met the Prince at the Caccia. He came to look at the pictures, and he talked about polo.'

155

A woman's voice called out from behind them in the queue, 'Gabriella.'

She turned. An elderly woman with white hair piled high under her tiara leaned forward and pecked her on the cheek. 'My dear, you look as beautiful as ever – or rather, I should say, even more beautiful than ever.' To the man at Gabriella's side, she inclined her head. 'Minister,' she said, as he raised her gloved hand to his lips. There had been a faint note of interrogation in the woman's intonation, as though it was a surprise to her to see him – and it had irritated him.

'This is an evening for politics as well as society, Marchesa,' he replied. 'Their Prime Minister is also visiting.'

'Of course,' she said. 'I saw the Englishman's arrival on television last night. He looked exhausted.'

Slowly they mounted the stairs. When Gabriella made her curtsy, she noted the look of approval in the Prince's eye and when she had passed, she heard him enquire of the Ambassador who she was. She moved slowly on towards the main reception in the ballroom, pausing at the door for Giulio Salvatore to join her.

'For the life of me,' said the Marchesa to her husband as they too mingled with the crowd in the ballroom, 'I cannot understand what that beautiful woman sees in that creature.'

'He's rich,' said her husband.

'Because he's a minister?'

'Of course. At least he's a Christian Democrat, not a Socialist.'

'Is he a Neapolitan?'

'No, Sicilian, from Palermo. But of no great family.'

'One can tell that. He makes me feel uncomfortable.'

'He's no different, my dear, from them all.'

Gabriella was standing with Giulio among the throng when a tall, bald-headed man squeezed through the packed room, making for them. 'Minister,' he said when he had got to them, 'I was looking for you. How good to see you here.'

He spoke in Italian, but Giulio replied in English. 'It is good to see you in Rome, Sir Piers. I heard you would be attending the conference.'

'Just one of the lackeys in attendance, ready to prevent the great men from doing or saying anything too foolish.' He smiled at Gabriella.

'Allow me to present Donna Gabriella Fontini,' said Giulio. 'Sir Piers Grenwich.'

Piers Grenwich bowed. 'If I may be permitted to say so, Donna Gabriella, you look enchanting. I fear you must be finding this evening a very English occasion and therefore very dull. No music, no dancing.'

Gabriella laughed. 'My tiara would topple off my head if I danced! Anyhow, it's far too hot.'

'It is, but perhaps a little Monteverdi in a corner of one of the salons would have made it more agreeable.'

'If one could have heard it,' replied Gabriella.

Piers Grenwich turned back to Giulio. 'Tomorrow the great men fly home and my duties are concluded. It is my last governmental conference. In one week I shall have left official life for ever and started a new life as a businessman. And then,' he twinkled at Gabriella, 'I shall be very much richer.'

'I heard from your brother George that you are joining his board after your retirement. I am meeting him and his associates from my country tomorrow in Salerno.'

'So George told me, and he invited me to join you.'

A young man tugged at Sir Piers' arm. 'What is it, Jamieson?'

'The Ambassadress would like a word.'

Piers Grenwich turned back to Giulio and Gabriella. 'Do you imagine that there is some royal crisis? Whatever it is, I'd better go to her. *À demain*.' He bowed to Gabriella and pushed his way through the throng.

'What was the significance of that?' enquired Gabriella.

'His brother's company, which Sir Piers will shortly join as their new Chairman, has gone into partnership with some of my friends in Salerno. They need some development permits, so they've asked me to lunch with them tomorrow.'

'Was this evening's encounter arranged?'

'He knew I would be here. Doubtless his first task on the Board is to encourage me to grant them their permits. He little knows that it has already been decided.'

'They will get their permits?'

'As I said, the people in Salerno are my friends – good friends.'

She looked at him. 'Of course.'

They began to make their way through the main reception chamber to an outer room where they found two seats, and sat sipping champagne. 'Tell me, how is your Englishman?' Giulio asked.

'He has gone south.' She inclined her head to a passing couple. 'He is staying at the Villa Margherita. Lucia, my maid, is keeping an eye on him.'

'That is very advisable.'

Two men strolled past. Giulio rose hurriedly, and the two stopped. 'Foreign Secretary,' said the elder of the two in English, 'may I present one of my most important colleagues, Signor Giulio Salvatore. He is our energetic Minister for Redevelopment.' Giulio bowed. 'And his decorative companion is the Donna Gabriella Fontini.'

'Charmed,' said the British Foreign Secretary. 'Charmed, I'm sure.' Gabriella bowed. 'It is a great crush here. Is it not your experience, Signora, that ambassadors when they entertain always ask too many people? I suppose it's because they are not themselves paying the bill.' The English minister laughed jovially, and the two passed on. Giulio resumed his seat.

'Charmed, charmed, I'm sure! Gabriella mimicked. 'What a common little man.'

'He is said to be clever – or rather, as our people say, devious. But to return to the Englishman, his enquiries intrigued me.'

She turned her head and looked at him steadily. 'And me,' she replied, 'I found him most intriguing.' She rose. 'Come, we must circulate.'

They walked from the main room out on to the landing at the

head of the stairs. The receiving was, by then, over and they remained strolling and chatting for another hour. Then they left, separately.

At the end of the reception, the British Prime Minister slowly climbed the stairs of the Embassy to his rooms. He heard a voice behind him and, pausing, turned. To his annoyance he saw the Foreign Secretary mounting the stairs below him.

'That was a most successful conference, Prime Minister. A good meeting, crowned this evening, in nearly every sense of the word, by a splendid reception.'

The Prime Minister was exhausted, and looked even more tired than he had on the day before when the Marchesa had seen his arrival on television. He resumed his slow climb. 'Yes, Rex. It went well.'

'Some broken fences mended, eh?' The Foreign Secretary, now at the other's side, gave one of his jovial laughs.

At the landing, the Prime Minister put his hand on the handle of his sitting-room door. 'Yes, Rex, some broken fences have been a little mended.' He opened the door. 'Good-night, Rex.'

'Can we have a word, Prime Minister, before we turn in?'

The Prime Minister groaned inwardly as the Foreign Secretary followed him into the room. He looks worn out, the Foreign Secretary thought with satisfaction.

'It's about C. I told you the other evening at No.10 that I'm very concerned about the performance of James Kent as Head of MI6.'

The Prime Minister lowered himself into a chair. There was a decanter of whisky on the sideboard and he longed for a nightcap, but he did not want to offer any to his visitor as he did not wish to prolong the interview which had been forced upon him. 'He was your choice, Rex. You recommended him when Burne left only eighteen months ago,' he said wearily.

'I did, Prime Minister, I did. And, I confess, it was a mistake. None of us is infallible.' He laughed happily as he sat on the sofa.

The Prime Minister closed his eyes. But only for a moment.

It was wise to be on one's guard when talking with or listening to his Foreign Secretary.

'As I told you earlier in the week, Prime Minister, I'm satisfied that James Kent is not up to it. He made an error over removing the protection from the fellow in Cambridge, and he's not exercising proper leadership of the service. So I believe we must find a successor.'

'Immediately?'

'Yes, immediately.'

'It's very soon after Burne's departure.'

'I know, but the post is so important.'

The Prime Minister examined the Foreign Secretary under heavy eyelids. He longed for bed, but considered he would get there the sooner if he let the other do the talking. Rex, he thought, has some scheme. He was always scheming. He's going to propose someone to take over from Kent, and it would be wise to hear who it was.

'I talked with Dick after Cabinet, and he agreed that Kent ought to go. That bombing business was a scandal, and landed Dick in a very uncomfortable debate in the House.'

The Prime Minister nodded. He had been present to show support for his Home Secretary, who had handled a tricky Parliamentary situation very well. Rex, he knew, had not chosen to demonstrate his support for Dick.

'We both thought we ought to replace Kent with someone outside MI6, a diplomat, someone from the Office.'

The Prime Minister remained silent. He would check with the Home Secretary what exactly had been said after Cabinet on Thursday. Dick and Rex were not exactly bosom friends.

'I think I have the ideal man. What would you say to Piers Grenwich?' went on the Foreign Secretary.

So that's who it was. Presumably because Grenwich would suit him. But after his failure over Kent, anyone whom Rex recommended would need to be considered carefully, very carefully indeed.

'I know Piers well. He's just finished a very successful tour at

NATO but wants to retire early from the service. He's got plans to go into commerce, but if we were to offer him MI6, I'm sure we'd get him. He's shrewd, a man of the world, and he undoubtedly possesses the charisma that, after Kent, is sorely needed. His time in the NATO post would prove useful in the new job.'

Still the Prime Minister said nothing. The poor old bugger's half asleep, thought the Foreign Secretary, who went on, 'I've a very high regard for Grenwich. I thought he was particularly helpful at the conference this afternoon, didn't you?'

But the Prime Minister was by no means half asleep. Grenwich, he remembered, was the bald-headed, self-satisfied official who had chipped in a little too often and too lengthily at the afternoon meeting between the heads of government. It had been Rex, he now remembered, who had brought Grenwich into the discussions, and the fellow had taken the opportunity to read them all a lecture. He obviously thought a lot of himself. Odd for such a one to be Rex's choice. A more amenable type would have been more likely, so there must be some less obvious reason for Rex's selection. He would have to look into that carefully and talk to Dick when he got back to No.10.

The Prime Minister got to his feet. 'Well, when we get home, I'll consider it. It will be important to get it right this time, after what you say above the failure with Kent. It will need a lot of soundings. Now I must get to bed. Good-night, Rex.'

He's in very poor shape, thought the Foreign Secretary as he closed the door, very poor shape indeed. In his dressing-room, he tugged at his white bow tie and flung off his coat. The old fellow hardly took in a word of what I was saying, he thought. It can't be long before he goes. But it would be convenient to get Grenwich into place before the transition. Things, the Foreign Secretary thought as he composed himself to sleep, are going nicely – very nicely indeed.

Many miles to the south, the boot of the car was opened. Jakes lay curled in her sweat and body filth, her arms and feet bound and her mouth closed by tape. Her eyes stared up in terror as a rug was swiftly thrown over her and she was lifted from the car and carried into a house. Mark, she thought, oh God, Mark! What have you done? Why is this is happening to me?

NINETEEN

After spending the morning researching Grenwich Industries in the City of London, as Kent had instructed, Brereton arrived in Naples late in the evening. At his hotel, he made a number of telephone calls and then took a taxi to a bar in the Via Capodimo, arriving there at one o'clock in the morning. He kept the taxi, and on entering the bar walked to a table in the corner away from the door.

'I am very happy. The English are back, and you're keeping me busy,' said Alessandro, stroking his moustache, as Brereton drew out a chair and sat down. 'It is most welcome, because I and my family were almost starving.'

Brereton examined Alessandro's stout little figure and well-nourished face. 'I am truly sorry to hear that. I like to relieve the poor and the unfortunate.' He handed Alessandro a slip of paper. 'This is the name,' he said. 'I want the face, not the mask.'

'We all wear masks,' said Alessandro, looking at the note. 'Who needs to see anyone's naked face?'

'I do,' Brereton replied. 'At least I want to see this man's face. And by tomorrow night.'

Alessandro tore the paper into shreds which he burned over the ashtray, stirring the ash with the butt of his cigarette.

'You will know about him. Or you will be able to find out. You may even have known him – once,' said Brereton.

Alessandro smiled. 'No, I came from Castelvetrano, over the mountains from Palermo. This one was never one of the friends of my youth. Now he is rich and powerful.' He smiled again. 'But you and Mark Somerset are good to your friends – and generous.'

Brereton gave him money. 'Where is Mark Somerset?'

Alessandro shrugged. 'That mad one! I saw him today, and we meet again tomorrow.'

'Where is he now?'

'He did not tell me.'

'I have to be in Salerno tomorrow. Tell him I'm looking for him. Tell him I shall be at the Hotel Caracciolo tomorrow night, and I must speak with him.'

Alessandro shook his head. 'He will not listen. He has some mission. I don't know what it is, but he is mad.'

'Tell him it's urgent. I must see him.' Brereton rose from the table. 'We meet here, at eleven tomorrow night.' He turned on his heel and left the bar.

Next morning, Mark again drove to the city and left the car in the same garage. Near the Hotel Excelsior, he dodged through the traffic across the road to the side next to the bay, and walked past the gatehouse and between the walls along the two hundred yards of the causeway which led out to the towers and battlements of the Castel dell'Ovo. At the end of the causeway before the entrance to the castle, he turned down some steps and along the edge of the small marina to the cluster of trattorie and cafés. At the end of the quay next to the sea-wall and the bay, Alessandro, a newspaper propped against a coffee-jug, was sitting at a table under the awning of a café. He was facing the town, looking over the narrow strip of water of the yacht basin to the busy street Mark had just crossed. He had chosen a table with a view across the marina and the street to the entrance of the Hotel Excelsior.

Mark pulled out a chair and sat beside Alessandro, who lit a cigarette and poured him a cup of coffee. The sun was already warm. 'I saw your colleague last night,' said Alessandro.

'Who was that?'

'Brereton. He wants to see you. He's in Salerno today, but he'll be back in Naples tonight. He'll be at the Hotel Caracciolo.'

Mark nodded. He would not meet Brereton. Brereton would only have a message from Godfrey ordering him home. He had come this far, and nothing was going to stop him now. 'I like watching boats,' he said. Alessandro grunted and returned to his newspaper, and Mark took his small field-glasses from his pocket and made a show of swivelling round and training them on the great ochre walls and towers of the castle directly behind them. Idly he turned again to look at the bay over the sea-wall to his right, then to the little marina immediately in front of them.

'Where is he when he's not in Naples?' Mark asked, still holding the glasses to his eyes.

'Scario.'

'Where is that?'

'South of Salerno, near Sapri, on the Gulf of Policastro.'

They sat in silence. Mark lowered the glasses and drank some of his coffee. Suddenly Alessandro nudged him. 'Now. By the Excelsior.'

Slowly Mark raised the glasses to examine a small dinghy with an outboard motor pushing its way out of the marina, and then raised them casually so that he could see the road on the other side of the strip of water. There were two of them, two men standing on the pavement outside the hotel entrance. One was very fat, as fat as Rosetti, dressed in a crumpled grey suit; the other slim, with dark brushed-back hair, wearing a blue shirt and white slacks. Mark could even make out the chunky gold chains at his wrist and round his neck. He was carrying a blue baseball cap with a peak.

'He's younger than I expected,' said Mark.

There came a gap in the traffic, and the two men began to cross the road towards the shore side. When they were in the middle of the road, the traffic began again and the younger man took the older one by the elbow and made him trot to safety before the cars rushed past behind them. On the pavement the fat man stood for a moment blowing, and the other laughed before leading him to a gate under a wooden arch.

'The entrance to the Yacht Club,' said Alessandro, as the

two men disappeared down some steps. 'They will come out on the quay.'

Mark kept his glasses trained on the water's edge where the boats were moored, and the men reappeared at a point on the quay where a motor-launch was tethered. The slim man jumped on to the launch, turning to give a hand to his companion, laughing again at the other's clumsiness. When they were both on board, a crewman cast off and the launch moved slowly out of the small harbour into the bay. Gathering speed, it made off towards the south-west.

'They'll be making for Capri,' said Alessandro. 'If you're fool enough to follow, take a taxi to the vaporetti station at the Molo Beverello.'

'The merchandise?' Mark said.

Alessandro pushed back his chair and lowered the newspaper on to his lap. Behind it, he put his hand in his pocket and transferred something heavy into Mark's. 'The magazine's full,' he said.

'Another,' said Mark.

Alessandro looked at him, shaking his head. But he repeated the movement, and Mark heard the chink of metal against metal as another magazine was dropped into his pocket. Mark handed over money and left him.

Two hours later, he disembarked from the vaporetto in Capri. He strolled up and down the quay, examining the yachts and craft but there was no sign of the launch. After half an hour, he climbed the steep steps up to the Piazza Umberto, where he leant on the rail overlooking the harbour and with his glasses began to scan the larger yachts anchored further out in the Marina Grande. Dinghies and rubber boats with outboard motors fussed around, and speedboats towed skiers between the yachts.

Then he saw the launch. It was alongside a large seagoing motor-yacht with a dark blue hull and white superstructure, about a hundred and forty feet long, flying the colours of the Monaco principality. She had all the radar and equipment required for a long passage. Her cruising speed, Mark calculated, could be about fifteen knots.

As he watched, the launch, with a single sailor at the bow, began to move slowly from a companionway amidships on the starboard side of the yacht towards the stern. White-clad crewmen swung out davits and the launch was winched on board. Moments later they began hauling up the anchor in the bow, and the motor-yacht swung so that Mark was able to read her name on the stern: *Phydra*. And, below: Monte Carlo. When the crewmen had lashed the launch high up in the stern, they went for'ard, and two figures came from the cabin and stood together on the stern deck. Through his glasses Mark could make out the blue shirt of one; the other was tall and lean, with a short dark beard, dressed in white, and wearing a white panama.

By now the yacht had weighed and began to steam slowly to the entrance of the harbour. When she was beyond the headland, he saw her turn to port and disappear – making for the south. As Genaro was on board, the south could mean the bay of Policastro and his home at Scario.

Mark put away his glasses and descended the steps to catch the vaporetto back to Naples. Tomorrow he would drive to Scario, to find Guido Genaro's home.

In Salerno, Brereton parked, and walked through the narrow streets away from the port into the town until he came to a tall building just off the main square. He mounted the stairs to the third floor, knocked on a glass-fronted door and entered a small office. He was shown into an inner room, where he was greeted by a woman with grey hair severely brushed back from her forehead and secured at the back of her head by a tortoiseshell clasp.

'I am not ready for you yet. I shall have what you want later today,' she said.

'The man is important.'

'He is well enough known.' The woman rose from her chair. 'Return at three o'clock.'

Brereton walked back to the car and drove up the hill to Lloyd's Bahia Hotel, where he booked a room for the night. After he had left his bag, he descended to the foyer and chose a seat with a small table in an alcove from which he could see the hotel entrance. He ordered coffee, and took from his briefcase a file of papers which he laid on the table in front of him. Other groups, mostly businessmen, were sitting at nearby tables. Standing by the porter's desk was a tall, well-built man whom Brereton knew, from the photographs he had studied in London, was George Grenwich, managing director of Grenwich Industries and the brother of Sir Piers, the retiring British Ambassador to NATO, in whom James Kent was so interested.

After a few minutes a short, dapper man, with dark hair shot with silver, an olive complexion and immaculately dressed in a pearl-grey suit with a pearl tie-pin in his black tic, came through the swing doors of the hotel. He stood in the entrance, at his shoulder a square, burly man who looked carefully around the foyer. George Grenwich immediately left the desk, advanced towards the man in the grey suit and shook him warmly by the hand. The burly escort turned on his heel and disappeared through the swing doors, while George Grenwich led the newcomer to a sofa in an alcove on the far side of the foyer, a little beyond where Brereton was sitting. A document was produced, and the two studied it. A few minutes later, Piers Grenwich emerged from the lift and joined them. After a short conversation, the three walked towards the entrance. As they passed Brereton's table, the man in the grey suit said in English, 'This little expedition, Sir Piers, will give you some idea of the scope of our local operations.'

'We shall be back in good time for lunch with the minister,' he heard George Grenwich say. Brereton gathered up his own papers and followed them.

Outside the swing doors, the doorman was speaking into the telephone from the kiosk by the front door. 'Signor Bussento's car.' He replaced the receiver, and said to Brereton, 'Yes?'

'A taxi.'

The taxi came before the car. At the port, Brereton paid it off and walked along the esplanade to a café and ordered lemonade. After a quarter of an hour, he was joined by a slim young man in a white shirt and black trousers, carrying a leather handbag which he put on the table. Brereton eyed it, but the man shook his head.

'No,' he said. 'There will be nothing in writing.'

They stayed at the café for an hour, and then parted. Brereton walked to the port and stood for a time watching the cranes unloading a freighter, then he collected another taxi and was taken back to the hotel. At the dining-room, he reserved a table for two and went to the newspaper booth. He bought a paper and stood reading it near the lift. At twelve-thirty, the three he had been observing earlier re-entered the hotel.

'I'm going to my room to wash. Where are we lunching?' Piers Grenwich asked as the three entered the lift.

'In my suite,' replied his brother.

Two minutes later, a handsome silver-haired man, smartly dressed in a neat, dark suit and black tie, strode down the foyer, escorted by a senior hotel clerk and two aides. As they passed Brereton, one of the aides said, 'I have ordered the car, Minister, for two-thirty.'

They disappeared into the lift. Three minutes later, the escorts reappeared and the two aides went to the dining-room. Brereton followed.

To the head waiter, he said, 'My friend is delayed. I shall eat alone.'

There were not many lunching, but he was shown to a table across the room away from the two who had accompanied the minister. Brereton lingered at his table until the minister's aides rose to leave and then strolled after them. He was in time to see them join the minister, who appeared out of the lift accompanied by the man in the pearl-grey suit. The two stood talking by the swing doors, beyond which Brereton could see the black limousine waiting. The minister shook hands and, accompanied by his aides, climbed into the car and was driven away. The other car followed.

At the desk, Brereton told the cashier that he had been called away; he would not need the room, but would, of course, pay. When he had got his bag, he summoned his car and drove to the port. At three o'clock precisely he entered the office he had visited in the morning.

The woman began immediately. 'The report has been typed on plain white paper as you asked.' Brereton nodded. 'The deal has been finalised. They were at the lawyers' yesterday for the formalities.'

'What is being said about it?'

'That Grenwich needs cash, and the Calcestruzzi Salerno e Sarpi Spa to diversify. Financial circles here are welcoming it, although it is being said that Grenwich needed it more than Calcestruzzi Salerno, for the English company has much debt. The Calcestruzzi cash is being described as a life-saving infusion.' She handed him the file across the table. As he leafed through it, she went on, 'As you will see from the report, the Salerno company services much of the construction industry from its eighty-five ready-mix concrete plants and it owns thirty local quarries or gravel pits, as well as a number of greenfield sites. Before they can start the excavation of these, the company requires planning permission from the ministry.'

'Why have they agreed to a deal so advantageous to Grenwich?'

'The company is cash-rich and for some time has been searching for a European partner. The merger is attractive because it will help its core business through Grenwich's industrial connections in the United Kingdom and the Netherlands.'

Brereton looked at her across the desk. 'To launder its profits?'

'I have not used that term in my report.' She stared steadily at Brereton while he read on. Then she added, 'The merger on the face of it fits their strategic interests. The headquarters of the new group will be in London.'

'Has the Salerno company any formal association with any major construction company?'

'No, but it is a major supplier to the whole of the construction industry.'

'The name I gave you?'

'Yes, the Chairman. He is a greatly admired local figure, well known throughout Calabria. He has many friends in government,' she went on, 'and has excellent relations with the other political parties. For this reason, the company is expected to obtain the permits to develop the greenfield sites which it owns without difficulty from the ministry.'

Brereton took the papers she had given him from the file and put them in his briefcase. The file he left on the table. 'His personal life?'

'A wife, children. Signor Bussento is well respected.'

'Any link with the Contreras?'

She looked at him steadily. 'My report does not refer to them.'

Brereton persisted, 'They too have interests in the construction industry?'

'So it is said.' She stood. 'I cannot help you further. He has many friends, especially among the Christian Democrat ministers.'

Brereton slowly got to his feet. 'I understand,' he said.

A half-smile briefly crossed the woman's face, but she said nothing. He paid her in cash, which suited her and suited him.

He collected his car from the garage where he had left it, and set out for Naples.

Kent's courier came to the hotel at midnight and waited while Brereton completed his personal report, which concluded: 'His home is in Praiano, near Amalfi, where he lives with his wife and six children. It is not generally known, but he has also a villa in Sorrento which he visits, accompanied by his mistress, Angelica Reni. She is from Scario further to the south and is married to the brother of Guido Genaro, with whom he is friendly.'

The courier would be in London by noon the next day and Kent would have what he wanted by the afternoon.

TWENTY

The tall grim-faced woman brought a a slice of bread and a bowl of thin black coffee, laced with a sedative, to the room at the top of the tall house in which Jakes was imprisoned. The room was dark, the only light filtering in from between the slats of the shutters nailed across the window. From beside the door, the woman switched on the light, a single bulb hanging from a wire high up in the ceiling. Jakes, barefoot and dressed now in a long grey shift, sat on the edge of the bed. Her left ankle was manacled to a thin chain padlocked to a radiator. The chain was not long enough to allow her to reach the light-switch by the door.

The woman remained standing silently until Jakes had finished the coffee. She did not touch the bread. By now she was very drugged. When the woman picked up the hood to place it over her head, Jakes pushed it aside. 'No,' she said. 'No!'

The woman hit her, first a slap and then harder, with the back of her hand. Jakes fell on the bed. The woman leaned down and pulled her up. 'Do as you're told,' she said in English. Jakes could smell the garlic on her breath. 'Do as you're told or you'll really get hurt.'

She put the hood over Jakes' head, went to the radiator and unfastened the padlock. Holding the chain, she led Jakes out into the corridor to the bathroom, waiting with the door open. When Jakes was back in the room, she refastened the chain to the radiator, removed the hood and waited until Jakes had got on to the bed. Without a word, the woman left, switching off the light and locking the door behind her.

Jakes lay in the half-light, staring up at the patterns made by the small strips of sunshine on the flaking plaster of the ceiling.

It was twenty-four hours since she had been taken. No one except the woman had spoken to her since she had been lifted, trussed, from the boot of the car and carried into this room where the bonds and the tape had been removed and the woman had ordered her to remove her clothes and had handed her the shift. When Jakes had protested and asked why they were doing this to her, the woman told her to be silent or they would tape her mouth. She had been given a drink, which tasted bitter, but she had been forced to finish it and immediately had become drowsy – as she was now, after the coffee. Throughout the hours of darkness she had mainly slept, sometimes waking not knowing where she was, and then, when she did, trying to stop herself from screaming, for she knew if she did they would put back the tape.

The hours she spent awake were the worst. She kept asking herself how this terrible thing could have happened. But she knew why it had. It was because of Mark; because of what he was doing. And now she was the prisoner of the people he had been looking for. Was he, too, a prisoner, lying chained in another room of the house? She kept thinking about the hostages in Beirut. They had been kept chained in some hot, filthy room for year after year. She would not survive that. She would die. But perhaps she was going to die. Perhaps they were going to kill her.

She tried to think of other things: of her home when she was a child, where the garden stretched down to the harbour and where, each morning before she went to school or university, she used to swim. She imagined her limbs moving through cool, clean water while she lay with her whole body filthy, her hair greasy from the boot of the car in which they had put her and of the vomit in which she had lain when she woke from the ether and before they had taped her mouth. She had thought in the boot of the car that she was going to die, from terror as much as from the stench and the heat.

When they arrived and she had been carried up all those stairs, they had not allowed her to wash. Just to use the lavatory –

with the woman standing there, watching. It was part of the treatment, to turn her into an animal. But what use was she to them? She knew nothing. If she hadn't agreed to come with Mark, she would now be in London. Mark had said that it wouldn't be dangerous – 'Not for you,' he'd said. 'Not in the least for you.' Now this had happened. Where was he? Where was Mark?

It began to grow stifling in the airless room and the sweat began to run from her body. She rolled over and buried her head in the pillow. Soon the drug took over, and she slept – fitful, broken sleep, with wild disturbing dreams, but dreams which, happily, did not waken her until it was once again dark.

In London that same morning, Tabbitt went to the mews house to see if Jakes had returned. He hoped she had, because he needed funds, and he would rather get the money from her. To get it from Adrian, he would have to do what Adrian wanted, and though he submitted, he did not like it. He preferred what he did with Jakes.

But there was no answer when he rang the bell. She must still be with Mark, he thought. So it would have to be Adrian. He wandered away.

Mark parked among the other tourist cars in the square at the top of the hill in Scario, a few yards from the steps which led up to the twelfth-century cathedral. From where he stood beside his car, he saw the sea below him, over the roofs of the houses. A large bus drew up, and a crowd of tourists dressed for the beach filed out and flooded into the small square. Mark joined them, and in his blue-and-white check shirt and khaki canvas trousers, with his dark glasses and a camera slung round his neck, he mingled easily among them as they began to make their way out of the cathedral square and down the hill to the port of Scario itself.

Chatting in his fractured Italian to the children, Mark went with them along the lane which twisted and curved down the steep hill. It was only after they had turned the last bend that they caught their first glimpse of the harbour. And there, taking up almost the whole length of the small jetty alongside which she was moored, dwarfing all the fishing-boats bunched together at the end of the quay nearest to the town, they saw the blue-and-white hull of a large motor-yacht. The children immediately ran ahead to the sea-wall. They were joined by the grown-ups, Mark among them, and they all leaned on the wall, gazing at the vessel which so dominated the small harbour.

The launch was still hoisted high up in the stern; there was no sign of activity on board, and after a few minutes the group of tourists moved off down the road that ran along the sea front. On their left was the harbour wall, on their right, the houses, shops and cafés with gaily striped awnings. They strolled in the middle of the road because a notice in various languages forbade all vehicles from using the road during the summer months, other than those belonging to residents or delivering supplies. Some of the group went into a shop and emerged with great cornets of ice-cream. Mark did the same, and wandered along among them, licking his ice. A little further on, they came to a corner where another lane, similar to that down which they had come from the Cathedral square but straighter, ran at right-angles up the hill into the centre of the town.

At the corner where this lane met the road along the front stood a tall four-storeyed house, grander and larger than any other, with an eighteenth-century façade the colour of burnt sienna. A high wall enclosed the side of the garden by the lane. On its other side, a narrow alley separated it from its smaller and meaner neighbours. On the street side, beside a wide, oaken front door beneath a portico, tall windows with narrow balconies behind rails of intricate iron-work overlooked the harbour, the windows open to let in the cool breeze from the sea. The top floor of the house, however, appeared to be unused, for here the windows were shuttered, and the shutters apparently nailed fast. It was so much larger and so much grander in design that it dominated all the other houses on the sea front just as the yacht, *Phydra*, dominated the fishing-vessels in the harbour. The home of Guido Genaro? Mark wondered. It looked grand enough.

As the tourists strolled past, the front door opened and a tall, dark woman came out and walked hurriedly down the street to a chemist's shop ahead of them. The group ambled on until they came to a café with tables set out beside the road. Leaving the others, Mark took a seat at one of the tables and ordered beer. The woman who had entered the chemist's now reappeared walked past him, and disappeared into the large house. He sipped his beer and watched the *Phydra* lying moored against the jetty some two hundred metres away. The sun was very warm and his drink very cold. If it hadn't been for his purpose in being there, he would have enjoyed basking so pleasantly in the sun.

At the top of the tall house not five hundred yards from where Mark was drinking his ice-cold beer, the woman came back into the room with the nailed-down shutters. She did not switch on the light but came to the bed and pushed roughly at the sleeping figure.

'Wake up.' Jakes stirred, her eyes still heavy with the drug. The woman shook her and pulled her up until Jakes was seated on the edge of the bed. The woman put the hood over Jakes' head. Through it, Jakes could see that the light had been switched on and heard the footsteps of others entering the room.

'I'm sorry you are so uncomfortable.' The voice was that of a man, soft, even gentle, speaking with a pronounced American accent and she thought of the 'Godfather' films she had seen with Mark. 'But it is, for the present, necessary.'

'Why are you doing this to me?' said Jakes, her voice scarcely audible beneath the hood.'

'Louder, please,' the voice said. 'Speak louder.'

'Why are you doing this to me? What do you want?'

'Some information. I will make you more comfortable when you have told me about your friend, Mr Somerset.'

'It's because of him you're doing this to me?'

'Of course. Tell me, what is Mark Somerset doing in Italy?'

'We came on holiday.'

'I don't believe you did. I repeat – why is Mark Somerset in Italy?'

'I told you. We came on holiday.'

Something was said that Jakes could not hear. The next moment the woman slapped Jakes' face through the hood, jerking back her head.

Jakes put her hands up to the hood over her face. 'Don't do that, don't do that.'

The woman grabbed Jakes' wrists and held them. The soft voice went on. 'She will do that every time you do not tell me the truth, and if you persist in lying, we shall do far worse. No, the holiday was a pretence. You came to Rome to search for a girl. Why?'

'I don't know anything about a girl. Mark never told me anything about a girl.'

'I think he came to find a girl? Why?'

'He didn't tell me anything. He just brought me on holiday.'

The woman hit Jakes again.

'Don't lie to me. How did you and Somerset come to Rome?'

'By car.'

'What kind of car?'

'What do you mean, what kind of car?'

The woman hit Jakes for the third time, harder than before, and beneath the hood she felt the blood in her mouth. She fell back on the bed, but the woman yanked her up and hit her again.

'Stop hitting me!' Jakes shouted. 'Stop!'

'She will, if you tell me the truth. What was the make of the car, its colour, and its registration number?'

'I don't know its number. We hired it in Nice.'

'What make is it?'

'It's a Renault.'

'What colour?'

'Grey.'

'Does Somerset still have this car?'

'I don't know. I suppose so.'

A silence followed. Then the voice went on. 'Yesterday you went to the airport to catch a plane to London. Were you going home to report what your friend had discovered?'

'No, of course not. I don't know what he'd discovered. I was just going home.'

The woman knocked her back on to the bed, then pulled her up and shook her so that Jakes' head rolled back and forward.

'Leave me alone, leave me alone!' Jakes shouted again, struggling.

'I warned you that you will be punished when you lie to me. And a few slaps are not the worst that could happen to you. We know how to persuade people to tell us the truth. So I would advise you to be sensible. I shall try again. You were going home, and you were leaving your friend in Rome.'

'I only came to Rome to be with Mark on the journey. You're making a mistake.'

'I don't think I am. Why was Mr Somerset so interested in finding the girl?'

'If he was looking for a girl, it was because someone killed his brother in England.'

'The man who died in England was called Hamilton, which is different from Somerset. So why pretend that Hamilton was Mark Somerset's brother?'

'He was his brother, his half-brother. Their mother was the same.'

There was silence. Jakes could hear whispering. Then the questions began again. 'But why was he searching for a girl in Rome? What did he think she had to do with the death of his brother?'

'He thought the girl might be able to tell him why his brother was killed and who was responsible. He thought she'd been used to get at Edmund's car.'

'So he did come looking for a girl?'

'He told me that later, when we were in Rome. He asked me to come with him on holiday.'

There was another pause. The woman was still holding Jakes' hands.

'Is Somerset working for the English government?'

'No, I don't know what he does.'

This time the blow was not from the woman but from someone else. It was not a slap, but a blow from a fist on the side of her face. She was left to lie for a time on her back, holding her head through the hood, moaning and turning and twisting on the bed. She felt the blood pouring down her neck. Then they pulled her up again. She struggled to get her hands free.

'You bastards!' she cried. 'Stop doing this to me! I don't know anything.'

'Keep still, or it will get worse,' said the voice. 'I'll try once more. Is Mark Somerset from the English government?'

'No! No, he's not. I'm sure he's not. He's on his own. He says the police aren't doing enough to discover who planted the bomb which killed Edmund. He wants to find out who did. I know Mark's not working with the government.'

There was a long silence. Then the woman let go of Jakes' wrists and pushed her roughly back on the bed. 'Lie still,' said the woman. Jakes heard the footsteps of people leaving the room and then the woman's voice from beside the door. 'You can take off the hood.'

As she raised her head to pull off the hood and put her hands to her bruised and bleeding face, Jakes heard the door closing. Her lip was split and her nose was pouring blood. There was no one now in the dark, half-lit room. The key turned in the lock and the bolts were pushed into place. She pulled the edge of the dirty blanket and held it to her face and chest, wiping at the blood. She sat up and began to rock to and fro.

'Damn you, damn you!' she shouted.

The door opened. 'Stop that!' said the woman as she took Jakes by the shoulders and shook her and then flung her back on the bed. 'If you make any more noise, I shall tape your mouth and strap you to the bed. And I'll turn the men on you.'

'Leave me alone,' Jakes mumbled. 'I don't know anything. I can't help them. Leave me alone.'

'If you know what's good for you, you'll keep quiet.' The woman stood above the bed while Jakes turned on here side and brought up her legs to lie curled on the bed. 'I shan't warn you again. If you don't keep quiet, you'll be sorry.'

TWENTY-ONE

From the café where he sat watching the *Phydra*, Mark noticed a white-clad crewman appear in the stern, step ashore and begin to walk along the quay. He stopped by some fishermen mending their nets and offered them a cigarette. The fishermen ignored him and went on with their work. The sailor shrugged, and walked from the quay to the road and disappeared into one of the bars.

Mark beckoned the waiter. 'Do you speak English?'

The man nodded. 'A little.'

'Is it possible to hire a boat and sail round the bay?' He wanted to get nearer to the yacht and he could not risk walking down the quay.

'There's a trip from here to the next bay round the point. Every hour. From over there.'

The waiter pointed to the jetty where it joined the sea wall. A man was standing by the bow of a stout wooden motorboat, selling tickets. Some of the group from the bus were already filing on board. 'It leaves soon. You must hurry.'

Mark crossed the road and joined the people queuing for the boat. When about twenty had come on board, the sailor held up his hand. '*Pieno, pieno,*' he said, and then threaded his way through the seated passengers to the wheel in the stern. A young boy cast off, and the boat chugged slowly down the harbour. Mark had taken a seat facing the stern so that he could have a good view of the *Phydra* as they sailed past and out into the bay.

When they were alongside her, a fisherman in a dinghy was shouting up to a crewman who was leaning over the rail. The fisherman was gesticulating angrily, but the sailor on the deck just smiled and waved him away. The man Mark had seen through his glasses talking with Genaro in the stern before the yacht sailed from Capri, appeared out of the cabin, apparently attracted by the shouting. Then the motorboat was past.

When they were clear of the harbour, the helmsman turned to starboard, rounded the point and sailed south along the coast. After about half an hour they came to a smaller bay with a stone jetty jutting out from a deserted beach. The boat steered alongside, the boy jumped out and made fast and the passengers filed ashore and began to walk towards the beach.

Mark stayed where he was, smoking. The helmsman called out to him in Italian. Mark shook his head and said in English, 'When I've finished my cigarette.'

He held out the packet, and the helmsman took one. 'Ashore?' he said in English. 'You go ashore?'

Mark held up his cigarette. 'In a minute. It's a good view from here.'

'We stay one hour and half,' said the helmsman.

'You have a fine boat,' Mark said. 'But not as big as the yacht in the harbour.' The helmsman spat over the side. 'I'd like a trip on that one,' said Mark. 'Where's she from?'

The man shrugged. 'France,' he replied.

'She takes up a lot of room. Do you get many of that size?' The man shook his head. 'She been here long?'

'No.'

'She's a fine boat.'

The man again spat over the side. 'She gets in the way. She'll be gone tonight,' he said with satisfaction.

'Where to?'

'Home, they say.'

Mark threw his cigarette into the sea and stood up. He nodded to the helmsman and climbed on to the jetty. On the beach, he lay on the sand as though dozing in the sun, surrounded by the children. Soon they left him alone. That tall house could be Genaro's house, and Genaro had been on the yacht at Capri with the man with the beard. So had the fat man, who could be the man with Rosetti in the night-club. Were they the South Americans with whom Genaro did business? If so, it was they who had planned Edmund's murder. So now it was the yacht which was important, and tonight, according to the helmsman, the yacht was leaving for home. And home for the yacht would be home for the South Americans, somewhere north, at Monte Carlo or one of the ports along that coast. But if she sailed south, in the direction of Sicily, he would have lost her. All would depend on whether the helmsman was right.

At the end of almost two hours a whistle sounded, and everyone gathered up their belongings and trooped back to the motor-boat. On the return journey, Mark sat amidships, one of the small children leaning against his leg, looking up at him. Mark smiled and lifted the child on to his knee and they were sitting like this when they sailed into the small harbour and passed the *Phydra*.

It was when they were going slowly past her and making for their mooring at the end of the jetty near to the town, that Mark saw, sitting in a chair on the stern deck, the black woman – whom the man at the garage had told him came from a château somewhere near Mougins.

At about four o'clock, while Mark was still on the motor-boat on the excursion, a blue police car turned through a gate into the paved yard of a house in the hamlet of Armenzano, about twelve kilometres in the hills above Assisi. The house, as they had been directed, was next to the locked and unused church. It was the only house in the hamlet.

It had taken them over half an hour from Assisi, and it was very hot. In the yard, the two carabinieri got out of the car and looked about them. The yard was paved and separated by a low wall from the road, almost a track, which had twisted up and down the hills through the dense woods. The house itself was an old stone building, obviously once a farm, for there were outhouses and a barn around the yard. Now, the policemen guessed, it was a pleasure house with a garden at its back. Over the wall they could see fields, the nearest thick with blood-red poppies.

They stood for a moment looking around and talking by the car. One strolled to the gate and looked up the village street. There was only the church, and beyond it a few dilapidated farm sheds before the road turned and meandered on down to the valley.

'There's no one about,' he said.

His companion went to the front door and pulled at the old-fashioned bell. They both could hear it ringing. When nothing happened, he rang again and this time banged the knocker loudly. The two men waited, shuffling their boots. One took off his cap and wiped the sweat from his forehead. Then the door opened.

'Signora Marreo?' the policeman asked.

Carla, dressed in a gardening apron over her light dress and wearing gardening gloves, looked at them, surprised. 'Yes,' she said.

'We've come from Assisi. We have been told to call on you.'

'How can I help you?'

'May we come in?'

For answer, Carla turned, and the two followed into the dark, cool hall. 'This way,' she said. They walked through the hall into a sitting-room, with open french windows leading into an unkempt garden. Beyond were the fields. It was a bright room, the chairs and sofa covered in flowered chintz. 'Please sit,' she said, taking off her gloves. 'I was in the garden when you rang the bell. What can I do for you?'

She remained standing by the french window. Seeing how uncomfortable they looked in their uniforms, their caps on their knees, she said, 'If it's too hot for you in here, we can go outside.'

'Thank you, no. It's cooler here in the shade.'

'Would you like some lemonade before you tell me why you are here?'

The first policeman looked at his companion, who nodded. 'We would,' he said. 'We would very much.'

When Carla had left the room, one of the policemen got up and walked around, picking up a photograph and then replacing it. The other, the one who had done the talking, took a notebook from his breast pocket.

Carla returned with a jug and glasses. She poured the lemonade and gave them each a glass. Then she sat. 'Well, what brings you out here to see me?'

'We've had a message from Rome, Signora. We've been asked to see you and enquire about an Englishman they think you know and whom they wish to question. He's called Somerset – Mr Mark Somerset.'

Carla drank from her glass. 'Mr Somerset? Yes, I've met Mr Somerset. He visited me a day or so ago at my house in Rome, in the Via Giulia.'

'So they told us. May I ask how you came to meet him?'

'Through a friend, another Englishman, an old friend who was visiting. Why? What is all this about?'

'When did you last see Mr Somerset?'

'When he called at my house that evening to see the other Englishman. I had not met him before. He was on holiday in Rome.'

'Have you seen him since?'

Carla looked at them and for a moment did not reply. Then she said, 'Why do you ask? What is this all about?'

'It's about murder.'

'Murder?'

The policeman looked at his notebook. 'The murder of a man called Giorgio Rosetti, in a night-club called Gianni's in the Campo dei Fiori in Rome on the night of Monday 15 July.'

'I heard something about that on my car radio on Tuesday. What has that to do with Mr Somerset – or with me?'

'The police in Rome believe that Mr Somerset may have been at the night-club on the evening Giorgio Rosetti was killed, and they would like to question him. They've been told that you may know where he is.'

Carla put down her glass. 'I'm afraid I've no idea. Whoever gave you the idea that I might?'

'It is Rome who are enquiring, Signora. They asked us to come and see you.'

'Well, I'm afraid I cannot help you at all. Mr Somerset, whom I'd never met before, came to my house last Sunday evening to see the friend of mine who was visiting from England. I imagine that Mr Somerset is now touring somewhere in Italy, for I know he's on holiday. Whoever could have given Rome the idea that I might know where he is?'

'I don't know, Signora. All I know is that someone told them you might be able to help locate Mr Somerset.'

'Well, I cannot. He was staying, I believe, at the Hotel Raphael.'

'He has left there now. He left on the morning after the murder. Do you know if he has a car?'

'I presume he has.'

'The hotel thinks so, but as they've no garage, they never saw it. They think he'd put it in a public garage while he was staying at the Raphael.'

'Well, I cannot help you at all. I know nothing about him. I assume he has a car because he said he would be touring. He came to my house at the invitation of my other English friend. They both happened to be in Rome at the same time. The English friend who was staying with me left Rome for London on Monday morning.'

'What was the name of the English friend who was staying with you?'

There was a pause, and then Carla said, 'He is an old friend who spent a few days at my house. Why do you need to know his name?'

The policeman looked at Carla's white hair. But she's still very handsome, he thought. He said gently, 'I don't wish to embarrass you, Signora, but this is a murder enquiry, and Rome believes the information would be helpful.'

Carla looked from one to the other, and then got to her feet. 'Do you know who my late husband was?'

'No, Signora.'

'Then go back to Assisi and speak with Rome. He was a very important official, of whom the Rome police will have heard. Ask them, and tell them that all I'm prepared to say is that I have no idea where Mr Somerset is. If they insist upon continuing this interrogation, come back tomorrow. Now, if you will excuse me, I shall go back to my garden. I am not often here and there is a great deal to be done.'

She walked out of room and the two policeman followed her. She opened the front door. 'I have no telephone, so if Rome insists, you can return tomorrow.' She stood in the doorway, watching as the car turned out of the small yard on to the road to Assisi.

When it was out of sight, she went back through the sitting-room and sat in the garden. She had little doubt that they would be back, perhaps bringing a more senior officer when they had learnt of Paolo's position in the SIMI. But it would give her time to think.

Someone had informed the police that Mark Somerset had been at Gianni's on the night Rosetti had been murdered and that she, Carla, knew Mark Somerset. Whoever it was must have had him watched and followed, probably from the day he arrived in Rome. So they would have known he had gone to the south. But as they had not told that to the police, it meant that in the south they had no need for the police. In the south, they would be able to take care of Mark Somerset themselves.

She rose and went into the house. Mark was now in real danger, as she had always feared he would be since the moment when he had told her he was going to Naples to follow Genaro. Mark Somerset should have listened to her. He should have obeyed Godfrey.

The woman unlocked the door and switched on the light. Jakes, lying in her drugged sleep, did not move. The woman shook her roughly, and Jakes stirred. She could feel the caked blood in her nostrils.

188

'Sit up,' said the woman, and when she had roused Jakes, pulled her up so that she sat on the side of the bed. She went to the radiator and unlocked the padlock. When she came back and unlocked the chain from her ankle, Jakes saw she was carrying the clothes she had been wearing when they had taken her. 'Get dressed,' the woman said, throwing the clothes on the bed. 'You're going home.'

When Jakes began to speak, the woman interrupted her. 'Be quiet, or you'll stay here – for ever.'

As Jakes struggled out of the shift and began to pull on her clothes, she saw from the shutters that by now it was night. 'Can I wash?' she asked.

'No. You can piss on our way out.'

Jakes saw that the woman was now cutting strips of broad sticky tape. 'What are you doing that for? Why are you doing that?'

'You're going on a trip, on your way home. This is to make sure you're quiet on the journey. If you struggle, you'll stay here.' Jakes let her bind her mouth with the tape. 'Now your hands.' When these were tied behind Jakes' back, the woman turned her round and took a scarf and bound it over her eyes. Two rubber earplugs were stuffed in her ears. Finally a cloak was thrown round her shoulders and the hood pulled over her head. The woman took Jakes by her arm and led her out of the room.

TWENTY-TWO

Mark stayed with the tourists as they climbed the hill to the Cathedral square, and he remained among them until they had boarded their bus. Seated in his car, he watched it move off and, having studied his map, he drove out of the town to a village on the hill above the harbour. He found a bar with a few tables on a small terrace from which he could see the bay and the *Phydra* lying alongside the jetty. He ordered an omelette, which came tough and dry. The lights came on in the town, along the quay and on the yacht, and he left the bar and drove a little way down the road, drawing up on the verge where he could still see the harbour. He sat there for over two hours, smoking, now and then dozing, waking with a start, anxious lest the *Phydra* might have sailed. It was at about ten o'clock, just after he had woken from one of his dozes, that he saw she had left the harbour and was in the bay. He watched anxiously as she gathered speed, waiting to see whether she would turn south towards Sicily, or north to France.

Then she turned north. The helmsman had been right. She was sailing home. He looked again at his map. His route back would take him past Salerno, Naples and Rome, and after Rome the road he and Jakes had taken on their drive down. It was motorway all the way. Then he calculated, roughly, the distance by sea from Salerno to Monte Carlo. If the *Phydra* cruised at fifteen knots and the weather was fair, it would take her about thirty hours to the south coast of France. He could travel faster, but he must not get there before her for he would have to search for her in the ports along the French coast. So tonight he could return to the villa, only two and a half hours' drive, and set off early the next morning.

Where the coast road joined the motorway, he found a telephone box. Lucia answered. 'I shall be back tonight,' he said. She did not immediately reply, and he could hear a voice in the background. The mother, he thought. 'Don't wait up. Leave the key for me,' he added. Again he heard a voice in the background. Then Lucia told him she would put the key in the pot of oleanders beside the front door, and rang off. He looked at his watch. He should reach the villa by one in the morning.

But because now and then he had dozed when he had been sitting in the car on the hill above the harbour at Scario, he had not seen another passenger being taken on board, a passenger who had come from the house on the front and who had to be helped along the quay by two figures. The passenger had often stumbled, and would have fallen but for the support of those on either side as they hustled their companion along the jetty towards the yacht. It was soon after the three had disappeared below that the *Phydra* had cast off and sailed silently out of the harbour and into the bay.

It was not easy going on the motorway. The flow of heavy lorries on their way north from the Strait of Messina made for tiring driving, and the lorries were travelling fast, usually in the centre lane, leaving little room between each. Many were new, gleaming with polished chrome, and although they had different names painted on their sides, Mark knew to whom they belonged. They were Guido Genaro's lorries thundering through Guido Genaro's kingdom.

During his journey to Scario that morning he had observed the poverty of the arid, rock-strewn land through which he had driven; he had seen the half-finished buildings scattered around in the scrubland beneath the hills, some several storeys high. He had noticed the uncompleted roads ending at a half-built bridge over a ravine or dried-up river-bed – and he knew the reason for all this useless construction. It was part of so-called regional development, designed to give the appearance of the start of an infrastructure, a show to attract more of the money the European Community had poured into southern

Italy. In origin, that aid had been a flood, but it had ended in a trickle; the bulk of the money had been diverted into the pockets of the local bosses through whom it had been channelled; and the bosses in this part of the world were Guido Genaro and his friends. They controlled the grant of planning permits, they owned the construction companies, they had built the useless roads and forlorn, derelict structures that littered the wild countryside like ruined tombs. Meanwhile the diverted money had gone to provide the finance for the real business – the trade in drugs, smuggled ashore in the Sicilian ports from the holds of ships from Colombia and Thailand, and now being carried in Genaro's lorries to the cities of the north where it would be sold to poison the youth of Europe.

For a few brief minutes there came a gap in the queue of heavy vehicles and Mark was past, driving along a clear stretch of road. His headlights lit up the back of a caravan towing a trailer carrying a small motor-yacht, a holidaymaker on his way home – and as he drove he thought again about the *Phydra*. She would not be one of the boats used for the drug shipments. She was too smart, too well known along the coast. She'd be used to bring the traders to visit the customers – and that was what she had just been doing, bringing the man with the dark beard to visit his client, Guido Genaro. Now he, Mark, was following her home, and if she was really heading home, she could be off the French Riviera by late tomorrow night or in the small hours of the following morning. Was it only five days since he and Jakes had left there on their way to Rome?

Jakes! He wondered how her journey home had gone. She would she now be in bed in the mews house. Then he thought of Gabriella in the Palazzo Borghese, sitting so straight in her chair under the frescos of nymphs and cherubs, half naked, fanning herself.

One of the juggernauts suddenly lurched across the road and veered into the fast lane just as he was overtaking, forcing him on to the verge until he was able to pull back into the lane as he drew ahead. In his rear mirror he saw the lorry move back into the centre of the motorway. The driver must have dozed. By now, he too was fighting to keep awake, but there was still an hour to go before he reached the villa. He lit a cigarette to keep himself awake, and eased the pistol in his waistband. He pulled into a petrol station and drank black coffee before he filled the tank, resenting the sight of the lorries which he had overtaken with such difficulty sweeping past. Then he was on his way again. He looked at his watch. It was nearly two o'clock. In London, Jakes would now be asleep, the poodle beside her. Not, he hoped wryly, Tabbitt.

It was half-past two when at last he turned off the main road at the bottom of the steep hill of the drive that led between the umbrella pines to the the Villa Margherita. At the circle of gravel in front of the house, he turned the car ready for an early start in the morning when it was daylight. He clambered out and stretched his stiff limbs, and looked across the garden at the moonlight shining on the sea far below. A light was showing above the front door. He went to the oleander pot and searched for the key. It was not there. Was Lucia still up and waiting for him?

For a moment he stood looking up at the silent house and then went to the front door and put his hand on the latch. It was unlocked. He opened the door, and stood blinking in the light of the hall.

Facing him, half-sitting, with both hands on the table on either side of her, dressed in black trousers and a low-cut white blouse revealing the curve of her breasts, was Gabriella.

On board the *Phydra*, Jakes lay on the bed where they had put her. Unable to see or hear, gagged and drugged by the sleeping draughts she had been given over the last twenty-four hours, she was totally disoriented. She had felt the cooler air on her cheek and had smelt the sea as she had been led stumbling along the quay to the companionway, and then the warmer air as she was helped down narrow steps and along a short passage before she was laid on a bed and left alone.

Throughout the transfer from one prison to another, she kept telling herself what the woman in the house had said – that she was going on a trip, and then would go home. From the time it had taken to lead her from her former prison, this place could not have been very far. As she lay, she could feel the throbbing of the engines but could not tell what it was. She kept telling herself what the woman had promised. She was going to be freed.

The first she knew that anyone was with her was when she felt hands fumbling at the back of her head and very slowly and gently the blindfold was removed. The sudden light blinded her, and she blinked and twisted her head to and fro until, gradually, her eyes began to focus and she was able to see above her a face. It was the grave, beautiful face of a black woman.

Then the earplugs were removed, and for the first time Jakes heard the noise of the engines but she did not yet grasp what the noise and the movement meant. The woman was looking down at her, resting her hand on her shoulder. 'Lie still while I take this off.'

She pulled the tape from across Jakes' mouth. As soon as it was off, Jakes mumbled through her sore lips, cut and bruised from the blows and from the gag.

'Don't try to speak,' said the woman, as she examined the bruises on Jakes' eye and her swollen nose with dried blood in the nostrils. She took a pot of salve from a cabinet by the bed, and began to rub it on Jakes' lips. Then she took another ointment and dabbed the bridge of Jakes' nose and, moistening a cloth, cleaned away the dried blood. All the time Jakes had her eyes on the beautiful face and the long fingers as they washed away the blood.

When the woman had finished, she said, 'Now turn,' and she undid the cord from Jakes' wrists.

When her hands were free, Jakes struggled to sit, and began to look wildly about her. 'Where am I? Where am I?' she repeated.

It was difficult and painful to speak through her cut lips, and the words came thickly. Gradually she took in the scene – the room with its square porthole, the movement and the noise and throbbing of the engine. She was on a ship, and the ship was at sea.

The woman took Jakes' wrists in her hands and began rubbing salve where the cord had bitten into the flesh.

'Am I free?' Jakes cried. 'Am I free?'

The woman paused in her rubbing. 'You must be quiet.'

'Why must I be quiet? They said I was going to be set free!'

The woman took Jakes by her shoulders and pushed her back until she again lay on the bed. 'You're not free – not yet.'

Jakes stared up at her. 'The woman promised,' she said.

The motion of the yacht had suddenly increased as the *Phydra* rounded the harbour wall and entered the bay, causing the woman to lurch and Jakes to slide on the bed.

'Where are you taking me?'

'You'll learn soon.'

'Who are you?'

'My name is Orianna.'

'Whose boat are we on?'

'The people who own it.'

'The people who put me in the car?'

'No.'

'Then who are they, and why aren't I free?'

Jakes tried to sit up again, but Orianna pressed her back on the bed. 'You're filthy. You must wash. You'll feel better then.' She went across the cabin.

Jakes called after her, 'I'm thirsty. It's the drugs they gave me in the house – and I can't think properly.'

Orianna opened the door of the shower-closet, turned on the water and came back into the cabin, carrying a glass of water. As she did so, she staggered a little from the movement of the yacht. 'Drink this, and then wash.'

Jakes drank. 'Where are we going?'

'A long way.'

'How long?'

'We'll be sailing all night, and then for another day and another night.'

Orianna helped Jakes from the bed, and led her to the shower-closet. She waited outside while Jakes stood under the stream of hot water, scrubbing at her hair and body, washing away the filth and dirt of the last days. When she had finished, Orianna gave her a nightgown and began to gather up her clothes. 'I have to take these,' she said.

The movement of the yacht had now increased, for the *Phydra* was out of the bay and in the open sea. Jakes stumbled across the cabin to the bed. 'The window, the porthole, is bolted,' Orianna said, 'but there is air-conditioning. The switch is beside the bed.' She crossed to the side table and placed some white tablets by the glass of water.

Jakes looked at them and shook her head. 'No, no,' she said. 'I won't take any pills.'

'As you like. They're seasick pills. The forecast for the night is not very good, but it will be better in the morning.'

'Where do you come from?'

'From Rio, in Brazil.'

'Why are you here, on this boat?'

'I am with them.'

'Why?'

'I am, that's all.'

'Why?' Jakes repeated. 'Why are you with them?'

Orianna suddenly leaned down and with both hands forced Jakes back on the bed and bent over her. 'You don't ask questions. You just do as you're told.'

'I only wanted to know why you are with the people who kidnapped me. You don't look that kind of person.'

Orianna straightened and stared down at Jakes. 'It's none of your business who I am, what I am. I'm with them. That's all you need to understand.' She bent down again, her face a few inches from Jakes'. 'Now, listen to me,' she said. 'Be sensible. If you're not, they'll send someone who won't be so gentle. Do you understand?'

Jakes did not reply, but turned her head away. 'Leave me alone.'

Orianna stood, and stayed looking down at her. Jakes' eyes were now closed. Suddenly Orianna put out her hand and very lightly touched Jakes' cheek. Jakes opened her eyes and looked up. Then Orianna swung round and left the cabin, and Jakes heard the key turn in the lock and the bolt being driven home.

Consuero and Andreas were sitting at the table in the saloon when Orianna entered.

'Well?' said Consuero.

'She is very drugged. I made her wash.'

'We should never have taken her. We should get rid of her,' said Andreas.

'Not yet,' Consuero replied. 'Not until we have found out more about Somerset. She could be useful.'

'How?' asked Andreas.

'As a hostage. She's Somerset's woman.'

'We should get rid of her,' Andreas repeated, 'and now's the best time. While we're at sea.'

'And have her body washed up on the coast past which we have been sailing?'

'Weight it down.'

Consuero shook his head, and said to Orianna, 'Tomorrow, make her think she'll be free when we reach port. Find out all you can about Somerset. I want to know if he's on his own.'

Andreas was looking at Orianna. Consuero stood up. 'I'm going to bed. Come, Orianna.' He looked at Andreas, who looked away. Consuero smiled. He raised his hand and crooked a finger, beckoning Orianna. 'Pleasant dreams, Andreas.'

Orianna followed him slowly down the companionway to his cabin, watched by Andreas. Neither of the men could see the expression on her face, which was the same as when Consuero had been having her on the morning he had returned to the château.

TWENTY-THREE

'You look as if you've seen a ghost,' Gabriella said as she rose from where she had been leaning against the table. She turned and led the way through the small library.

'Lucia never said you were here when I called,' Mark said as he followed her. In the drawing-room only two table-lamps were lit, and the room was mostly in darkness. The dustsheets had been removed from the furniture.

'I arrived earlier this evening,' she said over her shoulder. She had her back to him, busy at the table fixing a drink. 'You look tired,' she said as she brought him the glass. 'Come and sit down.'

'I'd rather stand. I've been sitting for a long time.' He took the glass and walked to the end of the room by the empty grate. He drank, and put the glass on the chimney-piece. When he turned, she was on the sofa, her legs beside her, sitting in the shadows. He could not see her face clearly. He thought of her on her bed in her apartment at the Palazzo Borghese. 'What brought you here?'

'It is my own house, Mr Somerset,' she said ironically, but with a smile.

'I'm sorry. I didn't mean that.' He drank more of his whisky.

'The police have been to see me. They told me you'd been seen leaving the Raphael earlier in the evening and later entering the club.' She spoke very coolly, as she had when he had come to see her before he left Rome.

By whom had he been seen? Who had been watching him? He had left Jakes at the hotel at half-past nine and had gone to the club well after midnight. Had they also seen him enter and leave the Palazzo Borghese? 'How could the police have identified me? And why should they have come to you?'

'I have no idea. But they did.' Then she asked, 'Have you come far tonight?'

'Two or three hours' drive.'

'And did you find what you were searching for?'

Before he could answer, he saw that in the shadows behind her, a figure had come into the room, so silently that it appeared to materialise out of the darkness. When it came into the pool of light behind Gabriella's head, he saw it was the man in the photograph.

'I thought I heard voices,' the man said in English. He had his hands now on the sofa on either side of Gabriella's head.

'Giulio,' said Gabriella without turning round, 'this is Mark, whom I told you about.'

The man bowed over the sofa and the light shone on the silver of his hair.

'We thought you would be here when we arrived,' Gabriella went on. 'We planned to surprise you.'

What time had it been when he had telephoned? Eleven? Mark remembered the voice in the background. Why had Lucia not told him?

Giulio now came round the edge of the sofa and sat beside Gabriella, who moved her legs to make room for him. He was wearing a flowered dressing-gown over an open white silk shirt. Both were now facing Mark, who still stood with his back to the grate. He could hardly see their faces.

'I hope you enjoyed your visit to the south,' Giulio said. 'Did you have a chance to visit the ruins of the Doric temples at Paestum?'

'No. I have friends with a villa near Sarpi and I went to see them. But they weren't there. The villa was let.' Mark finished his drink. 'I have to be off early tomorrow.'

'Where to this time?' asked Giulio.

'London.'

'Flying from Rome?' Giulio persisted.

'Yes.'

'You have been called home?'

'No. It's the end of my trip.'

'So many journeys.'

'So many questions,' Mark replied.

Giulio laughed. 'You are right. It is rude of me to be so inquisitive, especially when you must be tired. As I come from the south, I am always anxious that visitors should like it.'

Mark put down his glass. 'It's very late and I'm keeping you both up. It was good of you to wait up for me. If you will forgive me, I must go to bed.'

Gabriella swung her legs to the floor. 'Of course. We must all breakfast together and you can tell us then about your adventures. I'm sure you must have had some.' They followed him into the hall. 'What about your things?' she asked.

'They're in the car.' He went to get his grip.

When he came back, Gabriella said, 'You're in the same room.'

At the top of the stairs, he turned. They were both standing where he had left them, looking up at at him.

'Good-night,' he said.

'We'll talk tomorrow,' she called back.

In his room, he threw off his clothes and the moment his head was on the pillow, he fell asleep. But not for long. He woke with a start, and in the moonlight shining through the open window he saw a figure in white entering the room. 'Gabriella!' he said. But as the figure approached, he saw that it was not Gabriella. It was Lucia. 'Lucia, what are you doing here?'

'Shh,' she whispered. 'You must get up.'

'What do you mean?'

'Don't speak,' she whispered again. 'You must get up.'

'Why? What is it?'

'We must talk outside. Get dressed quickly. Someone is coming.'

'What are you talking about? Someone is coming? Who?'

'I don't know, but you must believe me. Be quick!' She went to the door and stood listening.

He swung himself out of the bed. 'What is all this?' he said.

'Hurry! You must hurry.' When he bent to put on the bedside light, she ran across the room and stopped him. 'No,' she said. 'No!' Where she now stood in the moonlight he could see her face clearly. She was deadly serious. 'Please do as I say.'

He pulled on his clothes, slipping the pistol back into his waistband, his wallet and passport into his jacket pocket. The grip he left on the floor by the bed.

'Follow me,' she said, and opened the door. In the passage she did not turn towards the stairs which led to the front of the house, but led him along the corridor through a swing door covered in green baize. The moonlight shone through a window at the far end of the corridor above a banister and more stairs. To their left was a door, and Lucia led him inside, leaving it ajar. He could see a bed with the white bedclothes tumbled back.

'We can talk here. It's away from the salon where they are. They arrived earlier, without any warning, and the Signora told me that if you telephoned I was not to say they were here. She said she wanted to surprise you. Later I heard them talking, and then I heard the Signor on the telephone. He was saying that the Englishman would be back soon and they must come.'

'They? Who are they?'

'I don't know. Could it be the police?'

He looked at her. Why should they send for the police?

'Whoever it is,' she whispered, 'you must leave. I know you're in some kind of danger. You must go.' He let her lead him back into the corridor and down the back stairs. 'When you're outside,' she said, 'slip round the side of the house through the garden to your car. But make no noise.' She unlocked the outside door, leaving the key on the inside. As they stood under the porch, she whispered, 'Go now,' and stood on tiptoe and kissed him on the mouth. 'Go now, quickly.' She disappeared into the house, closing the door silently behind her.

After she had gone, he stood motionless. What had she meant? Who was coming? And why had they sent for them?

How was he in danger? Then, very faintly, he heard the sound of a car approaching up the hill. He turned and crept through the garden to the front of the house and lay hidden in the shrubs. The car, without lights, came very slowly over the brow of the hill of the drive, turned on the circle of gravel in front of the house and drew up next to the Renault. Two men got out. One went to the Renault and walked round it, inspecting it. The other went to the front door and rang the bell. The door opened and the light from the hall flooded out. Gabriella stood framed in the doorway and the two men entered.

Mark waited for a moment and then crept to the Renault and opened the door on the driver's side. He released the brake and, with the door still open, began to push. The tyres crunched on the gravel as the wheels began to turn. Slowly he moved it the few yards to the end of the circle of the drive where the incline began. When the car began to roll, he leapt in, steering with one hand, holding the door with the other. There was enough light from the moon for him to see between the trees as the car gathered speed down the hill. At the bend in the drive, he put it into gear, pressing the clutch with his foot, free-wheeling until he thought he was far enough from the house. Then he released the clutch, the engine started, and still without any lights he drove out on to the main road.

He drove fast, very fast, for he knew it would not be long before they discovered that he was gone. The visitors to the Villa Margherita had not been the police. He had seen clearly who they were when Gabriella had opened the door, especially the one who had entered the house first. He was the man he had seen dressed in a blue shirt and white trousers boarding the launch to join the *Phydra* in Capri . . . Guido Genaro.

Jakes slept fitfully as the engines throbbed and the yacht heaved and swung in the open sea. She had not taken the pills Orianna had assured her were sea-sickness tablets, and after the darkness of her first prison, she kept on the lamp by her bed. She did not know whether it was night or day when the cabin door opened and Orianna entered, locking the door behind her. The movement of the boat had become steadier.

'You can have more, if you wish,' she said, putting a mug of tea and some dry biscuits on the table beside the bed. Jakes shook her head but picked up the mug and sipped the tea. Orianna sat on the bed. 'Are the bruises less painful?' Jakes shook her head.

'Where do you come from?' Orianna asked.

'Sydney, Australia, but I've been living in London. What time is it?'

'The evening.'

'How much longer on the boat?'

'They said it will take about thirty hours, and we've only done about twenty.' Then she said, 'Who is Mark Somerset?'

'You know who he is,' said Jakes.

'No, I don't. Nor do they. But they're interested in him. That's why they're keeping you. If you tell me more about him, they may let you go.'

'I told the people in the house when they were hitting me. Mark came to Italy looking for the people who killed his brother.'

'They think he's from the government.'

'No, he's not from the government. I told them that.' Jakes sat up and suddenly said loudly, 'Where are they taking me?'

Orianna put her finger to her lips. 'Speak quietly,' she said. 'We're going to France, to the South of France, near the mountains.'

'But they're Italians . . . Why are they taking me to France?'

'They're not Italians. If you're sensible, they may let you go when we get to France.'

'The woman in the house said I was going to be freed. Why did she lie?' Jakes stretched out her hand and took Orianna's. 'Please help me.'

Orianna looked at Jakes' hand in hers, then she said, very quietly, 'I can't. I can do nothing. I have to do what they tell me.'

'Why?' said Jakes, pulling her hand away.

'Can't you guess why?'

Jakes stared at her. 'Who are you? Where do you come from?'

'I told you. I come from Rio.'

'And you're one of them, one of the people who have kidnapped me?' Orianna sat looking at her. Jakes flung herself back on the bed. 'How could you be with such people! How can you be so wicked? They're going to kill me! You know they are. Why won't you help me?'

'I can't.'

'Why won't you try? Do you want them to kill me?' Orianna walked to the cabin door, where she stood listening. 'You don't seem the kind of person who would be mixed up with people like these. Why are you with them? Why?'

Orianna came back to the end of the bed and stood looking down at her. 'The man who owns this boat found me in Rio. He took me from the *favelas*. Do you know what that means?' Jakes shook her head. 'You don't know what a *favela* is? No, why should you. You've never lived in a *favela*.' Jakes remained silent, her arms wrapped round her knees. 'Well, a *favela* is a slum, a stinking, filthy slum, wooden shacks stuck together on the side of a hill, half a mile from where the rich people live in their fancy apartments and great hotels by Copacabana beach. Shacks, with corrugated iron roofs which let in the rain, and no sewers and the drinking water, if there is any, comes from a single tap in one of the paths which run with muck and mud and where the babies crawl and the children and the dogs scrounge for scraps. That's where I come from. And this man bought me and took me away from all that.'

She paused and looked round the cabin, while the silent Jakes sat staring at the slim, elegant creature standing at the end of the bed, with the gold ear-rings, the scarlet blouse and the white slacks. 'You asked me why? Well, now you know why. I don't have to like him. He's brutal and he's cruel, and God knows what he's done to hundreds of people, quite apart from what he's doing to you. So I hate him, and I hate what I'm forced to do. But it's the price, and I accepted it. Wouldn't you?'

For a time neither spoke, then Jakes said, 'Who is he?'

'He is a Colombian.'

'They're the ones who killed Edmund! They're the people Mark came looking for. They're going to kill me . . . You know they will! Unless you help me.'

'Shut up,' said Orianna. 'Shut up!' She turned and flung herself across the room. Then she came to the side of the bed and sat, quieter now. 'They mustn't know we've been talking like this. They've told me to get information from you about Somerset. And you must give me some.'

'Is that why you're telling me all these lies?'

'They're not lies. But you must tell me something that I can tell them, otherwise they'll stop me coming and one of the men will come. You would not want that. So you must give me something to tell them. What does Mark Somerset look like?' She saw Jakes hesitate. 'They know, because a man they used in Rome was watching you and Somerset, and he told the Italians who handed you over to the Colombians. But I don't, and you must tell me something about Somerset so that I can say you told me. What does he look like?'

'He's tall, dark hair, about thirty.'

'Is he your boyfriend?'

'Yes. He was. He still is.' Orianna took her hand, but Jakes pulled it away. 'No, no, you won't help me.'

'Where do you think he is now?' Orianna asked.

'I have no idea. He was in Rome.'

'When you last saw him, did he tell you where he was going?'

'He just said he was going to find the people who'd killed his brother. He said the police weren't doing enough. But he'd only got two weeks away from his work.'

'What is his work?'

'I don't know. It's an office somewhere.'

'A government office?'

'Not the government. I know that. He told me he was on his own and I told them so when they were hitting me. Mark brought me with him to make everyone think he was on holiday. We came from France.'

'Where in France?

'Valbonne.'

'That is near to where you'll be taken. Do you think he's gone back there?'

'I can't think why he should. We only went there when he was pretending to be on holiday.'

'Where does he live in London.' Jakes told her, and gave her the telephone number. 'He'll be back there in about a week.'

Orianna got up from the bed, and stood in the centre of the room. 'The weather's better. They say it'll be calm from now on. I must go, but I'll be back. I'll bring you some soup. You'll be able to swallow that.'

Jakes laid her head back on the pillow. 'You must help me. Please help me!'

For a moment Orianna stood looking at the figure on the bed, at the bruised face with the marks of the beating still upon it. Then she turned and left, locking the door behind her.

In the main saloon Consuero was sitting alone at the table, reading, a yellow oilskin on the chair beside him, a glass in one hand. In a ring on the side of the table to keep it from sliding from the movement of the boat was a bottle of brandy. His face was flushed. He'd been drinking for some time. 'Have you got anything useful out of her?' he said.

'She gave me Somerset's address in London where she was going when she got back.'

'Anything else?'

'She's still very drugged. She described Somerset. He's her lover. He brought her with him to make it look like a holiday. She's certain he's not with the government. She says he came on his own, looking for his brother's murderers because the English police weren't doing enough. She said he only has a week before he has to be back in London.'

'Give the address to Andreas and tell him to have it radioed to London for Manolis. Our fat Turkish friend is at present a little the worse for wear from the sea. He must come from a long line of brigands, not pirates. But perhaps that's the Greeks, and he's not a Greek.' He laughed. 'But he'll be better now it's calmer, so tell him to have the message sent.'

As she turned to go, he said, 'Stop.' He closed his book, drank, and looked her up and down. She knew what that look meant. 'Our fat friend fancies you.' When she did not reply, he smiled. 'Has he ever touched you?' She shook her head. 'He wants you. He wants you badly, although God knows what he'd do to you if he got his hands on you. He spends his time imagining what you and I do together. Would you like to have him?' She shook her head, staring at him. 'No? Not at all? Not as an experiment, an experience? You've heard what the Turks get up to, haven't you? Do you think we ought to let him?'

She looked back at him steadily, with no change in her expression, standing perfectly balanced, hardly moving from the slight roll of the boat.

'Do you think, perhaps, we ought to do a kindness to a loyal and devoted servant – make him a gift, or rather a loan, as a reward for faithful service?' He smiled. 'The weather will be calm tonight and so the brigand may be up to it.' Then his mood changed, and he gestured, abruptly dismissing her. 'Go and tell him to send that message and then go to my cabin and wait for me.'

Without a word, she made her way down the companionway to Andreas' cabin.

Carla was drinking coffee in the kitchen at the back of the house when she heard the car. It was seven-thirty in the morning. The police, she thought, had returned very early. When she opened the door, Mark, haggard and unshaven, stood in the sunlight, swaying with exhaustion. 'At least, this time,' he said, 'I'm visiting in the daytime.'

Behind him she saw the grey Renault. Without a word, she turned back into the hall and returned with her keys.

'Quick,' she said and ran past him to the barn at the other side of the yard. She opened the double door and reversed her dark blue Alfa-Romeo out into the yard. 'Put your car in there,' she called.

When he was closing and locking the barn doors behind the Renault, she asked, 'Did you pass anyone on the road from Assisi?'

'No. This place is not easy to find. I only got here by luck.'

'We're going to need plenty of that,' she said grimly. 'Come inside, quickly.'

In the kitchen she made more coffee, took a bottle of brandy from the cupboard and poured a stiff measure into a mug. She put the bottle on the table between them. He sat and drank, holding the mug in both hands.

'The local police were here yesterday asking about you, and they will be back today. The Roman police want to question you about Rosetti's death.' He nodded. 'Someone informed on you in Rome.'

He thought again of Gabriella sitting in her apartment in the Palazzo Borghese, and of her standing, framed in light, as she opened the villa door to welcome Guido Genaro. 'I know,' he said. Then he told her what had happened at the villa.

'You are certain it was Genaro?'

'Quite certain.' If it had not been for Lucia, Genaro would have killed him.

'The man staying with Gabriella is a government minister,' she said. 'He's her lover, and that's why I suggested we ask her to find out the information you wanted – which, as it turns out, was not very clever of me.'

'Had you any suspicions about him?'

'None. There have always been rumours about the Mafia and the Party, and he comes from Palermo. But there's been no gossip about him.'

'And about her?'

'Certainly not. She's well-known in Roman society.' She looked at him as he drank, and then poured him more coffee and brandy. 'What start do you think you have?'

'It depends upon how long it took them to discover I had gone. At the best, an hour, but it could be less.' He told her that he had pretended to Giulio and Gabriella that he would be flying home today.

'Then they would have expected you to go to the airport. If so, they would have left the motorway at Frascati and have lost you. Where are you heading for?'

'First, Monte Carlo.' He told her about the *Phydra*, how he had seen Genaro on board, and finally about the black woman from the château. 'Then I'm going to Mougins.'

She studied his drawn face. 'You're not going anywhere before you've slept. Follow me.' She took him upstairs to a bedroom at the side of the house overlooking the poppy-field, and drew the curtains. 'Lock the door and get into bed. Make no noise, and do not leave the room until I come for you.'

Then she left him lying fully dressed on the bed, the pistol beside him, and he slept.

At noon, the police were back. They drove into the yard and drew up beside Carla's blue Alfa-Romeo. This time the Chief of Police, the Maresciallo dei Carabinieri from Assisi, was with them. She took him into the sitting-room. 'They have told you what I said yesterday,' she said.

'Yes, Signora. Rome reminded me about your distinguished husband, but they insisted that you were seen again. It is, you understand, a murder enquiry.'

'It may be, but it cannot concern my visitor who had left Rome before the murder ever occurred.'

'The point is that your visitor . . .' He hesitated over the word. Like his colleagues the day before, he could see that although she might be of what was called, 'a certain age', she was still a very beautiful woman. 'Your visitor might be able to say – at least Rome thinks he might be able to say – where his friend Mr Somerset might be.'

'No, he could not have known. When he was with us, Mr Somerset said he'd be leaving Rome after the lady with him had flown home to London.'

'That was Miss Hunter.'

'You know about her?'

'Yes, the informant . . .'

She interrupted him. 'Who was this informant?'

'We do not know.'

'A man or a woman?'

'They did not tell me.'

'Well, whoever he or she is, they are merely making mischief. I told your men yesterday that I had never met Mr Somerset before he came to my house last Sunday evening. He had been invited by my visitor, not by me.'

'And you've not seen Mr Somerset since?'

Carla had anticipated that would be the Maresciallo's next question, so before he had begun to speak, she had risen from her chair and stood by the french window with her back to him. 'You must understand, Maresciallo, that my house guest from England, whose name Rome wants to know, is an old and very dear friend,' she said softly. 'He should not have been in Rome with me.' For a moment there was silence. 'You will, please, understand that.'

'Of course, Signora,' the Maresciallo said, 'But this would be entirely confidential . . .'

Carla swung round to face him. 'During the years when my husband had charge of the most vital state secrets, I learned that nothing remains confidential if it once appears on police files. I am not prepared to tell you his name – especially when his identity is quite immaterial to your enquiry into the death of a man who was murdered after my friend had left the country, a man who, by all press accounts, must have had many enemies.' She sat again, opposite the policeman. 'Personally, I do not believe for a moment that Mr Somerset could have had anything to do with murder, let alone the murder of a man like that.'

'It is said he was at the club that evening.'

'It is said by whom? An anonymous caller on the telephone. Mr Somerset at a squalid night-club when he was visiting Rome with his friend, Miss Hunter? This is all nonsense, Maresciallo, and I will not involve my friend from England.'

The policeman sighed. 'Signora, your visitor knows Mr

Somerset, and Rome considers, quite reasonably, that he might have some idea where Mr Somerset could have gone after he suddenly left Rome the morning after the murder of Giorgio Rosetti.'

'He did not leave Rome suddenly or unexpectedly. He said on the evening he was at my house that he would be touring when Miss Hunter had gone home, although he did not say where. Accordingly, my visitor could not possibly know where Mr Somerset went.'

'I have to tell you that after the information about Mr Somerset had been received, it was followed by enquiries from important government circles. That was why the Rome police were obliged to follow it up.'

'Then tell the police in Rome to go back to their government circles and ask them what they know. But the name of the gentleman who was staying with me cannot be of the slightest help in tracing Mr Somerset.'

'Well, Signora, I've done what Rome asked. I was told I was not to insist if it really would embarrass you, but it was hoped you would co-operate and I was to try to persuade you.'

Carla smiled at him. 'And despite your charm and courtesy, Maresciallo, you have failed.'

He got to his feet. 'I am personally very sorry to have caused you this trouble.'

Carla rose, and he followed her to the front door. One policeman was sitting on the wall of the yard, the other leaning against the barn door, smoking. When they saw Carla and the Maresciallo, they walked back to their car.

'Good-bye, Signora. I'm sorry we had to trouble you.'

He saluted, all three got into their car and Carla remained standing in the doorway while it turned in the yard. Before they drove through the gate, she saw the driver say something to his chief, and the car stopped.

The Maresciallo leaned out of the side window. 'One last matter, Signora. Is that your car?' He jerked his head towards the Alfa-Romeo standing in front of the door.

'Of course it is my car! Who else's car could it be? You can see the registration number and if you don't believe me, you can check with Rome.' She went into the house and slammed the door.

'You bloody fool,' said the Maresciallo to the driver as they swung out on to the Assisi road.

About an hour after the police had gone, Carla set off to walk in the direction of Assisi. Half an hour later she reached the next village. She put through a call to England from the post office. When she got through, Godfrey was not at Hans Place. He'd be back later, the porter told her. She left a message. 'Make sure you have it right,' she said. 'It's very urgent.' She made him repeat it before she walked back.

It was very hot, and a storm appeared to be building up to the south. As she let herself into the house, she heard the first rumbles of distant thunder and saw stormclouds gathering far away over the hills.

TWENTY-FOUR

In London, when Godfrey received Carla's message, he spoke immediately to Brereton in Naples. 'I have news of Mark Somerset.'

'The last I heard of him, he was heading south.'

'Carla left a message. Somerset is on his way back to France, looking for a chateau near Mougins. Something about a black lady who lives there. I can't make head or tail of it, and I can't get back to Carla as she has no telephone. You go to Nice, and I'll join you tomorrow. Contact me at the Hotel Terminus.'

Then Godfrey thought of Jakes. She had been in the South of France with Mark and might be able to throw some light on what Carla had meant. He decided to go round to see her. When his taxi drew up outside the mews house, Tabbitt was standing outside the front door. Godfrey walked over to him.

'If you're after Jakes,' Tabbitt said. 'She ain't here.'

'When do you expect her back?'

Tabbitt shrugged. 'Dunno.'

'I understood she'd returned five or six days ago.'

'I told you, she ain't here. She's still with her fella.'

Godfrey returned to Hans Place. So Jakes was with Mark, and tomorrow they would be in France. But Carla's message had said nothing about Jakes. So was she with him? If she wasn't, where was she? It was time for him to get there himself. But, first, he would speak with his friend Bernard de Tourneville, the Head of the French Intelligence Service, the DSGE. If Mark was going to get into trouble in France, Bernard should be warned.

*

Carla left Mark sleeping until six o'clock, when she roused him. They ate in the kitchen, by candle-light for she had drawn the curtains. The thunder was no louder; the storm seemed to have stayed in the south, over Rome.

'Your car has French number-plates,' she said. 'Where did you hire it?'

'From Hertz, in Nice.'

'You must take mine. The police don't know what car you have, but the others may. I'll take yours and leave it somewhere in Rome and get Hertz to collect it.'

'What shall I do with yours?'

'Leave it in the garage at the Negresco Hotel in Nice, and give the keys to Georges, the hall porter. Tell him I, or a friend, will pick it up next week.' She began to put away the dishes. 'You go north to Perugia, on to the motorway near Arezzo, then all the way past Florence, Spezia and Genoa to the border.'

He remembered the drive down with Jakes, and wished she were with him.

'It's about six hundred kilometres, and, after Arezzo, it's all motorway. I've done it in nine hours. If you leave here at seven, you'll be at the frontier by daylight.'

When he had locked up the barn after she had reversed out the Renault, he leaned through the window and kissed her cheek. 'Thank you,' he said simply. 'You've been wonderful.'

'I'm rather enjoying myself,' she said. 'But now, go home, Mark, and tell them in London what you know.' She drove away. A minute later, he too was on the road.

Carla ran into the storm in the outskirts of Rome, and the rain was so fierce, pouring down in sheets, that driving became difficult and dangerous. She did not want the car to be seen near her house in the Via Giulia, so she decided to leave it at the Gianicolo. She would drop in the keys to Hertz and they could collect it on the following day.

She stopped at a telephone-box, running to it in the rain, and told the car-hire firm to send a car to collect her in an hour from the Gianicolo and take her home. Then she ran back to the

Renault and sat mopping the rain off her short hair, her wet jacket on the seat beside her.

When she arrived at the Gianicolo, she pulled up against the wall on the hill overlooking the city. Here, during the day, stalls and kiosks sold tourists ice-cream and balloons, and sightseeers leaned over the wall looking at the panorama of the city below. Now, late at night and in the lashing rain, the place was deserted. The lights of Rome were hardly visible as the rain fell in torrents and slashed across the windows and windscreen. Overhead the thunder crashed. Now and then flashes of lightning lit up the rain.

Carla stretched across the seat for her handbag. It was not under her jacket, or on the floor of the car. She remembered distinctly that she had taken it to the telephone kiosk for the change she had needed. In it was her money, all her credit cards and her house keys. She must have left it on the shelf in the call-box! By now, it would probably be gone, but when the taxi came, she would go back to the kiosk to see if, by chance, it was still there. If it was not, she prayed that her maid, Andrina, would be at home.

Carla heard the car draw up alongside, but could hardly see it through the rain on the side window. She reached across the seat for her jacket.

From the information beaten out of Jakes and from what he had seen when he had arrived at Gabriella's villa, Genaro knew that Mark Somerset was driving a grey Renault with Nice registration plates. When they had discovered that Mark had eluded them at the villa, they had raced to the airport at Fiumicino but found no trace of him. During the day, while Mark had been sleeping at Carla's house in Armenzano, Genaro's people had been watching for his car at all the entries into Rome. It was only when Carla was pulling away from the kiosk in the blinding rain after making her telephone call that they had picked it up. It was way ahead of them, and they could just make out the head of the driver in silhouette. With difficulty, they followed it into Rome and up to the Gianicolo. It was when Carla was drawing on her jacket that they opened fire at the figure sitting behind the wheel. The hail of bullets smashed the window, ripping through Carla's head and body, almost blowing off her head, making it unrecognisable as blood and brains were scattered on the seat beside where she was sitting. Then the car which had arrived so silently drove away through the storm.

When it was approaching dawn, Orianna came into the cabin with a glass on a tray. She walked stiffly, painfully.

'We dock in two hours. You're to take this.' She held up the glass full of a grey liquid.

'What is it?'

'It's to make you sleep.'

'No,' said Jakes. 'No!'

'If you don't take it, they will force you.'

Jakes shook her head. 'No!' she cried again.

'Listen to me. They'll have to carry you ashore, and it will be daylight. So you have to be asleep or they'll tape your eyes and mouth and gag you. There'll be a car to take us to the house. You'll have to be asleep.'

'I'll pretend . . . I'll pretend to be asleep.'

'That's too dangerous. If they saw you were not, he'd know I hadn't done what he'd told me to do. If you take this, I promise I'll try to help you.'

'You said you couldn't.'

'I have decided. When we're at the house, the château, I'll find a way. I'll get a message to your friends.'

'I haven't any friends. There is only Mark, and I don't know where he is.'

'There must be someone.'

'Only the man in London Mark asked me to ring when I got home. But if you're going to help me, why don't you go to the police?'

'I can't. I can't do anything by myself. They never let me out on my own. There's a man, Frederik. They send him with me all the time, everywhere I go. But I've thought of someone who might help – a friend. She would never go to the police, and even if she did, the police would never believe her. But she might send a message.'

'To London? The only person is this man, Godfrey, in London.'

'At least it's someone. Where is he in London?'

'I only know the telephone number.'

'What is it?'

'London 071 489 5000. His name is Godfrey.'

'Repeat it. I have to remember it.'

Jakes repeated the number. 'Do you think you could get a message to him?'

'I can promise nothing, but it's the only chance. If I can get to my friend.'

'Why are you now going to help me? Why?'

Orianna looked at Jakes, her eyes narrowing. Last night had made her decide. It was what they had done to her last night. Perhaps if Jakes was saved, they'd be destroyed – and she would be free.

Consuero had himself taken her to Andreas. He brought her, he announced, as he had said he would, as a gift, a loan, a reward for faithful and devoted service, for the success in Cambridge and in Rome. Amused, Consuero had suggested that he stay, but eventually, chuckling, he had left them alone. It was that, and what Andreas had forced her to do during the long hours of the night, that had made her decide.

'I have my reasons,' she said. 'Now you must take this.'

She put the glass in Jakes' hand and began to lift it to her mouth. 'There are worse things than being given a sleeping-draught,' she added.

Jakes stared at her, noticing for the first time Orianna's swollen lips, and the look in her eyes, those now wild eyes with dark hollows beneath them. She drank, and Orianna without another word took the glass and walked stiffly to the door and left the cabin.

*

They carried the sleeping Jakes ashore, wrapped in two blankets, one round her head like a cowl. No one was about and the car was waiting. It was four-thirty, and dawn was just breaking. There was no sign of Consuero or Andreas; the car would return for them later.

At nine o'clock, in an attic room with a low ceiling and a small, narrow window at the top of the east tower of the château, Jakes stirred. The sleeping-draught had been very powerful.

Orianna was sitting on the bed beside her with a cup in her hand and, putting an arm around her, helped her to sit up. 'I've brought you some tea,' she said, holding the cup to Jakes' lips.

'Where are we?' Jakes muttered. Her face was still very swollen, one eye now almost completely closed and the cut on her lip still open. Her nose began to bleed again, and Orianna took a cloth and wiped it.

'We are at the château.'

'What time is it?'

'It's morning.'

Orianna rose and looked down at her. Jakes had closed her eyes. Orianna left, locking the door behind her. In her own room she wrote on a slip of paper, which she pushed down the front of her dress. When she was descending the stairs and had reached the first floor, Andreas came from his room. He put his hand on her breast and fondled it. She stood silent, unmoving, praying he would not feel the paper. He dropped his hand and fondled her buttock. 'Tonight,' he said. 'Again.' Then he went back into his room.

Orianna went down to the dining-room where Consuero was at his breakfast. 'I cannot stop her bleeding,' she said. Consuero looked up, and she showed him the blood-stained cloth.

'So?'

'It could get worse. I must go to Opio.'

'Why?'

'To get salve from Leonie.'

'Your black friend who does the abortions?'

'She is a homeopath.'

'Why to her? You should go to the proper chemist, not that witch! The gendarmes will get her soon.'

'It may not be safe to go to the chemist. Leonie has the ointments, and they are better. I know how to use them.'

The telephone rang in the small library next door. Consuero got up hurriedly from the table. 'Very well. But we shall not be calling the doctor.' As he walked rapidly to the door, he said, 'Tell Frederik. Philippe will warn the gatehouse.'

Frederik sat beside the chauffeur as they drove through the forest to the gatehouse where the two guards looked into the car before pressing the button, and the electrically-controlled bar swung up and the iron gates swung back.

Orianna, with Frederik beside her, got out of the car in the main steet in Opio and walked to the small and dark shop in a narrow side street. Leonie, a massive figure, even taller than and as black as Orianna, was behind the counter. She wore a long blue gown and a pink bandana headcloth. She came from Martinique, and whenever she was allowed, Orianna liked to come and see her. But the man, Frederik, was always outside, waiting.

'I must come inside,' Orianna said to Leonie. And, to Frederik, 'The door will be open.'

Leonie raised the flap of the counter. In the inner room, Orianna put a finger to her lips. She had her back to Frederik, who was lounging on the counter in the outer part, reading a newspaper.

Orianna said aloud, 'I need something to stop the bleeding. It is very bad.' As she spoke, she took the piece of paper from her blouse, laid it on Leonie's table, and pointed. Leonie stretched out and the paper disappeared in her great hand.

'The friend who is bleeding is at the château,' Orianna went on. 'It is a bad nose-bleed. Have you anything which would help stop it?'

'I might.' Leonie turned and went to a corner of the room out of sight of Frederik and read the paper Orianna had given her. 'Telephone London 071 489 5000. Tell Godfrey that Jakes is at the Château du Forêt, near Grasse. She is afraid and lonely, and wants to see him.'

Leonie looked at Orianna, who again put her finger to her lips. She took a pot of salve and a pencil from the shelf behind her and came back to where Orianna was standing. She put the pot, the pencil and the paper on the table, pointing to a word.

Orianna took the pencil and wrote in capitals, JAKES. 'While I've been away, I have had trouble too,' she said. 'Of a different kind. Will you examine me?' She pushed the door half shut but left it unclosed. She lifted her dress, and bent over.

Leonie examined her and said, 'You need ointment too.'

When the two women came out of the inner room, Orianna was carrying two packets wrapped in blue tissue paper. Frederik was still leaning on the counter.

Orianna stretched and kissed Leonie's cheek. 'Thank you for your help,' she said, and went out.

Frederik followed her to the car and they drove back to the château.

TWENTY-FIVE

At Hans Place in London, Godfrey was in the hall waiting to give the porter the address where he could be reached in France. It was nine o'clock London time, ten o'clock on the Continent. He had decided to fly to Paris and visit Bernard at his office before flying on to Nice to meet Brereton. His bag was at his feet; outside a taxi was waiting to take him to Heathrow. But the porter was on the telephone. Godfrey stood impatiently. Eventually he picked up his bag and turned away. He would ring him from the airport. Then he heard his name, and looked back.

The porter had his hand over the receiver. 'I can't make it out, sir, but there's a foreign lady asking to speak to a Godfrey. Could that be you, sir?'

Godfrey took the receiver. 'Who is that?'

'Are you Godfrey?'

He could hardly hear the voice at the other end, the voice of a woman, speaking very quietly. 'I am. Who are you?'

'I have a message for you.'

'It is very difficult to hear you. Where are you speaking from?'

'Just listen. The message is from Orianna. Jakes is at the Château du Forêt, near Grasse. She wants to see you.'

He picked up the French accent, but there was something more. 'I can't hear you very well. Will you repeat?' He spoke in French.

The voice repeated the message, this time in French, and he got the intonation. It was Caribbean. 'She wants to see you very badly,' the voice went on.

'Where are you speaking from?' he asked, but all he heard was the sound of the receiver being replaced. He stood for a moment, the telephone still in his hand. Carla's message about the black lady. A Caribbean accent. Orianna. And Jakes had never got home.

He dialled James Kent's personal number at the office at Vauxhall Cross. A secretary answered. 'I must speak with C.'

'He's left instructions he's not to be disturbed.'

'Tell him it's Godfrey Burne, and it's a matter of life and death.' He held on. Then Kent came on the line. 'What is all this, Burne? You frightened the life out of my secretary.'

'Somerset has located the people who murdered Hamilton,' said Godfrey. 'They're at a house, the Château du Forêt, near Grasse . . .'

'What on earth are you talking about? Somerset's on leave, and he's in Italy.'

'He used his leave to track down the people who killed his brother. It was Consuero and the Mafia.'

'Have you taken leave of your senses? It was the IRA who killed Edmund Hamilton. It was an IRA bomb, and the man who planted it has been killed. We matched his fingerprints with some found on the car they used.'

'No, it was Consuero, and he's in France. I also believe they're holding Mark's friend, the Australian girl Jakes Hunter. You must do something immediately.'

'This is all nonsense, Burne . . .'

But Godfrey had rung off. He reached across the porter's desk, took a pencil and scribbled. Then he said, 'I've got to get to the airport. If I have time, I will ring Paris from there, but I want you to telephone this number in Paris and speak to Mr de Tourneville. Tell him it's now very much more urgent. I shall be on the ten-thirty from Heathrow, and ask him to meet me at Charles de Gaulle at twelve-thirty.'

As they swung into Cromwell Road to get to the M4 and the airport, Godfrey remembered the morning, less than two weeks ago, when he had heard on his car radio the news of the bombing at a house outside Cambridge. Now that telephone message could mean only one thing. They had Jakes.

He did not yet know about Carla. No one did. All the Rome police knew when they found the body in the car on the morning after the storm was that it was a woman. There was nothing to identify who she was; her face had been blown to bits and there was no handbag or any papers with her. The car, they discovered later, had been hired a week ago from Nice by an Englishman, Mark Somerset, the man they wanted to question about the murder of Giorgio Rosetti.

When Burne had rung off, Kent spoke to Morgan and told him what Burne had said. 'The man was quite hysterical. We know it was the Irish, but Burne ranted on about Somerset and the South Americans and a house in France. I thought you told me that Somerset was seen in Rome five days ago with the girl?'

'He was,' Morgan replied. 'Consuero in France? He's not been heard of for years!'

'It's nothing but one of Burne's ludicrous "hunches". And if we're not careful, he'll land us all in another disaster, as he did in Colombia. But you'd better check it out. Inform young Layton in Nice. Tell him to look into it. It's probably all nonsense.'

In this way James Kent dismissed Burne's fantasies. He had other things on his mind. For at any time now, he was expecting a development in the battle for his own personal survival.

Last night, or rather in the early hours of that morning, two anonymous reports in plain manila envelopes sealed with a circle of red sealing-wax had dropped, literally, on the mats of the offices of selected newspapers and television companies. No one subsequently ever discovered who had delivered them or how the deliverer could have gained access, in one case to an office on the fifteenth floor, and in every case past what had been thought were competent security checks. But someone had. In each case the envelope was addressed to the Editor, marked 'Personal, Confidential and Urgent', and each was found by the office staff when they had arrived that morning. They caused, as Kent had trusted they would, much interest and even more activity.

It was because of the developments that James Kent confidently expected would arise following the receipt of the envelopes that he had given instructions on this morning that he would receive no callers and no messages. It was only because of who Burne had once been and because Burne had so alarmed his secretary that he had accepted the call. But he had not taken Burne's story seriously. Morgan could deal with Burne's alarums. James Kent settled down to continue his vigil.

The Foreign Secretary had been at breakfast in his official apartment in Carlton House Terrace when he got the news. When he had first sat down and tucked his napkin under his chin, he had been feeling well. The previous evening he had spoken to the Conservative Wesleyan Group on 'Ethics in Public Life'. The speech had gone down well and a clip from it had been shown on the nine o'clock TV news. Later he had been interviewed on the subject on *Newsnight*, and his Parliamentary Private Secretary had congratulated him warmly.

'I'm glad you spoke out so strongly. There's a lot of talk about sleaziness in government nowadays, especially financial sleaziness. I'm glad you deal with it so firmly. You were so right when you said that ministers must be like Caesar's wife, above suspicion. It's about time someone claimed the high moral ground, and now you have. It needed saying. That'll do you a lot of good, Rex,' Jefferson had said.

So on this morning he was tackling his breakfast with more than his usual excellent appetite. But it was a breakfast that, for the remainder of his life, Rex Weston would never forget. He was, he would always remember, eating a kipper when the telephone was brought to the table and he was told that Randall Crauford was on the line from New York.

'Randall,' he cried cheerfully. 'How good to hear from you! Did you have a good journey home? But it must be three in the morning your time. Whatever are you up to at this hour? Have you been out on the tiles?' That was the last piece of cheerfulness Weston experienced for a long time.

Crauford was blunt and to the point. 'The Editor of the *Echo* has just woken me. The media, both newspapers and television, have received two anonymous reports.'

'Yes, Randall.' The Foreign Secretary pushed aside his plate with the half-eaten kipper and took a sip of coffee.

'The reports concern Piers Grenwich whom, it is said, you've been strongly pushing to replace the present man as head of your Overseas Intelligence Agency, MI6.'

There was something rather clipped in Crauford's tone, and a slight note of unease entered the Foreign Secretary's voice. 'Yes, Randall, that's quite right, I have. We are proposing to make a change, and it's true I have been recommending Piers Grenwich. He's an excellent fellow, just the man for the job.'

'The reports claim that he and his brother have gone into business with the Mafia.'

'What!' Weston almost choked on his coffee. 'What did you say, Randall?'

'The reports claim that Piers Grenwich and his brother George have gone into business with the Mafia.'

The normally rubicund complexion of the Foreign Secretary had paled. For the first time for many years, indeed since his maiden speech in the House, he was seriously alarmed. 'The Mafia!'

'Yes. The Grenwich brothers have a company called Grenwich Industries, of which Piers is, or is about to become, Chairman, and his brother George is the managing director. They have merged with a Salerno company in southern Italy. The purpose behind the deal, it is said, is to help the Italian company launder profits, probably obtained from the Mafia traffic in drugs.'

'I don't believe it!'

'The reports conclude,' Crauford went on remorselessly, 'with the assertion that the single biggest shareholder in Grenwich Industries is the Priory Trust, of which you, Rex, are the sole beneficiary.'

There was a stunned silence at the London end. Then

Weston said weakly, 'But this is absurd! I knew nothing of this, absolutely nothing. I had no idea what the Grenwich company was doing, nor that the trust was a shareholder in Grenwich.'

'Perhaps not, but you know well enough what some of the tabloids could make of it. So I thought I would warn you immediately.'

'But it would be grossly unfair to involve me. I knew nothing of all this!'

'Perhaps not, perhaps not. I'll stand by you, Rex. You can rely on the *Echo* to support you. Now I must go back to sleep.' And Randall Crauford rang off.

By midday the story had broken, and the offices and homes, the relatives and friends and the children of the relatives and friends of the Foreign Secretary, of Sir Piers Grenwich, of his brother George, and all the other directors and staff of Grenwich Industries, including their suspected mistresses and lovers, as well as the elderly and bewildered trustees of the Priory Trust, were besieged by an army of reporters and photographers. Despite the issue in the early afternoon of a dignified denial by the trustees that any beneficiary had any influence over the investment policy of the Priory Trust, the media kept up the pressure.

The *Evening Examiner* set the tone: 'This concerns the integrity of a public servant who has just been lecturing the public on ethics in government, and whom some were even demanding should become the Sovereign's First Minister,' ran the editorial printed on its front page.

There are questions which need answering. Did the minister know the character of the business in which his trust had invested? Did he know that Grenwich Industries was heavily in debt and that the merger with the Italians was the only way the company could survive? Was he aware that the Italians who were to save Grenwich Industries were associated with the Mafia? If not, why not? And how could the minister go around recommending Sir Piers Grenwich, Chairman-elect of Grenwich Industries with that company's dubious connections, for appointment to the most vital and sensitive national Intelligence post, MI6? Nothing will now satisfy the British people but an independent Public Inquiry.

At the start of the rumpus, the *Echo* made some attempt to support the minister. But not for long. The circulation of its rivals leapt. When told the figures, Randall Crauford had no doubts, no doubts whatsoever. Soon the *Echo* joined the pack hunting the Foreign Secretary.

'Rex Weston has let me down,' he told his Editor-in-Chief over the transatlantic telephone. 'I trusted him. I had plans for him. But he has betrayed me. This whole shoddy business only confirms my opinion that the public life of your country is corrupt and decadent.'

The embattled Foreign Secretary was now on his own. None of those he used to call 'his closest political friends' seemed anxious to be seen with him. When he entered the smoking-room in the House, hoping for comfort from his cronies, none came forward and soon the room gradually emptied. After a few minutes, Rex Weston swallowed his drink and silently left.

TWENTY-SIX

Six hours after Carla had died in his car in the Gianicolo gardens, Mark in her Alfa-Romeo crossed the frontier into Monaco. In Monte Carlo, he found a small hotel which was open, took a room and rested for three hours. Then he walked to the port. There was no sign of the *Phydra*. Anxious, he drove along the coast, turning off the main road to inspect the yacht-basins at Beaulieu and Villefranche, and making a détour around Cap-Ferrat. Nothing. At Nice, when he was satisfied that the *Phydra* was not lying in the harbour, he took Carla's car to the Negresco and handed over the keys to the hall porter. He bought washing kit, a pair of jeans and a couple of shirts. At a local car-hire office he hired a Citroën and drove west, searching every marina on the coast for the blue and white hull of the yacht.

At Cros-de-Cagnes, he thought again of Jakes. Here, a week ago, they had turned inland from Cagnes-sur-Mer on to the Grasse road and made for Valbonne. Now she would probably be at work in the studio. At Antibes, he turned under the arch into the car-park at the port beneath the walls of the old town. When he had parked, he walked down the quay past the bows of all the craft moored there – 'gin-palace' motor-yachts, tall schooners, converted minelayers, tough, sturdy fishing vessels. Until, right at the end, he saw the *Phydra*, which he had last seen sailing through the bay of Policastro.

He walked past her, turned and came back. There was no sign of life on board. She appeared to be locked up and deserted. A yawl with a French ensign was moored next to her and a man in white shorts with a bare hairy chest was standing at the end of the gangplank, smoking. Mark strolled up to him and asked if he'd seen any of his friends from the *Phydra*. He was hoping to meet them and wondered if the man knew where they had gone.

The sailor shook his head. 'They're ashore,' he said. He had heard her come in during the early hours, and looked out. They had someone ill on board and he'd seen them carry the patient along the gangplank to a car. Later in the morning he'd seen some of the crew, but he thought they'd all gone now. Gino, the only one he knew to talk to, had locked her up and walked into town.

'Do you think she'll be sailing today?' Mark asked. 'I don't want to miss them.'

The man shook his head. 'No, they haven't even refuelled. Try the café within the wall, Les Deux Colombiers. Gino's usually there.'

Mark walked back through the high gate of the harbour into the town and along the line of restaurants facing the wall. At the café to which he had been directed there was no one who looked as if he was a crewman, only families and English and German tourists eating lunch. He decided to go to Mougins to find the garage where he had seen the black woman in the Mercedes. If he failed, he would come back and keep watch on the yacht.

He drove through the old town and cut inland to Grasse, trying to retrace the route he had taken a week earlier after he had left Jakes painting up at Gourdon. He remembered he had gone from Grasse to Mougins. But where had he gone then? It had been a small garage, on a main road, with a single pump and a single attendant, probably the proprietor. It was not on the Mougins road, so he cut further inland towards the east. Perhaps it had been on the Cannes–Grasse road? Finally, near Opio, he found it. From the office, which was little more than a shed, came the same man who had served him before.

Mark leaned on the car as the man filled the tank. 'Business good?' he enquired. The man shook his head. 'I was here last week when I had a long wait. You were filling up a large white Mercedes. They take a lot of gas.'

'Mercs do,' the man said.

'This was very special, a beautiful car.'

'They make good cars.'

'I prefer these.' Mark patted the roof of the Citroën. 'But it was a very good-looking car. And it had a very good-looking passenger, an African woman, all in white.'

The man grunted. 'That one,' he said.

'You said they came from a château near here.'

'Foreigners, from the Château du Forêt by Roquefort. Good customers.'

Mark paid him and pulled away from the pump, and still in the forecourt, studied the map. The Commune of Roquefort-Les-Pins was north of the Grasse – Cagnes road, and on the map the Château du Forêt itself was marked. North of the château, across a valley, was the small town of Bar-sur-Loup; further north still, high on the mountain, was Gourdon. Suddenly he remembered the telescope on the wall – and the large house he had noticed in the forest. He checked the map. That could be it.

He drove fast to Gourdon. On his way up the mountain road, he passed the cliff from which the hang-gliders were launched. He had to stop behind a stationary van while traffic came past the other way, and he watched as one of the gliders with bright crimson wings took off immediately below him. The pilot ran to the edge of the crest and jumped, grasping the bar and pulling up his legs until he lay horizontally as the hang-glider swung upwards in the currents of wind, floating in ever higher circles above the valley of the Loup far below.

Half an hour later, Mark had the telescope trained on the isolated house on the far crest, half hidden in the forest. Suddenly the crimson hang-glider swam across the lens, and he followed it as it circled lower and lower until it disappeared. He could not see where it was going to land. When he drove back along the mountain road, he was flagged down by a man standing by the van. It had broken down, the man said. Could he have a lift to the village? In the car he told Mark that he was the companion of one of the hang-gliders and was due to pick up the 'pilot,' who would now have landed.

'Where would that be?' Mark asked, and was told that it was a meadow between the foot of the Gourdon mountain and the opposite hill. 'Is that the crest with the large house in the forest?'

'That's it. The Château du Forêt,' the man replied.

Mark offered to drive him to where his friend had landed and then take him on to the garage. On the way, he said, 'You must get a good view of the house as you come in to land.'

'You do. It's what we call a "château-fort", with battlements and two towers and a slip of lawn on the north side before the parapet and the cliff. It's very isolated, but you get a great sight from the air. And you can see it only from the air because it lies at the end of a long drive through the oak forest, and the occupants don't like people wandering through their woods.'

'Why not?'

'I don't know. They're foreigners. They've only been there two years. There's a lot of wild boar in those woods but they've scared off the hunters. They have keepers patrolling the woods around the drive. They're not very friendly.'

While the man ran across the meadow to talk to the pilot who was was dismantling the glider, Mark looked up at the thickly wooded cliff which rose sheer from the edge of the field. From where he stood, the trees hid any view of the house – but he knew it was there, on the crest, high above him. The man came back to the car and they drove to the garage in the village, leaving the pilot in the meadow sitting by the dismantled glider.

In the car, Mark said, 'I'd like to see that château. It sounds interesting.'

'You won't get far. There's a gatehouse and iron gates, and behind the gates a bar like a boom. And they have keepers patrolling the woods.'

'What are they afraid of?'

'Trespassers, sightseers, hunters . . . I don't know. But they keep up the festival all right.'

'What's that?'

'A local custom, hundreds of years old. It dates from the Great Plague. When the other priests had fled, one of the friars stayed in the village and looked after the sick. The Seigneur of the day took him into the château when he was dying. Each year the men from the village carry the statue of him on a platform with poles on their shoulders from the church in the village to the chapel in the château.'

'That still goes on under the new people?'

'Yes, and they're very good with the feast after the Mass. Plenty of food – and plenty of good wine. I helped to carry the statue this year. It nearly killed me. No, they're very friendly on the feast day. It's just they don't like people wandering through their woods.'

At the garage he got out of the car and shook hands through the car window. 'If you want to see the château, come and fly with us.'

Mark laughed. 'That's too dangerous for me.'

The man looked up at the sky. 'There's a storm coming. No more gliding this weekend. Thanks again for your help.'

Mark drove to Roquefort, past the little church, the shops and the Mairie and along the winding road through the forest to the start of the drive to the château. He saw the gatehouse, the tall iron gates and the bar behind them. When he got to the gates, he stopped the car, pulled out his map, and then began to turn in the narrow lane, as though he had lost his way. A man came from the gatehouse and watched. Two hundred yards beyond him two men, holding dogs on leashes, were standing talking in the drive. Both had sporting rifles, and gaiters above their hunting boots. Then they disappeared into the woods, one on either side of the drive.

Mark drove back the way he had come. He was going to take a look at the mysterious château, and he was going to climb.

All those who lived in that part of the Alpes Maritimes knew that another of the summer storms so common there was on the way. By early evening dark clouds had gathered over the mountains of the Gorges-du-Loup and sheets of lightning and the rumble of thunder had already begun when Godfrey Burne, alone in an unmarked police car that Bernard de Tournville had provided and fitted with a concealed location device, drew up before the closed gates of the Château du Forêt. It was seven o'clock in the evening.

While a storm of another kind was breaking over the head of the British Foreign Secretary in London, Bernard had taken Godfrey in an official plane from Charles de Gaulle airport to Nice, where they were joined by Brereton and Lloyd, the young man Morgan had been told by Kent to alert. At the Mairie in Rocquefort, four miles from the château, they met Commissaire Divisionaire Ange Corsini, the commander of the Groupement d'Intervention de la Gendarmerie Nationale, the GIGN.

Godfrey volunteered to go to the château to try to negotiate the release of Jakes Hunter. 'If it's Consuero, I've met him, and he will know about me.'

Bernard agreed. While Godfrey was at the château, Corsini was to place his men in position in the forests and hills around the house. There was to be no move by the gendarmes, Bernard ordered, before Godfrey returned.

'Unless,' Godfrey said wryly, 'I don't.'

A time was set for when Godfrey must be back at the Mairie. If he had not returned by then, the GIGN would move in.

At the gates, Godfrey blew the horn and a man emerged from the gatehouse. He looked at the car, then up at the sky, and went back inside. When he reappeared in a dark waterproof cape, the first heavy drops of rain had begun to fall. The man unlocked the pedestrian wicket gate and walked up to the car.

Godfrey lowered the window. 'I have come to see Señor Vincente Consuero.'

'I've not been told about a visitor.'

'Tell the Señor that Sir Godfrey Burne from London is here to see him.'

'No one's allowed through unless I have instructions.'

'That is why you are to telephone the house and tell the Señor that Sir Godfrey Burne has come from London to see him. It's important.'

The man walked slowly round the car. By now the rain was falling in sheets, and it had grown very cold. A second man, also in a cape, came from the gatehouse.

'Do as I say,' Godfrey called from the car window. 'It is very urgent.'

The first gatekeeper spoke to his companion and went inside; the other remained by the closed gate. The rain now turned to hail, and balls of ice, some the size of cherry-stones, began to rattle on the roof of the car and bounce on to the drive. The man by the gate ran back into the gatehouse. Soon the ground was white with a carpet of hailstones. For half an hour Godfrey sat waiting. Then the first gateman reappeared and came to the passenger side of the car. 'You are to go on up. I am to come with you,' he said.

The gates opened, the solid bar behind was raised and they drove in silence through the whitened oak forest. When they came to where the drive reached the cliff and turned at a right angle down the incline to the house, Godfrey slowed and then stopped. He peered through the windscreen at the spectacular view of the mountains which, despite the hail, he could see across the valley when the Gorges-du-Loup were lit up by great flashes of lightning.

'Go on,' said the man, and Godfrey drove down the hill and drew up before the double front doors.

'Wait.' The gateman got out and rang the bell. There was no portico or porch, and he stood with the hailstones bouncing off his cape and on to the ground at his feet.

When the door had opened and the manservant beckoned to him, Godfrey ran from the car into the stone-flagged hall. Frederik was lounging to one side of the fireplace. Philippe, the manservant, led Godfrey across the hall past the burly, lounging man into the salon. It was a double room, divided by an arch. The light was dim, relieved only by a single lamp on a table in the first part of the room. Godfrey walked into the inner half where the ceiling was decorated by a fading, peeling fresco. He was looking up, with his back to the door, when he heard the voice behind him.

'Good evening, Sir Godfrey. I hope you did not get too wet between the car and my front door.'

Godfrey slowly turned. Leaning in the doorway was Vincente Consuero. 'No,' he said. 'It is nothing.'

'The hail will not last. It will soon turn to rain, but we're in for a storm.' Consuero had not moved from the doorway. 'I understand you wish to see me? Well, now you see me.'

'See you again,' said Godfrey.

'Yes. See me again. That first time was a long time ago, when we were both much younger and both just beginning.'

It had been an evening reception at the house of a banker in Bogota; with an orchestra in a garden lit with coloured lights. Godfrey had been, officially, the Second Secretary at the Embassy; in fact, he was head of the MI6 Colombia station. Vincente Consuero, ostensibly the head of a merchant house trading in coffee, was emerging as one of the barons of the drug cartels, and Godfrey, learning that Consuero would be at the reception, had been interested to see what he was like. The meeting had been brief: an introduction, a few formalities with both men eyeing each other, both well aware of what the other was and did. They had spent the rest of the evening observing each other. Shortly thereafter, Godfrey had been moved. It was many years later that he had dispatched Edmund Hamilton to Colombia to investigate Consuero, by then one of the most powerful figures in the trade of drugs into Europe.

'I followed your career with interest, Sir Godfrey,' Consuero said, walking into the room. 'I heard you had been dismissed, or at least prematurely retired, as a result of your failure in Colombia. For which I must take the credit.' He now faced Godfrey, who had not moved from beneath the peeling fresco. 'But that's all in the past. Now we are both much older and both retired.'

'I am retired,' said Godfrey.

Consuero's place in the doorway was taken by the bulky figure of Andreas. 'When I heard you were at my gate –' Consuero bent to take a box of matches from a low glass table between the armchairs, and lit a cheroot – 'I had to remind myself that you were now only a private citizen – and not even a citizen of France. Nor yet, of course, a citizen of that other country in the hymn which Gustav Holst set so delightfully to music.' He smiled as he sat in one of the wide armchairs in the first part of the double room, and waved a hand. 'Please be seated, if you wish.'

Godfrey shook his head. Consuero went on, 'So, for what am I indebted by this unexpected, social visit?'

'The reason I have come is to take home someone you are keeping here.'

There was silence. 'That,' Consuero said, 'is a very extra-ordinary statement.'

'It is a perfectly clear statement, and I repeat it. I have come to take someone home.'

Godfrey saw the man in the doorway put his hand in his jacket pocket. It was now quite dark, with only a pool of light from the lamp and some from the hall, as much as was not obscured by the bulky figure of Andreas. A crash of thunder and a particularly bright flash of lightning caused the light to flicker wildly.

'These storms, I fear, can be very fierce.' said Consuero. 'They often affect our lights, even on occasion fusing them. I am sufficiently in the dark about the real reason for your visit here, Sir Godfrey, without being thrown literally in the dark by the failure of the electricity. While we still have light, perhaps you'd care to explain yourself.'

'I repeat: I've come to take someone home. It is the young woman you are holding here.'

Consuero shook his head slowly, as if in disbelief. 'I thought at first that I must be imagining. You, a private citizen of, let us remember, a foreign country, come to my house and first demand to see me and then demand to take home a young woman whom you say I am holding here? Have you taken leave of your senses?'

'No, and you know I haven't. You are holding here a young woman as a prisoner.'

Consuero sighed, and said, 'Andreas, be so good as to ask Orianna to come here.'

Andreas disappeared from the doorway. This, Godfrey thought, will be the black woman. The woman who had sent the message.

'I am normally a patient man, Sir Godfrey, but you are trying my patience – and my temper.'

'As you are mine.'

The two men gazed steadily at each other. Orianna appeared in the doorway, Andreas behind her. Godfrey looked at her, but her eye was on Consuero.

'What is your name?'

'Orianna.'

'How many women, Orianna, are there in this house?'

There was a slight pause, and then she said, 'Three.'

'For the benefit of my importunate and sadly confused visitor, let us go through them. First there is Pierrette. What is she?'

'She is the cook.'

'Then there is Madeleine. What does she do?'

'She cleans.'

'And the third is you, my companion. Any other?' Orianna shook her head. 'That then is three, the full complement of the distaff side of the Château du Fôret. This gentleman has a notion that we have another. I'll ask you again. Is there any other woman here in the château?' She shook her head again. 'Speak,' said Consuero softly. 'Speak, so that this gentleman can hear you. Is there or is there not another woman in this house?'

'No,' said Orianna.

Consuero waved a hand, dismissing her and she disappeared. He leaned towards the table beside his chair and stubbed out his cheroot. 'What is the meaning of this insanity?' he said very softly. 'Why are you here?'

'I told you. I have come to take home the young woman you are holding,' said Godfrey quietly. 'I think we should stop this play-acting.'

Consuero got to his feet. 'That is impertinent, Sir Godfrey.'

'If you let me take her, and provided you leave this place, I am authorised to say that will be the end of it.'

'Authorised? An end of what? This is becoming intolerable.'

'It is intolerable for the young woman to be kept here.'

'You are mad! Quite mad!' Godfrey could not see Consuero's face in the dim light but he heard the anger and fury in his voice. 'For the past two weeks, I am told that a young man has been following me, investigating me and my business. . .'

Godfrey interrupted him. 'I know very well what is your business.'

'You think you do, but you are wrong. You harassed me in South America, and now you harass me in France with a preposterous story of a young woman a prisoner here, in my home. You have had that young man follow me to Italy. You invent lies about me. Now you accuse me of holding in my house a young woman of whom I've never heard – all because you have some crazy fantasy about what I do and what I am. You were wrong in the past, when you had some authority, and you are wrong now, when you have none.'

'Let me take the woman, and that, for this time at least, will be the end of it,' said Godfrey quietly. 'If you don't . . .'

'And if I don't? If I don't do what I can't do because there is no young woman here, what then?'

'Then I shall go and . . .'

'Provided always I let you go.'

'You will let me go, for if you do not and I do not return, others, who do have authority, will come looking for me.'

Consuero remained silent. Then he shrugged. 'You made a fool of yourself once before in Colombia. That cost you your job. This time your interference will cost you more.'

'You mean my life? As it cost Edmund Hamilton his?'

Consuero turned and put both his hands on the stone chimneypiece, raising his head until he was looking up at the dark ceiling, his back to the room. 'Your life! What is that worth, Sir Godfrey? The life of an old, dismissed, public servant. I don't care that for your life –' he snapped his fingers – 'save for the trouble of taking it.' Then he turned round. 'I let you enter my home because I was curious to know what you wanted. Now that I've heard what you have had to say, I'm tempted to keep you here and hand you over to those who would teach you not to abuse private citizens in a country where you have not a shred of authority. But you can leave. When and if you return with those who may have authority, they can search every corner of every tower and every part of this house. They will find nothing. Nothing. And you will bear the consequences. Now get out of my house.'

Consuero flung himself back into his chair and Godfrey stood looking down at the figure sprawled in front of him. Then he crossed the room and stopped at the doorway in front of Andreas, who was barring his way. From his chair, Consuero waved his hand, and Andreas stood aside. Godfrey walked out into the hall. By the front door stood Frederik.

'He is leaving,' said Andreas to Frederik.

By now it was quite dark, except for the flashes of lightning, for the storm now raged directly overhead, although the hail had turned to rain as Consuero had prophesied.

Frederik walked with Godfrey to the car. 'Go with him to the gate,' he said to the gateman, standing in his cape by the car. 'And make sure he leaves.'

He stood in the rain in the light of the open door as the car turned and drove away. When he came back into the hall, Consuero, from in front of the fireplace, called to him from the salon.

'Telephone the gatehouse. Tell them to cut the telephone wires beyond the gate down in the forest and to delay the car at the gate. They are to say the storm has cut the elecricity and that it cannot be opened. They are to delay him there as long as they can, and then tell him the gate cannot be opened, his car will have to remain, and he is to leave on foot. If, later, the gendarmes come, the gatemen must break the mechanism so that their vehicles cannot get through. That should give us enough time. Hurry. And send Orianna here.'

He turned to Andreas. 'The gendarmes are probably in the village. It will take Burne some time to get to them in the dark. Now for the woman. She must be dealt with.'

'We should never have taken her in the first place.'

'She would have been useful if it had been Somerset alone. Burne is another matter.'

'How did he track us here?'

'I don't know, but I shall find out. We must act quickly.' Orianna entered the room. 'What is the state of the woman?'

'She is asleep. She is still suffering from the last drug.'

'Good.' To Andreas he said, 'There must be no bloodshed. No trace of her must be left. So no gun, no knife. Then she must be taken to the forest and you and Frederik must bury her.' He turned to Orianna. 'You will clean the room. There won't be much time, so go and get on with it.'

In the hall, Andreas said to Orianna, 'Get me a cloth!'

She disappeared through the dining-room to the kitchen, and came back with a crimson silk-coloured scarf. Andreas twisted it round his hands as, with Orianna behind him, he climbed the spiral stairs to the attic bedroom.

TWENTY-SEVEN

In the early evening when the clouds were gathering over the mountains and the thunder had begun to rumble, Mark was in Grasse, buying a heavy long-handled torch and a sheath-knife; from an outfitter, dark overalls, thin leather gloves and rubber-soled boots. Then he drove to a lane near the meadow where he had been with the men from the hang-glider and parked on the verge against a tall hedge. He stripped off his jacket, transferred his passport, driving licence and wallet with his credit cards and money to the breast pocket of the overalls, and pulled the overalls over his shirt and trousers. He put the gun, silencer and spare magazine in the right pocket, and sat, torch in hand, waiting for darkness – which, because of the threatening storm, came earlier this evening. When he judged it dark enough, he locked the car, crossed the meadow and entered the belt of trees behind which was the foot of the cliff he was to climb. As he pushed through the scrub up a slope to where the cliff rose sheer, the rain began, turning almost immediately into the hail that had rattled on the bonnet of Godfrey's car. But after a time, the hail turned back into rain, which fell in sheets, lit by the constant flashes of lightning.

With his torch, Mark examined the foot of the cliff. It was not sheer rock, save in a few places. Mostly it was a mass of broken rock, between which grew shrubs and trees, rising ever more steeply to the summit on which stood the stone walls of the battlements, and what the hang-glider had described as the outer parapet of the château bordering the slip of lawn under the main walls joining the towers at either end. The climb would be hard, but he had light from his torch and from the flashes of lightning; because of the trees, he would not be seen from either above or below.

After rubbing wet earth on his face to darken it, he set off, scrambling over the boulders and through the shrubs, pulling himself up by the branches and trunks of the trees as gradually he ascended higher and higher towards the summit of the cliff and the foot of the parapet. When he was about halfway into his climb, although he could not see them, two cars with men in black carrying submachine-guns drew up beside his in the lane by the meadow far below him. Three of the men walked round Mark's Citroën. One forced the lock and searched the empty car. Finding the jacket, he went through the pockets, searching for identification. When he found none, he spoke into his hand-radio, giving the number of the car. Then the men formed up in line and marched across the meadow to take up position in the belt of trees at the foot of the cliff, crouching in the undergrowth and sheltering as best they could against the rain.

High above them, Mark climbed on. The storm had now reached its height. Every now and then forked lightning struck a tree, splintering it and sending it crashing down against the side of the hill. After nearly an hour, he came to the final belt of rock and shrubs; above him he could see the foot of the parapet through the trees – and above that, as they became illuminated every now and then by the lightning, the towers of the château.

This was the hardest part of the climb, for now he had to scale the face of sheer stone of the parapet wall, slippery from the rain which poured in torrents from the plateau above. Slowly and laboriously he dragged himself up until his head came level with the top of the parapet. There he paused, and looked about him. Far to his right, he saw the lights of a car climbing the drive away from the house until they disappeared as the road turned at right angles away from the cliff-side and into the forest. They were the lights of Godfrey's car, making for the gatehouse two miles to the south.

Mark levered himself up, swung himself over the parapet and lay for a moment prostrate, gathering his breath. He saw that now he had no need of his torch; the lightning and the lights from the lower windows showed him where to go, and he crawled to the foot of the battlements across the narrow strip of lawn where many months ago Consuero had walked with Andreas and Manolis and planned the murder of Edmund Hamilton.

At the top of the spiral stairs in the west tower, Andreas stopped. 'When it's done, I will carry her down,' he said to Orianna. 'Then you clear the room. Make sure there is no trace of her left.' Orianna nodded. 'Now, open the door.' She unlocked the door and stood aside, one hand behind her back. He entered, holding the scarf in front of him, a hand gripping either end of the crimson silk which he had twisted into a single narrow band.

Earlier, Jakes had been woken by the noise of the storm. During the day she had slept, but now lay in the darkness listening to the thunder. When she heard the lock being turned, she sat up and switched on the small bedside lamp, thinking it was Orianna. As she did so, the door opened and she saw the bulky figure advancing towards her bed holding the scarf stretched out in front of him. She put her hand to her throat, and screamed.

At that moment the light flickered and went out – then came on again. Andreas was now nearly at the bed. Jakes raised her hands and turned away her head. He bent to brush away her arms and force the scarf round her throat. Suddenly he stopped, arching his back, jerking back his head. His hands with the scarf wrapped round his fists fell down across his thighs. He tried to turn, to look behind him, but his knees began to sag.

It was only then that Jakes saw Orianna behind him; Orianna with the blood-stained kitchen knife in her hand as she plunged it again and again into the side of the fat body. Now it was Andreas who screamed, a great high-pitched scream, louder than that of Jakes, as he sank to his knees and fell on his back. Orianna stood astride him, raised the knife once again above her head and then brought it down, stabbing at his belly and his loins. Once, twice – then she stopped. Her long black hair had fallen over her face. When she raised her head, Jakes could see her eyes glinting through the tresses. She flung them back over her head and Jakes could see the frenzy of hate on her face.

'Get up,' she said to Jakes. 'Get up!' Unsteadily, Jakes swung her legs off the bed. The blood from Andreas' body was now spreading across the floor, and she stood in it. Orianna, the knife still in one hand, grabbed her arm with the other. 'We must get to my room below. Your clothes are there.' She pushed Jakes towards the door. 'Hurry, hurry!'

On the floor, Jakes' feet left a trail of blood. 'Down the stairs,' Orianna said, 'Quick!'

Jakes had to hold on to the iron rail along the stone wall which served as a banister in this part of the tower. Orianna put an arm around her to support her. The lights on the staircase kept flickering, turning off and on again at each strike of lightning as the two women came slowly down the spiral stairs.

At the final turn, just before they came to the next landing, they came face to face with Vincente Consuero. He had a gun in his hand, pointed at them. 'Drop the knife,' he said, and it fell with a clatter to the stone step beside Jakes' bloodstained feet.

At the edge of the main battlement wall, Mark pressed flat against the stone, finding some shelter from the rain. His overalls had been ripped and torn during the climb, and his face scratched by branches so that the blood streaked and mingled with the mud on his face. In front of him, over the parapet and across the tops of the trees and the valley below, lit every half-minute by the lightning, he could see the great peaks of the twin mountains divided by the Gorges-du-Loup, like the backcloth to a stage set.

In the flashes of lightning, he saw that steps beneath the east tower led from the lawn to a terrace. The hang-glider man had said the main door and the drive was on the southern side of the chateau. He took out the pistol and, with the torch in his left hand, moved along the wall, up the steps to the terrace and around the east side of the chateau. Lights were shining in the narrow window of the ground floor of the tower at the corner, and he bent as he passed.

There was a sudden lull in the storm, a break in the noise of the thunder. Suddenly from the tower high above he heard a woman's scream. Then, seconds later, less high-pitched than the first, the scream of a man – the scream of a wounded animal. Then silence. Keeping close to the stone wall, he kept on around the corner of the east tower to the front of the house, making for the main door. Now, in the flashes of lightning, he saw it was only a few yards from where he was. The lull had not lasted; the thunder and lightning had resumed, and now increased with frightening intensity, sometimes sheet, sometimes forked. A strike like an explosion landed in the garden across the terrace, and a great oak swayed and then fell with a crash against the front of the chateau, its top branches smashing against the wall, breaking the window on the far side of the door, narrowly missing the door itself.

A moment later a floodlight from the battlements came on, lighting the terrace and the fallen tree. Pressed against the wall and only a few feet from the broad oaken door, Mark heard the bolts being drawn back and a moment later it was flung open. A man ran out, a gun in his hand, and looked first at the fallen tree lying against the house, then he jerked his head and looked straight at Mark as he crouched against the wall, now fully lit by the spotlight. The man shouted and raised his gun, pointing it at Mark. Mark fired, and the man fell.

At that moment another blinding flash of forked lightning struck the east tower. Every light in the château went out; masonry fell from the battlements and crashed on to the terraces. A stone thudded into Mark's left shoulder, knocking him to his knees. Another smaller piece of masonry struck him on the head, and he felt the blood running down his face. He knelt in agony in the darkness. Then he got to his feet. With the torch gripped painfully in his left hand and the gun in his right, he stumbled over the man he had killed and went through the open door into the darkened house.

A flash of sheet lightning revealed a stone-flagged hall, with a circular flight of stone stairs to his left, a small table to his right. Above the noise of the rain and between the claps of thunder, Mark heard what he thought was a sob, and then the sound of footsteps descending the stairs in the darkness. He moved back against the wall and crouched by the corner of the open doorway so that he would be hidden from the lightning which, at intervals, lit the hall. From the sound of the footsteps, he judged that more than one person was slowly coming down the stone circular stair. Now there seemed to be longer intervals between the flashes of lightning and the hall and the stairs were longer in darkness. Then a great flash suddenly lit the garden, the terrace in front of the house and the hall, and he saw them, just for a second, three of them, at the foot of the stairs – at the back, the head and shoulders of a man with a dark pointed beard, in front of him two women, one the black girl and, beside her, clad in a white nightdress, her hair dishevelled, her face bruised, blood on her bare feet – was Jakes. Then it was darkness again.

'Jakes!' he shouted.

Immediately a bullet smashed into the wall some feet in front of him. One of the women screamed, and then in the darkness the sound of footsteps, as though someone was running from the stairs to the door. Still in darkness, another shot came – and this time the sound of the bullet was more muffled. Another great flash lit up the scene. One of the women was now lying at the foot of the stairs and another halfway across the stone floor of the hall. The man was still on the stairs, crouching behind the balustrade, his gun raised ready to fire, searching for his target.

When the light had gone, Mark placed the torch on the ground beside him. With his right hand, he pulled up his injured arm so that he could hold the pistol in both hands. Then he raised it, pointing at the stairs.

With the women lying on the floor between them, Mark and Consuero waited for the light.

When Godfrey had been told that the storm had fused the

mechanism and that he would have to wait in the car until they repaired it, he guessed this was being done to delay him, and he knew Jakes' life depended upon how soon he could get the gendarmes to the château. So as soon as the men disappeared inside the gatehouse, he slid across the front seat and climbed out on the far side of the car. In the drive, he broke through the tangle of bushes and disappeared into the forest. Lit every minute by the lightning, accompanied by the sound of the thunder and falling trees, he struggled through the undergrowth, drenched from the rain, with the thorn bushes tearing his clothes. He heard shouts above the noise of the storm, and looking back, he saw that the gatekeepers had come from the gatehouse and switched on the lights of his car, presumably to illuminate the road ahead in order to pick him up in their glare.

Inside the forest and now guided by the beam of the car lights, he turned south, trying to move parallel to the road. Behind him he heard the noise of dogs and he remembered that the gendarmes had warned that gamekeepers at the Château, armed with sporting rifles, patrolled the forest. He struggled on as fast as he was able, slithering down the hill, comforted by the thought that the storm and the lashing rain would make the task of the dogs and his pursuers more difficult. But they hardly left the surrounds of the gatehouse, and soon the sound of the dogs had faded and the lights of the stationary car behind the gate vanished.

It was more than three miles from the gate to the Mairie in the village, but when he had driven up earlier, he had seen a house not far from the gate. Half an hour later, he was banging on the door. But no light showed and there was no reply. So on he went, still keeping within the forest but closer to the road itself where the going was easier. By now his hands and face were scratched, his breath came in gasps, every limb in agony. Half a mile further on, an armed, black-clad gendarme of the GIGN stepped out from the trees and Godfrey literally fell into his arms. Within a quarter of an hour, bloody, his clothes torn and drenched, he was sitting in the Mairie, drinking from Bernard's flask.

'You're a bit old for this, *mon vieux*!' said Bernard in English. He was a thin, silver-haired man, of Godfrey's age. They had been friends for twenty years.

Godfrey told him about the car and the gate. 'It has given Consuero time,' he said.

'So it is he?'

'Yes, and he has the girl; I am sure of it. God knows what has happened to her since I left.'

Bernard turned to the Commissaire. 'Are your men in position?'

Corsini called up the units in turn. Godfrey asked Brereton, 'Any trace of Mark?'

'We've had a description of an Englishman at a garage near Opio.'

Corsini turned to Bernard. 'They are all in position, above and below the château. They report that many trees are down in the forest and they think the house itself has just been struck. There are no lights showing.'

'Then let's go.'

Corsini and his personal escort of three armed gendarmes went in the first car, with a searchlight mounted on the roof. Bernard, Godfrey and Brereton came in the second, followed by two truck-loads of armed GIGN with oxyacetaline cutting equipment and motorised hand-saws. Layton they left with the gendarmes manning the radio in the Mairie.

The storm had by now abated. There were only occasional flashes of sheet lightning, the rain was less but still steady, and the thunder had rolled away over the sea to the south. When Corsini in the first car came to the gatehouse, the searchlight picked out Godfrey's car, its lights out, still stationary behind the locked gates and lowered bar. There was no sign of any of the gatemen.

Corsini called up more men from the truck and within seconds the gate was hacked off and the hinges of the pole cut. Godfrey's car was pushed aside and Corsini swept on, with Bernard close behind. Around the next bend, they came to a halt with a squealing of brakes before a fallen tree. They had to wait again until the saws had been brought up to cut a way through.

Godfrey sat behind Bernard. 'Please God,' he prayed, 'we won't be too late.' First Edmund – then the girl and Rosetti in Rome. Now Jakes. He still did not know about Carla.

At last the way was clear and they drove on. Suddenly, in the light of the lead car, they saw in the middle of the drive three figures. Two women, and behind them a man. Corsini and two others jumped out. In a moment, he was back at the window of Bernard's car.

'It's the servants,' he said. 'There's been shooting in the house. We may be too late.'

He ran back to his car and they swept on down the hill and drew up as near to the front door as the fallen tree allowed. Two sections ran past to the east tower, another to the west and others on to the lawn on the north. Corsini, with his three gendarmes, followed by Bernard and the two Englishmen, went to the front door. The driver drove the car on to the terrace and the searchlight shone on the front door as Corsini bent over the figure lying at its foot.

'He's dead – shot,' he called out.

The three gendarmes stood with their automatics at the ready as Corsini stepped over the body and tried the iron ring of the latch. He looked over his shoulder and nodded to the armed men behind him. Then he turned the ring and stepped quickly aside as the door swung open. The beam from the searchlight lit the stone-flagged hall and the foot of the circular stone staircase. Corsini, with his revolver in one hand and a torch in the other, stepped inside. Between the door and the stairs they saw pools of blood.

Corsini shone the torch up the stairs and beckoned to one of the gendarmes, who mounted the stairs. 'Nothing,' he called down. Corsini turned to a door immediately to his right. Watched by the others, he put his hand on the latch and, as he had with the front door, stood aside, covered by his escort.

Then, with Bernard and Godfrey behind him, he stepped into the doorway and shone his torch into the room.

The beam of light fell on the figure of a man sitting on a low stool before the empty fireplace, dried blood from a wound on his head caking his face. He was cradling in his arms a woman in a white nightdress, with blood on her bare feet.

Godfrey pushed past Corsini. 'Mark!' he cried. Mark raised his head and looked at him dully. 'Is she dead?' Godfrey asked.

'No,' Mark replied. 'She's asleep. The others are. They are in the other room. I put them there.'

TWENTY-EIGHT

Back in London, Jakes began to recover from her ordeal. Mark never left her. He did not return Kent's calls, and when Morgan, dispatched by Kent, came to see him, he slammed the door in his face.

Godfrey Burne went home to Wiltshire. He was sitting in the garden looking out over Angela's herbaceous border, now in all the magnificence of its July glory, when she called to him from the lawn to come and walk with her and Teresa in the woods.

'I'm a little tired,' he called back. 'For a man of almost sixty, I've had rather too much exercise recently. You go.'

While they walked, Teresa talked about Edmund, as she had talked about him every day since the morning two weeks ago when he had been blown to death by the bomb.

Godfrey was also thinking about Edmund – and about Carla. It was he who had got both of them involved in what had led to their deaths. As he sat in the sunshine in his country garden, it wasn't only the stiffness of his limbs and the pain from the scratches of the thorns that made him feel so old.

Two days after the storming of the château in the Alpes-Maritimes, the Prime Minister sent for Rex Weston to Downing Street. They sat side by side at the Cabinet table.

'As you know, Rex, the government at present is going through a decidedly nasty patch, and I'm afraid this matter of the Grenwiches has become very tiresome. It's not helping. It's not helping at all.'

By now there had been seventy-two hours of continuous media attention and questions in Parliament. The Prime

Minister had seen his chance, and was seizing it. There were two patches of livid colour on the cheekbones of his usually parchment-pale face.

'I hate doing this, Rex. Indeed it's most painful. You and I have been friends for so many years, but . . .'

'But,' said Weston, 'you want me to go.'

The Prime Minister nodded gravely, then said briskly, 'I think it's best for you, Rex. It will leave you free to take what action you like against those who have been abusing you.'

The two men rose. 'The usual letters?' the Prime Minister said, almost cheerfully. 'I'll show you mine before it's sent.'

As they went, he put his arm round the other's shoulder. 'We'll miss you, Rex, but it'll not be long,' he said. 'Just enough time in the wilderness to recharge your batteries, eh? Then you'll be back. You'll be back. I'm sure of it.' *Over my dead body you will!* thought the Prime Minister as the door closed behind the resigning but not resigned minister.

Brereton had been transferred suddenly to Beirut.

'It's urgent,' Morgan had said on the telephone. 'Kent wants you there as soon as possible. No need to come home. It's a rather difficult time there at present, so watch yourself. We've had reports of our people being targeted. C chose you to go as you're a bachelor.'

Brereton rang off without a word. He knew why Kent had chosen him.

Rex Weston had been succeeded by Dick Burnett, the Home Secretary. As was customary, one of the first tasks of the new Foreign Secretary was to send for the Chief of MI6. 'You may have heard, C, that my predecessor had decided to replace you?'

'Replace me, Foreign Secretary? I had no idea.' Kent looked at the Minister. 'But I've been in the post only two years, and . . .'

'Well, that's what he'd decided, but if you hadn't heard about it, so much the better. All I intended to say to you this morning was to put you at ease about your future.'

'Thank you, Foreign Secretary. Thank you very much.'

'That incident in France – the French seem to have dealt with it most sucessfully. You had one of your men there, I believe?'

'Two, actually, Foreign Secretary. One from Rome – he's now gone to the Middle East – and a young fellow from Nice.'

'Excellent. I'm glad we were well represented. So these were the villains who engineered the bomb that killed Hamilton? At one time it was thought it was the Irish.'

Kent smiled. 'Oh no, no. Never the Irish. It was those South Americans. No doubt at all.'

'You did very well, C. Keep up the good work.'

'Thank you, Foreign Secretary. May I say I am most gratified by the confidence you're showing in me.'

James Kent rose and, casting an eye at the portrait of George III above the fireplace, left the Foreign Secretary's room. He walked briskly down the staircase to his waiting car and was driven home to Hampstead.